SOMETHING TO MAKE US HAPPY

by Linda Crawford

"Funny, moving, always entertaining . . ."
— *Publishers Weekly*

". . . a charming, smiling, sweet, elegant book . . . it's a winner."
— *Kirkus Reviews*

Isobel and Will Claflin, mother and son, wrap their lives in fantasy — the kind of fantasy that only Hollywood can provide. Set in the early 1930s, this is a story that takes us back to the golden days of moviedom when stars were kings and queens and films provided the romance so lacking in Depression days.

(continued on back flap)

Something to Make Us Happy

Linda Crawford

G.K. HALL & CO.
Boston, Massachusetts
1978

Library of Congress Cataloging in Publication Data

Crawford, Linda.
  Something to make us happy.

  Large print ed.
  1. Large type books. I. Title.
[PZ4.C89916 1978b] [PS3553.R286] 813'.5'4 78-16495
ISBN 0-8161-6599-8

Published in Large Print by arrangement with Simon and Schuster, a division of Gulf & Western Corporation.

The writing of this book was made possible through a grant from the Ludwig Vogelstein Foundation, Inc.

Set in Compugraphic 18 pt English Times

For my mother and father

Why be so realistic? Let us go back to the golden path. We don't want life but something to make us happy. Let us live.

A fan writing to *Photoplay* in 1927

The day Will Claflin's father was buried, his coffin settling into the dark hole in the ground, Will's mother turned to him.

"Willie," she said in her thick Scotch brogue, "would ya take me t' see *Platinum Blonde?* It's at the Fox."

Will knew where it was. He'd taken her there to see *Platinum Blonde* twice in the last three days: the matinee on the afternoon of his father's death and the evening show on the night of his wake. The night after his father died they saw Gable and Garbo in *Susan Lenox: Her Fall and Rise* at the Adams, and yesterday afternoon they'd seen Garbo and Robert Montgomery in *Inspiration* at the Madison.

Last night Jamie, Will's oldest brother, had offered to take Isobel so Will could attend the wake.

1

"Ah'll noo go without Willie," she'd said.

Alexine, Will's sister, had tried insisting they both stay home.

"It will look very strange," she said. "I mean, how will it look?"

"Ah canna help the look," said Isobel.

"Well, at least out of respect for father . . ." Alexine began.

"Bertie'd understand," Isobel cut in. "Ask Riley t' bring the car."

Now, with his mother's hand resting on his arm, Will moved down the black canvas walkway that stretched from the grave to the automobile. Jamie followed; then Alexine, draped in black, supported by her husband Herbert; then Ian, the other son, and his wife Ethel, both dry-eyed and upright. The others, nonfamily, hung back slightly, separated from the Claflins by an invisible circle of grief.

Riley moved to the back door of the car and opened it for Isobel. Before she could get in, Alexine separated herself from Herbert and, squalling, rushed toward her mother. Isobel spread out her tiny arms and Alexine leaned down so they might encircle her neck. She stood, bent almost double in the effort to reach her mother's shoulder, and sobbed against it.

"It'll pass," Isobel murmured, patting her daughter somewhat distractedly. "It'll all pass."

"Let us ride home with you." Alexine's words rose and fell with her cries. "Herbie and I would like to come with you."

"Willie's takin' me t' the Fox," Isobel said.

Alexine's head snapped up. She stared at her mother.

"It's *Platinum Blonde*."

Alexine's silent stare continued.

"The new Harlow picture," Isobel added.

Herbert moved forward and took his wife's arm. "It's all right, Mother Claflin. I'll take care of her."

"Ya'll noo call me mother, Herbert Bonine, and ah'll noo remind ya again." Isobel's voice rose slightly.

"Yes, Isobel, yes," Herbert stammered. "Dear, come now." He jiggled Alexine's arm, trying to get her attention.

"Alex." Jamie took his sister's other arm and he and Herbert began propelling her toward another car. For an instant she was docile but then she whirled away from them and back toward her mother.

"But you've already seen it," she shrieked at Isobel's back, retreating into the car. "Twice!"

Jamie and Herbert got hold of Alexine again and bore her away, her wails trailing in the air behind her like a long black veil. Will climbed into the car beside his mother, turning immediately to stare through the window at the hill that held his father's body.

"We'll call later, Isobel." Ian reached his hand into the car and touched his mother's shoulder.

"Aye," she said. "Tell Riley t' start up before the others get here."

Ian closed the door and signaled Riley into the driver's seat. The motor began to purr. Isobel put her small gloved hand on Will's and leaned toward him.

"It's Loretta Young ah'm goin t' see this time," she said. "And we mighta

4

missed somethin', Willie. Ah wasna quite myself.''

He nodded, enclosing her hand in both of his. The car began to wind through the cemetery's narrow lanes. Will felt himself moving away from his father, leaving him behind. He had an impulse to throw himself from the slow-moving car, to run back up the hill where his father lay and cover the box with his warm body.

''Her marriage just broke up, ya know.'' Isobel's tone was confidential.

''Yes, I know,'' said Will. ''And I quote: 'I regret more than I can say that my marriage with Hal Rosson didn't work out.' ''

''Ah'm noo talkin' about Jeannie.'' She gave his arm a playful little slap. ''Loretta . . . Loretta and Grant Withers. Didna last a year.''

''That's rough,'' Will murmured. ''Really rough.''

As the car passed through the cemetery gates Will turned to look back but he saw only a sea of anonymous gravestones.

''Willie.'' He felt his mother's hand on his arm. ''He'll noo find the Fox from

5

here. Would ya tell im the way?''

When Isobel Claflin was Isobel McShane, a young girl growing up in Glasgow, she had a single dream: to quit school. When that came true and she went to board with an aunt to sew finery for gentler women than any she knew, her only dream was to secure a glance from Arthur Greenlees, a young man who worked at the bank where she deposited her pennies. But the day she laid eyes on Robert Claflin, she stopped banking altogether — keeping her pennies in a sock beneath her mattress — and dreamed of becoming of his wife. That was accomplished on June 25, 1899, her seventeenth birthday.

He was four years older than Isobel, fifteen inches higher off the ground and almost as beautiful, with coal-black eyes and curly hair that matched them exactly. He was six feet tall, moved with an easy grace and, as his sister Bess used to boast, every one of his 180 pounds was "hard." Isobel's eyes were a brilliant blue, her hair the same color as Robert's. When they

6

stood together, the top of her head falling just below his shoulder, they presented a truly splendid picture.

Bess alone, it seemed, was immune to their radiance. They'd been married only a week when she began haunting their flat each day before supper.

"He'll noo eat it," she'd say to Isobel, gesturing toward a pot on the fire, screwing her face into wrinkles of distaste. "Bert doesna fancy a thin soup."

At first Isobel remained silent and occasionally even took one of Bess's suggestions. After a few months of feeding Robert to his evident satisfaction, however, she began to fight back.

"It's veal he loves the best," Bess would say.

"Kidney," Isobel would whisper.

"What's that?"

"Ah said kidney."

"Veal's the favorite . . . no question there."

"Kidney," Isobel would whisper again.

She seldom had the last word but she became a bit more voluble with each encounter. Six months into her marriage, she and Bess were hollering at each other by teatime everyday. Nine months after her wedding day she was begging Robert to keep his sister away. On their first anniversary, Isobel threatened to leave him if he didn't arrange for them to leave the country.

He promised he would take her to America within five years. Not soon enough, she said. Then three, he said — he'd have her standing on American soil within three years. She agreed, on one condition: Bess must never be allowed to visit them. The day Isobel left Scotland she wanted to know she would never have to see the woman again. Robert promised.

In the autumn of 1902 he journeyed to America ahead of his family, going first to Baltimore where he learned the trade of iron-molding in the foundry of an old family friend, and then to Philadelphia where he found a house for his family and employment in a shipyard.

"Bessie'll noo come round if ah'm gone," he'd assured Isobel before leaving.

But, just in case she did, Robert arranged for Payton McDonald, his very good friend, to come and share the supper hour each night with Isobel and James Robert, whom she'd called Jamie from the moment of his birth two years earlier; Alexine, a new infant; and the unknown, unnamed child in Isobel's womb.

Bess stayed away for nearly a week. When she stopped in one night and found Payton there, however, she resumed her regular visits. Even a letter from Robert, which Isobel solicited, explaining that he'd requested Payton's presence at the flat, couldn't convince Bess that Isobel and Payton weren't joined in some dark purpose. She never voiced any specific suspicions but was given to decidedly ominous, although vague, mutterings.

"There's no eye like an open one," she'd say, apropos of nothing at all. Or: "Canna hurt t' look about," her eyes flashing furtively from Isobel to Payton and back again. Or: "Ah've nothin' t' hide . . . not me."

Isobel, who could tolerate Bess now that the end was in sight, changed her tactics. She no longer struggled against her, no longer raised he voice. Instead, she poured graciousness over her sister-in-law like warm syrup on a bread pudding. It made Bess frenzied.

"Ya're so right, Bessie dear," Isobel would say.

"What's that?" Bess would croak.

"About the eyes."

"What about em then? What's right about em?"

"T' keep em open. It canna hurt."

"What eyes're those?"

"Ya're so right, Bessie. That's no mean head ya're wearin'."

But when Isobel boarded the ship for America in the spring of 1903, looking toward the knot of family and friends gathered on the dock to see her off, it was Bess's face that made her cry. And once she'd started she couldn't stop. She cried for one solid week of the voyage. She cried in the cabin, which she, Jamie and Alexine shared with another woman and her two young children. She cried on deck where she went to escape their cramped quarters. She cried during meals and was unable to eat more than a few bites at any sitting. She cried at night, squeezed between her two children in a narrow bunk. And as her tears flowed, her milk dried up and Alexine began to cry along with her. When Isobel stopped crying at the end of a week, her milk did not return and Alexine bawled the rest of the way across the Atlantic Ocean. By the time Isobel was reunited with Robert, she resented him terribly for what she'd had to endure.

Isobel gave birth to a son that summer and named him Ian Angus in an acute nostalgic seizure that enraged Robert.

"Ah brought ya where ya wanted t' be and now ya're lookin' back," he accused her.

"It's only a name," she protested.

"It's no name a'tall," he thundered. "It's a sign."

"Jamie and Alexine were your names," she pointed out.

"James and Alex," he roared. "A sign."

"What kind a sign?" she asked.

"That ya're noo happy here."

"But ah am, Bertie. Ah swear it. It's just that the trip was so rough."

"The trip's over, fer God's sake! Ya

live here now.''

But she didn't quite and Robert knew it. When she first arrived the rigors of the journey clung to her like a garment she wouldn't let him strip away. After Ian's birth she couldn't bear to be touched at all for several months. Then she began slowly to accept Robert's caresses but only when they were playful and light. If she felt any true ardor in them, she turned quickly away.

Robert was patient.

''Ah understand, Issie,'' he crooned to her. ''It'll take some time.''

While he waited, Robert took occasionally to treating the pain of rejection with alcohol. During his spells, as Isobel referred to them, she drifted even further away.

''Ah liked ya better in Scotland,'' she'd say to him.

''Ya didna push me away in Scotland either,'' he'd reply.

''There was no need, Bertie. Ya werena reeky.''

It took nearly five years, an abstinence pledge, a move to Detroit where Robert

12

became a day-shift foreman of an iron foundry and able to afford a house with a somewhat private master bedroom, and lengthy and delicate negotiations before the carnal aspect of the Claflins' marriage was restored.

The result was Will, born March 4, 1909, the day William Howard Taft was inaugurated as President of the United States. Isobel compromised on this one: William for the President and Dudley for the town in England where her great-grandfather had been born.

JUNE 13, 1932

Caught by the eye of Ian's camera in a spill of early morning sunlight, Isobel and Will stood out sharply against the glossy black Graham-Paige parked at the curb.

The brim of her high-crowned cloche cast a band of shadow across the frameless spectacles resting on her nose, the rouged circlets on her cheeks. Her mouth, fully lit, was solemn. The pale blue, densely patterned dress she wore fell to just above the ankle; its sleeves came down to her wrists, meeting there with gloves that matched the polka dots in her dress. Her hands were always covered, a vanity begun when she was a quite young woman and mistook a freckle for an age spot. Her gloved fingers were overlaid with rings; her neck was draped in ropes of beads and metal; her bosom glittered with brooches; her wrists were ringed with bracelets. A long fox fur ran across her shoulders, its head resting on one side of her body near the waist, and its tail trailing down the other to her hip. Her instep puffed out slightly around the edge of her snug black shoes whose three-inch heels brought her close to five feet.

Will's jaunty pose — one foot on the running board, one elbow cocked into an open window, smile flickering at one corner of his mouth — contradicted the hesitation in his eyes. The same bright blue as his mother's, they were clearly visible despite an unruly spiral of brown hair meandering onto his forehead. His lean frame was covered in layers he could peel off, or not, according to the weather: white shirt and chocolate brown tie, beige crew-neck sweater, dark flannel jacket. The stockings running from his short boots to his cream colored knickers were the same brown as his tie. He clasped tan leather driving gloves and a soft felt hat in the hand farthest from the car.

"Just one more," Ian called from behind the camera.

Isobel and Will remained frozen.

"Perfect." Ian slipped the camera strap over his shoulder and started toward them. "Well, I guess that's it. You'd better get started now. You've got a big day ahead."

Isobel, already settled in the passenger seat, brushed her gloved fingers against Ian's cheek as he bent down to say goodbye. Crossing to the driver's side, he admonished Will to drive carefully.

"You're carrying precious cargo, you know."

The motor's ignition filled the silence left by Will's wordless nod.

"And don't forget that."

Will pushed down on the gas, causing the engine to roar.

"Okay, okay," Ian laughed. "Get going

. . . enjoy yourselves."

He stepped aside as the car glided away from the curb. Waving, watching the automobile move down the street, Ian thought he may have seen Isobel's hand through the rear window, rising in a small royal wave. He was certain, however, despite the light dappled by the canopy of trees, that neither Isobel nor Will looked back.

Diary

BY

WILLIAM D. CLAFLIN

Concerning the westward journey of one Mrs. Isobel Claflin and her son and their sojourn in and around Hollywood in this summer of 1932.

MONDAY, JUNE 13

The Good Ship Mary (named for Miss Pickford, who else?) set sail at eight o'clock sharp this A.M. in quest of adventure with Captain Isobel in the navigator's seat and yours truly at the helm. Ian was the last loved (?) one to bid us adieu. Jamie, Alex, and Horrible Herbie (or Beastly Bonine — you can take your pick) said their cheerios last night.

We struck our course southwest through Indiana, stopping for lunch on the other side of Elkhart. The Captain insisted on a light repast: melba toast and Coke. Steak 'N' Spuds for our hero to keep up his energy for driving. And did I need it? I'll say. Four hundred fifty-nine miles to the Hotel Abraham Lincoln in Springfield, Illinois.

This was Abe's (Mr. Lincoln to youse guys) home for many years and the good folk hereabouts ain't about to let you forget it. They've got his puss plastered everywhere: on the walls, the upholstery, the stationery, the dishes. When Isobel picked a bite of chicken off her plate, she jumped. Said she felt she was being watched and promptly put the morsel back on Abe's eyes.

After dinner for a short stroll, then to postcards, then to bed. Am I lucky?

———————————

Isobel's tolerance for the rigors and banalities of life as a struggling young wife and mother, never high, plunged lower than ever upon Will's arrival. Away from the tasks of infant care for several years, she found them even more unpleasant and demanding than she'd remembered. And, as she had before when she'd suffered from reality, she blamed Robert, her censure no less potent for being unconscious. She'd designated him her protector. When she felt violated, it was his failure. To reprimand him, she withdrew. To assuage his agony, he drank again. And the cycle they had arrested was animated once more.

Isobel, reluctant herself to accept Robert's amorous advances, developed a terror that he might direct them elsewhere. She feared especially, though inexplicably, Miss Margaret Goodenow, a maiden lady at the church.

"Ah see she fancies ya," she'd hiss when Miss Goodenow passed by their pew, nodding. "She's noo leerin' at *me*. Ah'm sure a that."

"That was no leer, Is," Robert

whispered. "The woman's smilin', fer God's sake."

"It's a bum name fer that viper. *Good*-enow indeed!"

"What's she done?" Robert asked.

"Ah'm noo as innocent as ya are, Bertie Claflin. Ah know what's in er head."

"What is it, then? Tell me."

"She canna fool me. Ah dinna know why she tries."

Isobel's storms of jealousy and Robert's "spells" looked quite different — hers were volcanic, his deathlike, still — but the children treated them exactly alike. Jamie detached himself, vanishing into his room with a book. Alexine fussed over the distressed party, offering cold cloths and warm potions. Ian asked incessant, and unanswerable, questions. Will exhibited quiet bewilderment.

One Sunday evening in 1911, after a spell of his that lasted several days, and a rage of hers that consumed the better part of an afternoon, Robert took Isobel, as a peace offering, to see the photoplay of *Cinderella*. She was transfixed.

"Bertie," she said afterward, when she

finally found her voice, "ah think they're really in love."

"Aye, Is. It's a love story, after all."

"Ah mean the players."

"Dinna ferget it's make-believe," Robert teased. "Just pictures."

"Ah think they're in love, Bertie," she repeated. "Ah really do."

JUNE 14, 1932

"Ah'd noo put the dump right on the road," Isobel remarked as clusters of refuse began appearing along the edge of the highway leading out of Springfield.

Forced to stop at an intersection, Will looked to his right. Amidst the pieces of old cars, the packing cases, the wooden crates, he saw human movement. While he continued staring the refuse redefined itself and he realized he was peering at people in their homes, a series of shelters fashioned from debris.

"It must be a Hooverville." Will's voice was quiet with astonishment.

"What'd ya say, Willie?" Isobel stared straight ahead.

"The dump . . . people are living in there."

"Are ya daft?" She glanced through her side window. "It's rubbish."

"Don't you see the people?"

"There're a few pickin' about t' see if there's aught they can use. Times aren't as good as they were, ya know."

A horn sounding behind Will caused him to look back at the road and drive on. They traveled the next few miles in silence, except for soft snatches of "Tiger Rag," which Isobel hummed to herself.

"It's hard to believe they really exist," said Will, looking now at the golden wheat fields streaming by on either side of the road.

"What's that, Willie?"

"The Hoovervilles. I'd heard of them but I never thought they'd be like that."

"No man, woman or child is livin' in that dump, Willie Claflin. Ah can tell ya that. If they were, d'ya suppose the President'd put is name on em?"

21

TUESDAY, JUNE 14

We hoped to have a look-see at Abe's old home but being as how they don't even open the doors until noon, we nixed it and set off across the mighty Mrs. Ippi. In Hannibal we toured the home of Mrs. Clemens' boy Sammy, lunched, postcarded and plunged back into the corn.

The Cap's already settled on her favorite Burma-Shave: "The 50¢ Jar / So Large / By Heck / Even the Scotch / Now Shave the Neck."

Our roost this eve is St. Joseph, Mo.'s, Hotel Robidoux. Its one claim to fame, as far as we can see, is that Jesse James slept here and methinks even that may be bunk. Even if it ain't, we give the Robidoux one loud raspberry.

Spring and summer Sunday outings were a custom in the Claflin family when Will was a child. And they unfolded, it seemed to him, with an inexorable precision.

When she returned from church, Isobel dressed Will in his sailor suit — middy blouse, short trousers, stockings to the knee — and combed out his long fair hair. Then picnic lunch and family were settled into the carriage that Robert drove into the countryside. Once underway, he and Isobel discussed the picture they'd seen the night before.

"It was a mite brutish, Bertie," said Isobel.

"Scared ya, did it?" Robert asked.

"What was it?" Alexine asked from the back seat where the four young Claflins were squeezed together.

"*The Spoilers,* lassie. About the gold rush in Alaska and a wee bit rough fer yer mum."

"Were you scared?" Will asked his mother.

"No, laddie," said Isobel.

"Why is it then . . ." Robert glanced over his shoulder and gave his children an enormous wink . . . "why is it ya were squeezin' my arm till the blood stopped runnin'?"

"Why were you scared, Mother?"

Alexine asked.

"They were tearin' and clawin' at each other." Isobel shuddered. "A terrible fight. Ah think they were Scots too."

"Only the characters, Is. It's only a story."

"Glennister and MacDonald," said Isobel. "Ah dinna know what else they'd be."

"Ya canna be fooled by a name," said Robert. "Look at Wilson."

"The poor man . . . buryin' is wife."

"She'd noo be buried if she hadna married im."

"You rhymed, Papa . . . buried and married." Alexine's chiming in from the back seat did not deter her parents from their running argument about President Wilson.

"He didna kill er, Bert," Isobel pointed out.

"A livin' death's what it would be with that man. The poor woman's better off in the ground."

"And he's left behind t' grieve."

"He'd noo grieve at is own mother's grave. The man's ice . . . frozen solid."

"Poor thing," Isobel murmured.

"So James," said Robert, moving with perfect cadence into the next passage of their Sunday symphony, "now that we're on our way are ya glad ya decided t' come along?"

"I didn't exactly decide," said Jamie.

"Dinna pick at the words, lad. Tell yer mother ya're glad ya decided t' join us."

"Ah dinna care, Bertie," said Isobel.

"Speak up, lad. Dinna ya like t' be out in the air?"

"I have nothing against the air, Father. If I'd stayed home to finish my reading I would have done it outside."

"Ya'll get sick always shut in yer room with a book, never gettin' any sunlight or breathin' anything fresh."

"I went swimming yesterday," Jamie said.

"It's noo healthy t' be starin' at a page every minute. Yer limbs'll wither up."

"Let im be, Bertie," Isobel said.

"Tell yer mother ya're glad ya decided t' join us."

"Yes, Mother," Jamie said.

When they arrived at their picnic spot,

Robert issued instructions before anyone left the carriage.

"James, ya'll bring the lunch and blankets. Alex, gather some flowers fer yer mother. Ian, help yer mother doon and carry er umbrella. And Willie, ya'll get a ride. Hop on now."

As his brothers and sister climbed out one side, Will vaulted onto his father's shoulders from the other, one part of the routine he relished.

After they'd eaten and the luncheon things were cleared away, Robert stretched out, his head in Isobel's lap, her parasol shielding both their faces from the sun. He dozed. She watched him and the children as they played in the tall grasses of the surrounding field.

Sometimes they huddled together, at some distance from their parents, and Jamie told stories. But if he'd managed to smuggle along a contraband book, he went off by himself and lay down in the grasses to read. Alexine and Ian, Will bobbing between them, scouted for new flowers or edible berries or colorful rocks or they sat braiding the long grasses together, forming bracelets, baskets, or what Alexine referred to as "designs." These she took home to hang on her bedroom walls where they grew rather forlorn as they dried and drained of color.

If Ian decided they were going too far afield for Will to come along, Jamie kept Will with him. While Jamie read, Will made a great effort to lie still beside him, squeezing his eyes until the sunlight formed kaleidoscopic bursts of color beneath his closed eyelids.

When Robert awakened, he summoned his children back to the blanket. Sometimes he sang — Alexine always requested "Annie Laurie" but Isobel often vetoed it because it made her cry. Sometimes he told stories — Ian's favorite involved Bess, and Isobel was even more adamant about keeping it to a minimum. But no matter what transpired, it always led to a dispute between Robert and Jamie. And the dispute invariably ended with Robert thundering at his eldest son:

"Well, ya've certainly cast a cloud over this day, thank ya very much! Gather up the things. We're goin' home."

On the way home, while Robert muttered darkly and took an occasional verbal swipe at Jamie, Isobel dozed. Jamie rode in the corner of the back seat directly behind his father. If he had a book with him, he took it out and read. This gave Alexine and Ian uncontrollable giggles, causing their father to begin fuming at them as well. And in the far right corner of the back seat, Will felt the wind play over his face, tossing about his father's words, and wondered why things always turned out the same.

JUNE 15, 1932

Arising in St. Joseph, Isobel and Will followed what had very quickly become their morning routine. When the wake-up call sounded she slid out of bed and into the lavatory to begin her toilette. Will took the call, ordering the porter to their room in half an hour. By the time Isobel emerged, Will was dressed to the waist, ready to shave. While he did that, Isobel dressed, closed up her bags and took down from the mirror two handkerchiefs she'd washed the night before and hung there to dry. She tucked one in her glove-top and one in her purse. They were the only two hankies she'd brought, a bit of frugality she explained by saying: "Ah've noo fergot m' roots."

While she descended to the lobby with the porter and their bags, Will finished dressing, meeting up with her at the ubiquitous lobby scale where she liked to begin her day. A penny always brought her a reading of eighty-four pounds, or six stone, as she preferred to call it, and a fortune in which she put great store. Today's read: "You are determined to see things your own way."

For breakfast she had one piece of dry toast brushed with a whisper of cinnamon and sugar. As particular about this as she was about most edibles, she explained it patiently to each waiter.

"The toast should be medium, not too dark. Dinna butter it. Put sugar and cinnamon in a wee bowl, mix it and sprinkle it on the toast. Move it about like so." Isobel made a circular motion on the table with her gloved hand. "Then pick it up and shake it off."

"Shake off the cinnamon?" the waiter asked.

"Aye," she reassured him. "What's left is just right."

Will's instructions were slightly less mysterious but just as precise. He liked one slice of Canadian bacon "very thin and fried until it begins to pucker along the edge," two warm blueberry muffins with six pats of soft butter and a large glass of freshly squeezed orange juice poured over ice. Isobel had half a cup of tea, the only time she drank anything other than Coca-Cola.

When Will packed the car in the morning, the first thing he checked was the Coke supply, never setting off with less than six full bottles. Isobel wasn't sure their stopping places in the countryside could be trusted to have it on hand.

"Even if they had it, Willie," she observed, "they could always run out."

WEDNESDAY, JUNE 15

The Robidoux could learn a thing or two from Hotel Stamey, out here in the sticks of Kansas (Hutchinson, to be exact). Our room is big enough to hold a dance at a dollar a couple, pay the orchestra and still show a good profit. Swanky it ain't but plenty comfy. And after 382 miles, most of them on lou-say roads, that's all Capt. Isobel and your scrivener ask.

We stopped this afternoon in Junction City, "the geographical center of the U.S.A.," postcarded and Coked at a local jernt just about exactly 1,100 miles away from hearth and home. And if the Captain doesn't send winging over those miles some of the postcards she scoops up everywhere we go, we'll need a trailer to carry them. However, as she pointed out to me, if she sends 'em, she won't have 'em. Could I argue with that? No, siree.

When Will was six his mother gave birth to her fourth son and insisted he be named Francis X. after Mr. Bushman.

31

From the moment she'd first glimpsed him in *The Magic Wand,* Isobel had been smitten.

"He was named Most Handsome Man in a contest," she told Will. "Ah've never seen anyone more beautiful."

She was also enamored of the love she sensed between Mr. Bushman and his leading lady, Beverly Bayne. And when they got married she was positively triumphant. "Ah told ya, Bertie! Ah knew it. Ah knew they were really in love."

"It's a lassie's name," Robert protested, looking down at the tiny new boy lying beside his mother.

"Mr. Bushman's no lass." Isobel was indignant. "And what's Alex then? What kind a lassie's name is that?"

"It's noo the same," said Robert. "My father was Alex."

"And dinna ya call im Frank," said Isobel.

"Aye," said Robert and as long as Isobel was within hearing range he complied. When she was not, he called his youngest son Frankie.

"Still," he confided to Alexine, "it

coulda been worse. She coulda settled on Woodrow."

Mr. Bushman was not the only luminary in Isobel's firmament. In 1915, the year of Francis X.'s birth, she had also an extravagant enthusiasm for "Little Mary," as did most American movie-goers. Her single dark thought about America's Sweetheart, as Miss Pickford was so aptly called, concerned Mary's mother, a Mrs. Charlotte Smith.

"Ah think Mary works too hard," Isobel said. "And it's the mother that pushes, ya know. She wants enough for Lottie and Jack and herself . . . all from the sweat a Mary's brow."

Isobel was delighted when Mary that year re-signed her contract for more than $100,000, but her doubts about Mrs. Smith were unallayed.

"Ah hope that'll satisfy er," she she muttered, "but ah doubt it."

She adored "wee Mabel" Normand, the Gish girls, Clara Kimball Young, Norma Talmadge and William S. Hart. The latter, she was always quick to note, had been "on the stage."

"As a young lad he was doin' the Bard, ya know," she'd say.

She had been very taken with Blanche Sweet when, in *The Lonedale Operator,* she held an entire gang of payroll bandits at bay until help arrived. But since hearing Blanche was often difficult on the set, she'd gone off her a bit.

She thought Jamie bore a marked resemblance to Wallace Reid and that Pearl White was the most courageous human being alive. Devotion to her theater favorites, Gaby Deslys and Elsie Janis, only strengthened when they moved onto film and she had an absolute mania for anything to do with the Barrymores. "Dear Jack" was her special favorite ("We were born in the same year") but Ethel and Lionel had no reason to feel slighted.

Isobel's aversions were as distinct and as passionate as her admirations although she wasted little breath on them. She performed her dismissals with pith and dispatch. Annette Kellerman, swimming champion turned motion picture performer: "Ah hate the muscle." Earle

Williams, *Motion Picture Magazine*'s 1914 popularity contest winner: "looks like a raccoon." Florence Lawrence, first of the photoplay's stars: "coarse around the nose." Owen Moore, Little Mary's husband and frequent player opposite her: "flat as an old scone." Theda Bara, America's first vamp: "the dregs."

Francis X.'s arrival coincided with Will's beginning school, a combination of events that caused Isobel to begin to allow Will's passage from baby to boyhood. She packed away his sailor suit, shortened his hair and hoped he would like school more than she had. Since Jamie was downright bookish, Alexine a very good student and Ian a popular and conscientious pupil, she felt this was certainly possible. Her hope was in vain. Will hated school from the moment he entered.

Robert was now managing the foundry for owner Frederick Blackwell, who suffered from what Isobel insisted on calling "slack face."

"It's a muscular weakness, Is," Robert corrected her every time.

"Ah only know how he looks, Bertie,"

she always said.

The salary Blackwell paid was substantial enough to provide a nursemaid for Francis X., leaving Isobel free during the day to go about as she pleased. On Will's seventh birthday she kept him out of school and took him with her to the movies. They saw *Joan the Woman,* with Geraldine Farrar, Wallace Reid and Hobart Bosworth, at the Capitol Theatre.

As the lights dimmed, Will's excitement was acute. But the moment the picture began he forgot his excitement and everything else. The world on the screen absorbed him completely, a world of thousands of people in strange and wonderful costumes. They fought with swords and blew on elongated horns and swirled enormous banners and it was absolutely thrilling. Isobel whispered to Will when the writing came on the screen. Sometimes he heard her over the piano, but even when he couldn't it didn't seem to matter.

That evening, at his birthday celebration, Will jabbered nonstop about what he'd seen.

"Ah wish ya showed as much gusto fer yer schoolin'," Robert finally remarked, causing Will to fall silent.

"It's the lad's birthday, Bertie."

"Ah know what day it is," he grumbled.

"Pop's just tired of little Willie chatterbox," said Ian.

"Ah dinna need an interpreter," said Robert.

Ian was stung. "Well, he hasn't stopped talking since he came home."

"Ah'll speak fer m'self, thank ya very much," Robert bellowed. "It's twaddle ah'm tired a hearin' . . . twaddle."

"Leave yer father alone," Isobel said to no one in particular. "Ya'll drive im t' a spell."

"Tell about Geraldine Farrar, Mother," Alexine urged. "You like her, Papa. Tell about when she went to Hollywood."

"Ah dinna care about the Farrar woman," Robert began, his voice rising, "nor about spells, nor about any a the rest a the twaddle ya may dream up. Ah'm goin' back t' the foundry. James, make sure ya stoke the furnace. Ian, ya'll

37

come with me.''

Robert shoved his napkin through its ring and slammed it onto the table as he got up. Ian followed directly behind him. Jamie rose a moment later and left the room. Alexine, hesitating a few beats, finally ran out after her father, wailing and calling to him. Will felt sick to his stomach.

''Geraldine was singin' with the opera when Mr. Lasky decided t' bring er out t' Hollywood.'' Isobel cut a piece of cake and handed it to Will. ''Fer appearin' in just three pictures, he paid er $20,000 . . . a great deal a money, Willie.''

Will nodded and bit into his cake.

''And it wasna only the money,'' Isobel continued. ''He gave er a mansion t' live in, servants t' wait on er hand and foot, and a motorcar t' go about in.''

''Did he give her a driver too?'' Will asked.

''A driver too,'' said Isobel. ''And fer the journey from New York t' Hollywood he hired a private railroad car fer just er t' ride in. She had the whole car all t' erself.''

"How did she get meals if she was all by herself?" Will asked.

"Servants could come in t' bring er things but they'd noo ride in the car with er . . . unless she asked, a course. And Willie . . ." Isobel paused while she slid her chair closer to Will's. "The whole time she was in town, Mr. Lasky bought er groceries, too."

Will finished his cake and he and Isobel split another piece, discussing *Joan the Woman* as they ate. Then it was time for Will to go to bed.

"Give us a kiss, Willie," said Isobel.

Will wrapped his arms around his mother's neck, pursed his small lips and placed a soft kiss on her mouth.

"Thank you for taking me," he said. "It was the best birthday I ever had."

THURSDAY, JUNE 16

The G.S. Mary covered 440 miles today — with only one flat tire, this while traveling through a glass field near Ulysses, Kan. Didn't know they grew the stuff out here! Our hero managed, however, to refrain from putting the jack handle through the windshield even though his nerves were a mite frayed by the end of the hour it took to change the blankety-blank thing.

The day was not all black, I hasten to add. Whilst cooling our heels at a R.R. crossing, Isobel was very impressed with an exercise in good old American ingenuity. While the train was stopped, and the R.R. gents were occupied, such activity you never saw on the open coal cars! Out of nowhere came a bunch of fellas who scrambled up the sides of the cars like Doug scaling a castle wall and started pitching the stuff onto the ground. And down below, picking it up as fast as it landed, were the gals and kiddies. The Captain allowed as how they were smart to eliminate the delivery man cuz he's always late anyhow. We say it's one slick system. Orchids for the guys what thought it up and onions for the hard-boiled so-and-sos who came along and told them to scram.

Tonight we rest at The Toltec, Trinidad, Colo., not a bad spot for a one-night stand. I swear I felt the West begin as we entered Colorado and that put me in mind, of course, of Arthur Chapman's ode, a piece of which I quote here:

> Out where the handclasp's a
>   little stronger,
> Out where the smile dwells a
>   little longer,
> That's where the West begins.
> Out where the sun is a little
>   brighter,
> Where the snows that fall are a
>   trifle whiter,
> Where the bonds of home are a
>   wee bit tighter,
> That's where the West begins.

Californy, here we come!

In the spring of 1917 Robert was summoned to Frederick Blackwell's sickbed to solicit his opinion of Dylan Doyle, Blackwell's son-in-law.

"Well . . . he's no foundryman," said Robert.

"That's right, Bert," Blackwell said. "That's why I need you in on this. I'm not going to get any better." He lifted a limp hand and gestured toward his drooping face.

"Aw rubbish, Freddie. Ya'll come around and . . ."

"Never mind that. I don't need to hear that. What I need is to know you'll keep this place going after I'm gone. It's for the sake of Janie and the kids, not for any love of Doyle. I want my girl's future assured."

"Ah understand," said Robert.

"Doyle's so windy and so full of himself he'd never keep steady employment. Who'd have him?"

"Ah understand, Freddie . . . but m' capital's a wee bit short at the moment . . ."

"Hang your capital, Bert. All I want from you is a promise, a promise that you'll keep Doyle as half-owner as long as my daughter insists on keeping him as her husband."

"Ya've got m' promise but ah wouldna feel right makin' no investment a'tall,'' Robert said.

''Your word's more valuable to me than gold brick. I don't need money. I need security for my Janie.'' Blackwell's voice cracked and a tear crept out from under one of his languid lids.

''Ya've got it, Freddie. Ya've got m' word.'' Robert clasped both his hands around one of Blackwell's.

''As far as Doyle knows it's a straight business deal,'' said Blackwell. ''You bought in for half and I leave my share to him. I've drawn up two sets of papers, but he'll only see one.''

''He'll see one set a papers and none a m' money.''

''I've taken care of that, Bert. He'll never know it's anything but a straight sale.''

Robert signed the papers at Blackwell's bedside. A week later the United States entered the war and business boomed. Two weeks later Blackwell was dead.

JUNE 17, 1932

As Will and Isobel drove into New Mexico, the sun was relentless. No cloud crossed it and threw even a moment's shadow in their path. An occasional arid breeze caused puffs of dust to curl up from the dry roadbed but these only made the day seem hotter. Isobel finished four full bottles of Coke before noon.

But despite the heat she insisted they stop when a patch of bright yellow flowers sprang up from the parched land. Her fondness for flowers transcended almost anything.

"Pour me another Coke, Willie," she said, alighting from the Graham-Paige and opening her parasol. Wobbling slightly whenever her very high heels slid into the cracked ground, she picked her way toward the golden tract. Once there, she bent over and gathered several blooms. Watching her return, blurry in the heat-shimmered air, she became to Will a young girl with an armful of heather crossing some distant moor, softened by its mists.

"Ah dinna know the name a these," she said, handing him the bouquet as she climbed back into the car, "but ah've got em on a card. Would ya hand me last night's bundle, Willie?"

While she looked through a batch of postcards, she sipped her Coke and hummed softly, swinging slightly her legs, which were demurely crossed and dangling just short of the floorboards.

"Ah've two a em," she said finally. "It's wild buckwheat, Willie. Ah'll send one to Alexine."

Will stood beside the passenger door, holding Isobel's parasol, the flowers and the Coca-Cola. She reached into her purse and pulled out a small gold pen covered with brightly colored stones.

"I've just picked some of these," she wrote. "Our waitress yesterday looked just like Janet Gaynor. Have you ever thought of wearing your hair like that? The way it was in *Seventh Heaven*."

FRIDAY, JUNE 17

Isobel's fortune this A.M.: "Don't let minor setbacks deter you. There's a reward ahead."

She figgers the reward is this jernt *(only* Albequerque's finest, The Franciscan) and the fact that *Arrowsmith* is playing down the block and our first mail in five days, with news from Alex that she and Shmerbie are infanticipating. Isobel prays the child will favor Alex. Don't we all!

Lots of our favorites in *Arrowsmith:* Charlie MacArthur's gal Helen (Miss Hayes to you mugs), Connie Bennett's dad Dick, Ronnie Colman (if he were any smoother he'd slide right off the screen), and that bonny lassie Myrna Loy. I could go on but I am summoned to the arms of Morpheus. And besides that, I'm darned sleepy. So there!

Roughly sixty hours from now (give or take a few for the time change and the caprices of life on the open road) we'll be laying our heads to rest in HOLLYWOOD! Who says I'm not lucky?

Jamie enlisted. Will, the nursemaid and Francis X. were the only ones in the house when he came home that afternoon. Isobel was at the new neighborhood theater, which was running a Chaplin film. She'd promised, if Will brought home good reports from school this week, that she would take him with her Saturday evening.

Jamie told Will his news and extracted an oath of secrecy from him.

"I'm sure there'll be a big fuss," Jamie said, "so I'm going to wait to tell them until the night before I leave."

"Will you fight the Kaiser?" Will asked.

"Well, not directly, Willie. I won't fight anyone for a while. First I'll go down south and they'll teach me how to become a soldier."

"What d'ya know about soldierin'?" Robert roared when Jamie made his announcement. "Ya can't learn how t' fight from a book, ya know."

"I don't know anything yet but I'll learn," said Jamie.

"Well, ah've never been able to teach ya anythin' . . . not one bloody thing."

"Watch yer tongue, Bertie," Isobel said. "Aren't ya a wee bit young, Jamie?"

"A course he is, fer God's sake . . . why he's naught but a weanie compared t' the men who'll be fightin'. Did ya lie t' em, James? What sort a cock-n-bull story did ya trump up?"

"What difference does it make?" said Jamie. "I'm going and that's final."

"Ya didna fib did ya, Jamie?" Isobel asked.

"Final, is it?" Robert bellowed. "We'll see about that!"

"There's nothing you can do, Pop. You can't lock me up."

"He's accusin' me a tryin' t' imprison m' own son!" Robert's face reddened and his neck began to swell above the sharp edge of his collar.

"That's exactly what you've done to me all my life." Suddenly Jamie was hollering back. "Always wanting me to be something I'm not, always dissatisfied with everything I do. Why do you think I want to get out of here?"

"Jamie," said Isobel, "ah'd noo talk t' yer father that way. It's a brash lad that'll . . ."

"It's not brash, Mother." Jamie's voice softened as he addressed her. "It's the truth."

"Is it *me* yer tryin' t' get away from then?" Robert was genuinely puzzled and hurt.

"That's part of it," said Jamie.

"Oh God, James." Robert lowered his head, shaking it slowly back and forth. Then he raised it and looked directly at his son. "Ah know ah'm gruff, laddie . . . and maybe ah've been a wee bit hard on ya. But ah've loved ya. Ah swear it. And ah've counted on ya too. Who d'ya suppose ah've counted on t' help me out at the foundry? Not Dylan bloody Doyle, ah'll tell ya that. He's more hindrance than help. Ah'd as soon have yer mother doon there."

"Ah'd noo be much help, Bertie," said Isobel. "And watch yer tongue."

"It's you ah've counted on," Robert repeated to Jamie.

"But I'm not interested in the

49

foundry, Pop."

"Ya're a bright lad, God knows. Ya could learn anythin' ya'd a mind to."

"But I'm not interested," said Jamie.

"And ya're *in-ter-es-ted* in bein' a soldier, ah suppose?" Robert's voice began to rise again.

"Well . . ." Jamie hesitated. "It's not that simple."

"Ya're *in-ter-es-ted* in learnin' how t' shoot a gun? Is that where yer *in-ter-est* lies? Is it? Ya're noo *in-ter-es-ted* in the foundry but ya're *in-ter-es-ted* in gettin' yerself killed?" Robert's shriek hung in the air as he brought both fists down on the table. "Well, if that's the truth ya're either dense or daft and ah've misjudged ya. Ah dinna know ya a'tall. Ya're a stranger t' me and ya can do what ya bloody well please."

Robert left the room, his passage through the house marked by the echoes of a series of slammed doors.

"Ya could change yer mind, Jamie." Isobel's voice held neither a question nor a plea.

"No, Mother, I couldn't," he said,

rising and then bending to place a kiss on top of her head. "I really couldn't."

Will was inconsolable when Jamie left early the next morning. He spent most of the day in his room, experiencing alternating bouts of abandoned sobbing and silent shaking with terrible chills. Alexine tried several times to comfort him. Although he submitted to her efforts, they didn't really help. He was certain he'd never see Jamie again.

That evening Isobel kept her promise and took Will to see *The Little Tramp*. Robert, Alexine and Ian came too. Riding to the theater, their presence only made Jamie's absence more apparent and Will wished they had stayed home. But as soon as he was seated in the theater and the lights went down, it didn't matter who was there — and who was not.

SATURDAY, JUNE 18, 1932

Our sixth day out and our longest and hardest. We kept spirits high by working on our very own hotsy-totsy rendition of "Ain't We Got Fun." When Hollywood hears us we'll probably be besieged with offers — I'm not saying what kind!

On account of the quantity and quality of towns in this here part of the U.S. of A. (I'm not just cracking wise when I say they'd make Podunk look like a metropolis), we lunched al fresco (that means outdoors, you louts) on cookies and Coke.

Arrived at the south rim of the Grand Canyon about 6 P.M. How can one describe what oughta be one of the seven wonders of the world? This numbskull can't, except to note the massiveness, the vivid coloring, the awesome quiet. A truly overwhelming sight and one never to be forgotten.

And if *it's* one of the seven wonders, we guess El Tovar, Fred Harvey's little hostelry a mere stone's throw from the Canyon rim, must be the eighth. The place fairly reeks with atmosphere and good taste. And besides that, it's terrifically comfy. Could we ask for more?

We didn't — but we got it anyway when we strolled Canyonward after our evening's repast: the most glorious sunset

I have ever seen. We felt they'd rolled it out especially for us and, believe me, a more appreciative audience they never had!

Perhaps it was because she had a son who was a soldier or perhaps, as Robert contended, it was because Mary Pickford was an Honorary Colonel in the army. Whatever the reason, Isobel was fervent in her support of the war effort. She adhered rigidly to meatless, wheatless and heatless days. She superintended the children's planting and tending of a Victory Garden. She went to the pictures only twice a week and set aside the money saved for Liberty Bonds.

Robert was pleased by her new interests and by the fact that she was home more often. He made a point of fussing over vegetables from the garden and abundantly praised her meatless and wheatless dishes even when the quality was questionable. She made one concoction the children referred to, out of her hearing, as Mother's Horrible Pudding.

She would never divulge its ingredients, but speculation was wide-ranging and always accompanied by fits of laughter. It included such possibilities as old dishwater, their father's favorite all-purpose liniment and Francis X.'s diapers. The only time they didn't giggle about it was when it was before them at the dinner table. Then they suffered in agonized silence while Robert applauded it.

"Mmmmmm," he would murmur approvingly, chewing the first bite.

"Very tasty," he would pronounce after he'd swallowed. "Very tasty indeed."

After every third or fourth mouthful he would reiterate this judgment and when he'd finished he'd say: "That was very savory, Is . . . a right gusty dish."

When Will protested once that he couldn't eat it because it tasted like spit up, Robert sent him to his room and, later, spanked him with the strap.

Isobel's support of the war also extended to the foundry and she endeavored to cultivate relations with Dylan Doyle and his wife Jane, telling Robert to invite them to Sunday dinner.

"Why would ya want me t' do that?" he asked, dumbfounded.

"Bertie," she said, rather severely, "he canna be that bad and ya'll noo profit by stayin' at odds with im."

"Ah suffer im all day long, six days a week," Robert whined. "Must ah have im Sundays too?"

"Aye," said Isobel and that was that because Robert couldn't bear to refuse her anything and because, secretly, he was delighted by her interest.

She took special pains with the meal and the table setting although Robert insisted all the effort would be wasted on Doyle.

"Ya could give im a bowl a potatoes t' eat on the back stoop and he'd noo know the difference. He's Irish, fer God's sake."

"There're fine Irishmen as well as the other, Bertie. Hold yer tongue."

When the Doyles arrived, the children were standing behind their parents in the entry hall. Glimpsing Dylan, Alexine whispered to Will: "He looks just like Mack Swain."

And he did bear a remarkable resemblance to their Keystone favorite although he was perhaps fifty pounds lighter. Still, he nearly filled the doorway. His eyes, face and body were completely round. He had two chins and his mustache rose from his upper lip until it encircled the base of his nose. His pitch-black eyebrows would have touched his hairline had it not receded a few inches. He had a gruff and very loud voice.

"Good afternoon, Mrs. Claflin . . . Robbie. May I present my wife, Jane. Course you know Rob, Janie. Say hello to the missus . . . and the kiddies. Well, well, well . . . isn't this nice? Why haven't we done this sooner, Robbie? I can't imagine. Isn't this nice, Janie?"

While he struggled to peel his overcoat from his bulk, his wife gave out small and random bursts of greetings and smiles. Robert helped her out of her coat and then led her to the parlor. Dylan settled himself in a chair he filled entirely, shifting his buttocks about in an effort to fit.

"Well, well, well . . . isn't this nice?

Fine-looking children you've got here, Robbie. Our two are with their grandmother today. They're fine-looking children, Mrs. Claflin. Yours, I mean. Course ours are too. Isn't that right, Janie? But aren't we missing one here? Besides the boy who's off to fight the Huns, I mean. You must be proud of him, Mrs. Claflin. Isn't there another one missing? Well, of course. The baby. I don't see the baby. Little Frankie."

"Francis X. is sleeping," said Isobel.

"Well, maybe he'll finish his nap before we go. Janie'd hate to miss seeing him, wouldn't you, Janie? I don't know why we haven't done this sooner, Robbie. Isn't this nice?"

Dylan Doyle did not stop talking until he sat down at the table and began to eat. Conversation at dinner fell into a distinct pattern. When Dylan had food in his mouth, everyone else stopped eating and talked very quickly among themselves. When he was between mouthfuls and talking, they ate very quickly so they'd be ready for his next silence. After dinner he held forth again in the parlor until they departed in midafternoon.

"Ah didna realize he was quite so chatty," said Isobel as Robert closed the door and turned to face his assembled family.

"Well, well, well . . ." Will lowered his voice and puffed out his cheeks. "Isn't this nice? I wish we'd done this sooner, Robbie."

"Dinna make fun a the man, Willie," said Isobel, trying to suppress a giggle.

"Ah, let im be, Is. Let im prick the bag a hot air."

"Ah dinna know how ya stand it, Bertie. Day after day."

"Ah've told ya," said Robert. "Ah don't."

And neither could Isobel, war or no war. She had Jane to tea a few times after that, along with her children, but she never again invited Dylan to the house. The Doyles invited the Claflins to dinner four times but each time Isobel fell ill as the day approached and she was forced to cancel. Eventually, the Doyles stopped asking.

SUNDAY, JUNE 19

For the record, let it be known that any heat encountered heretofore was kid stuff compared to today. Ronnie Colman, Neil Hamilton and Ralph Forbes could not have sweated (you should pardon the expression) any more in the Arabian sands of *Beau Geste* than we did in the furnace that was Arizona this day. Real burnoose country, this!

We crossed the California line at four, still so hot even at this hour that we couldn't give a hurrah — too parched. The instant we reached Needles, I ensconced the Captain in quarters at the Gateway Hotel, surrounded her with buckets of ice and frosty bottles of Coke and set out to inquire about the desert crossing that lies ahead. The natives, I am told, prefer four bells in the ayem as their starting time. We'll go 'em one better and set out at 3:30. Anyway, who could lie abed until four knowing that beyond the desert lies the town of a thousand fortunes, the town of a thousand dreams, the town the movies built:

HOLLYWOOD!!!

Isobel said she'd never be able to sleep tonight. I'll have to remember to ask her how come she kept her eyes closed all those hours. And your scrivener? Shut-eye eludes me as yet but who cares? Tomorrow Dreamland and to blazes with everything else!

During Will's ninth summer, Ian was running errands at the foundry and Will begged to be allowed to share these chores. Robert, however, decreed that Will be given household tasks to perform instead, promising that he would reconsider Will's request the following year. Will's tasks, often shared and always overseen by Alexine, frequently took all day and cut severely into his movie-going. When he pointed this out to Robert, Robert said that was exactly what he'd intended.

Will did manage though to see at least two pictures a week. Those featuring Wallace Reid were always his first choice because they assuaged somewhat his loneliness for Jamie. He agreed that his brother looked just like the movie star. Alexine also recognized the resemblance but couldn't bear to see it on the screen. When Will was going to a Wallace Reid picture, they parted company at the theater door.

"Why don't you come with me, Willie?" she'd say.

"I want to see this one."

"I'll even give you a choice. We could see *Headin' South* with Douglas Fairbanks or *Tarzan of the Apes* or *Mickey.*"

"This is the one I want to go to."

"Mabel Normand's in *Mickey.*"

"I want to see Wallace Reid."

"It's morbid," she'd say. "It's morbid and you're morbid."

"He's good," Will would protest.

"Well," Alexine huffed, "I'm going to see something that's fun! I'll pick you up after."

And she would flounce away, her retreating back giving off waves of rebuke. When they met afterward, Alexine always told in great detail the story of what she'd just seen but refused to listen to anything about Will's movie.

He had seen Wallace Reid in *Believe Me, Xantippe* and Alexine had gone to *Bound in Morocco,* starring Fairbanks, one day late in the summer. She was still going on about a scene in the teeming marketplace as they came up the front walk toward the house. Robert, looming in the doorway, stopped her abruptly.

"Here ya are then," he said, holding the door aside.

Both Alexine and Will froze near the bottom of the front steps. Robert was never at home in the daytime unless it was Sunday. The sight of him, they felt, was prelude to something awful.

"Come on," he said quietly. "Come on in the house."

He directed them into the parlor, a room belonging strictly to visitors. Ian was already seated there, making everything stranger still.

"Now lads and Alex," said Robert, after carefully closing the door, "yer wee brother's very sick. The doctor was just here and gave yer mother somethin' t' make er sleep. The bairn's got this influenza and ya'll all turn up with it if we're not careful. So ya'll noo be goin' upstairs a'tall. Ya'll be makin' yer quarters here till the lad's better and ah'll appreciate anythin' ya do t' make this easier on yer mum."

For the next few days the children's world was confined to the lower floor of the house. They were not allowed to go outdoors. They saw only their parents and only for very brief periods. They tried to guess at the meaning of the mysterious and muffled sounds that occurred overhead or beyond the closed parlor doors but the only ones they were sure of were the arrival and departure of the doctor, who came twice a day.

At the end of the fourth night, Will was awakened just as daylight began to slide in under the curtains, certain he'd heard a sound. But now, sitting up on the sofa, listening intently, only Alexine's and Ian's sleepy breathing was audible. Then, just as he was lowering his head, it came again. It came from above him, a long, sharp, mournful wail that ran through his body and left it filled with fear. When their father came and told them Francis X. was dead, Will was relieved to feel the fear recede and a smooth and soothing sadness take its place.

Robert refused to allow Francis X.'s body to be removed from the house and Isobel refused to come downstairs as long as it remained.

"Ah'll noo say goodbye t' the lad before ah hafta," said Robert. "That's final."

"Ah'll noo live with is wee corpse," said Isobel and stayed upstairs.

Quiet surrounded her room. The only sounds the children heard from behind its doors came during an argument between their parents on the afternoon of Francis X.'s death.

"Ah said ah wanted er out." Isobel was adamant in her resolve regarding the nursemaid.

"But, Is," Robert pleaded, "she'd be helpful now with the others . . . at least fer a few days."

"Out," Isobel shrieked. "She brought death t' this house and ah want er out."

"Ya dinna know she carried the germ . . ."

"Out!" The sound was frightening as it spilled into the hallway.

"All right, she'll go." Robert's voice began climbing. "But let me recall one thing. She'd noo have been here in the first place if ya'd been a true mother yerself."

"While we're recallin' . . ." Isobel's voice cracked. "While we're recallin' first places, who was it wanted the lad? Who was that?"

"It was so we'd come closer. Ah see now how wrong ah was."

A door slammed and the children heard Robert descend the stairs and go into the parlor. Quiet again encircled Isobel's room.

They did not see her until the next day and she seemed then to be quite collected. The only evidence she gave that this day was extraordinary was her request that the children not address her as Mother. And they accepted this as a mysterious but temporary aberration caused by grief. Not one of them slipped during the ten minutes they spent with her.

Robert's grief was much more evident. Tears rolled freely down his face as he ushered three of his children into the room holding the body of a fourth. All of them cried together as they stood in a knot at one end of the parlor before Francis X.'s tiny bier.

Will knew exactly what it meant that his baby brother lay in a small box lined with blue silk. He also didn't know at all. And he couldn't understand how these two things could coexist. He was certain, however, of two things: he had never seen Francis X.'s face filled with such sweetness and his heart would break if he looked at it a moment longer.

Robert lifted Will in his arms as he turned away. He lifted him and carried him to a chair at the opposite end of the room. He hugged him tight against his body, crooning soft sounds next to Will's cheek as the boy's tears formed a damp circle on the shoulder of Robert's jacket.

The four of them stayed in the parlor for several hours that night. Robert sang ''Annie Laurie'' and ''Roamin' in the Gloamin','' the children joining him for choruses of the latter. He told stories. They all talked about Francis X. And off and on, throughout their vigil, they wrapped their arms around each other and cried.

Robert left the parlor only to dismiss the nursemaid and to pay brief visits to his wife. Alexine took over the kitchen. Ian appointed himself keeper of the door when people began to arrive to pay their respects. Will did whatever anyone asked.

By the morning of the burial, Robert's face reflected every moment of sleep he'd lost and the path of every tear he'd shed. He looked ill. All the children exhibited a certain facial puffiness. Alexine's was accompanied by extremely red eyes, Ian's by a giant sore on one side of his nose, and Will's by a sallowness of skin. The ordeal had marked them all distinctly.

Their departure from the house was set for ten o'clock. A few minutes before the hour, Robert and the children and a few close family friends gathered in the front hall. One of the men would assist Robert in bearing his son's coffin to the carriage outside. The children and friends would follow. Other people awaited them at the church. After a brief service there, Francis X. would be buried in the graveyard that lay behind it.

A rustling sound caused the group in the hallway to look toward the staircase. Isobel, swathed in dark silk and heavily veiled, stood at its head. As she began to descend, her black-gloved hand gliding lightly along the banister, Robert moved to the bottom of the stairs and awaited her there. No one knew if he'd expected her or not but once she appeared he moved in concert with her as if following a carefully rehearsed plan.

When she reached him at the base of the stairs, Robert wound her hand around his arm and placed his other hand on top of it. He guided her forward and as she passed her children she touched each of them gently. Robert spoke quietly to one of the waiting men and he and another detached themselves from the group and entered the parlor.

When they emerged, Francis X.'s coffin was between them. Robert and Isobel followed it out the front door, Isobel's body fiercely erect, no part of it leaning against Robert's. The children followed, each carrying a sheaf of flowers that had lain on their brother's bier.

At the church, Isobel's composure never wavered. She held her head up and looked straight at the box that held the body of her youngest son. Alexine and Will sobbed aloud throughout the service, Ian only at the beginning and at the end. Robert's body shook visibly when the minister, standing behind the coffin, spread his arms and intoned: "And Jesus said, 'suffer the little children to come unto me.' "

As the family filed from their pew, following Francis X. into the graveyard, Isobel again took Robert's arm but more for decorum than support. Not until she saw the dark brown box vanish into the ground and heard a handful of dirt spatter against its forever-closed lid, did she break. The sound was the same one Will had heard on the morning his brother died. It came in waves that broke over the group surrounding the grave and then moved beyond to hang in the late summer air. At the end of the third wave, Isobel fell to her knees and into silence. She lowered her head and clasped her hands before her in an attitude of prayer although her lips were unmoving. For a few moments she rocked gently, soundlessly, back and forth. Then she reached out toward Will, the child nearest her, and took from him the flowers he was holding. Still kneeling, she tossed them softly, one by one, into her son's grave. When they were gone, she rose, rested her hand lightly on her husband's arm and turned and walked away.

JUNE 20, 1932

Rising in the dark in Needles, Isobel and Will were within several hours driving time of Hollywood. The desert ahead seemed unimportant, their abbreviated sleep trivial. Ordinarily, Isobel was slightly off balance if she didn't begin a day with her usual breakfast. But today she was sipping her first Coke on an empty stomach at 4:30 A.M., surrounded by darkness.

They pulled up in front of the Roosevelt Hotel at exactly noon.

"Ah'll have m' fur, Willie," she said as the car stopped.

He took it from the back seat where she'd carefully laid it out and placed it around her shoulders.

Isobel's door flew open and a gloved hand extended in toward her. She placed her own on it and emerged onto Hollywood Boulevard.

"Mrs. Robert Claflin," she said to the doorman, who bent down to hear her. "We'll be stayin'."

"Very good, madam," he said. "I'll see to your luggage."

"The luggage and the automobile," she corrected him.

"Yes, of course. The luggage and the automobile."

"Aye," she said and, taking Will's arm, she swept into the hotel as if she were the biggest star of them all.

MONDAY, JUNE 20

So we have ar-ee-vayed! That means we is here — and is we ever! First a word about this jernt known as the Roosevelt

71

(Republicans, please note: it was not named for F.D.). It's a lulu. Anything you could want in the way of comfort, courtesy or cuisine (that's food to youse dolts), they have it. Plus hot and cold running bellboys and a darn good closeup of a movie star every now and then.

For instance, as we emerged from the hotel this afternoon, who should drive up and be deposited practically at our feet but Greta Nissen. For our readers in the sticks who might need their memories jiggled, she's the Scandinavian lass with the limpid eyes. You saw her dark-tressed in *The Wanderer* with Wally Beery and Bill Collier, Jr., or wearing her own natural gold in *The Popular Sin,* among others. Talkies have been tough on her but did she look swell today! So we discovered right off the bat that they *are* human. But I digress.

Immediately upon engaging the room, we sent all our clothes to be pressed, lunching in number 708 while awaiting their return. Refreshed and fresh pressed, in mid-afternoon we stepped across the street to Mr. Grauman's palace and saw

Grand Hotel, a truly superb picture. Mlle. Garbo was never lovelier; Jack and Lionel right on the mark, as ever; Beery's always jake in my book and this was no exception; Lewis Stone — could the pitchers exist without him?; Joan Crawford giving a fine performance (Mrs. R. Claflin begs to disagree, being as how she's still sore at her for marrying Doug, Jr. She insists Joan's an upstart trying to crash The Royal Family and no amount of gab from yours truly can lower her dudgeon over the matter).

After the flicker, we strolled the Boulevard a bit, postcarded, and then back to the Roosevelt for dinner on the Patio Roof. There are Terpsichorean rites (ya can't make me tell) nightly on the Roof with a Mr. Henry Halstead furnishing the music but we gave them the go-by in favor of *Blessed Event,* a stage play starring Reginald Denny, and a darned good one.

And on our way home, after this very long and very eventful day, who should we spot to top it all off but Myrna Loy. Nize? The Cap'n told me, as she does whenever we see Myrna, that she's at least half Scotch and probably closer to three-quarters.

And now your scrivener must to bed. If things were any more copacetic, I'd be sure I'd died and gone to heaven.

Will's stomachache began during the ride from the graveyard back to the house. By the time the Claflins and several guests were ready to sit down to a midday meal, he was doubled over in terrible pain. The doctor who'd attended Francis X. was among the guests. He told Robert he should prepare to dig another grave.

"Are ya out a yer bloody mind, man," Robert roared at him. "What're ya tellin' me? The lad was fine an hour ago."

"Well, he's not now," the doctor said. "It's hit very fast."

"What's hit? What's bloody well hit? Are ya tellin' me it's the same thing? The damned bloody flu?"

"Well, we knew there was a certain risk . . ."

"Ah, damn yer risks. This one goes in

the hospital where he's got a chance . . . and he goes now."

"It's not that easy to find space, Mr. Claflin. You have to understand . . ."

"Ah understand ah put one lad in the ground today and ah'll noo put in another, thank ya very much. And ah understand ya'll come t' the hospital with me and make the space."

Within an hour doctors were removing Will's ruptured appendix and fighting to save his life. When Robert learned the Claflin family doctor had made a mistaken diagnosis, he ordered him out of his sight and out of his life.

"Ah dinna know if ya've Frankie's death on yer hands," he said, "but stay away from me in case ah decide ya do."

Will was in the hospital nearly six weeks because of a series of complications that beset his kidneys and intestines. At the time of his release, as he was still very weak and required special care, Robert suggested engaging a nurse. Isobel became quite agitated.

"Ah'll noo have another stranger in m' house," she insisted.

"But the lad needs a great deal a lookin' after," Robert pointed out. "It's a big task."

"Ah'll noo allow it, Bertie. Dinna push me."

"He needs special foods and bedpans and medicines and . . ."

"Ah repeat," Isobel broke in. "Ah'll noo have anyone in here."

"And who'll tend im?" Robert's voice was hard. Isobel didn't answer. "Ah'll arrange fer ya t' speak t' em yerself so ya'll find one t' yer likin'."

"Ah'll noo talk t' em," Isobel said quietly. "Do as ya please."

Isobel's misgivings never completely vanished but when Robert found a woman named Farnum, she was somewhat appeased. Anyone who shared a last name with Dustin and William must have something to recommend her. And, eventually, a quite comfortable relationship developed between Isobel and Miss Farnum. She treated Isobel exactly as though she were a patient — diagnosing, prescribing treatment, administering it — and Isobel responded with gratitude.

"You're looking a little gray around the gills, Mrs. Claflin," Miss Farnum would say when Isobel came in from an afternoon at the movies. "I think you could stand to take off your shoes, put up your feet, drink some tea and nibble something delicious. Let me get that for you."

And she would make up a tray with a pot of tea and several small cakes and bring it to Isobel in the living room.

"I think this is just what you need," she'd say. "You'll feel much better when you finish this."

"Aye," Isobel would agree. "Thank ya, Nurse Farnum." And she ate the cakes and drank the tea, exactly as directed.

She seldom said more than this to Miss Farnum and she only once mentioned her to Robert. It was at dinner one evening when the nurse had been in residence about two weeks. Isobel looked up from her plate.

"Ah think she'll work out," she said. Then she resumed eating.

In addition to Miss Farnum, Will found other changes when he returned home from the hospital. The house itself was different. After Francis X.'s death and Will's hospitalization, Isobel had moved about the old house like a ghost. She gave no indication of being plagued by grief. She simply seemed absent. Feeling a change in surroundings might be therapeutic, Robert moved his family to a new house. It was much grander than the old, memory-filled one, and Isobel seemed pleased with it although it had not so far produced any noticeable change in her behavior.

Another change Will noticed immediately was Isobel's renewed insistence that he not call her Mother. She'd allowed him to use the appellation while he was in the hospital, apparently feeling he deserved a special dispensation. But she revoked it the moment he came home. He was to call her Isobel just as the others did. When Will asked why, she simply said: "It's m' name, Willie."

And another distinct change was that each night, when Robert entered Will's room to kiss him goodnight, a sharp, unpleasant smell came in with him. When

Will asked Alexine what it was, she told him it was whiskey.

JUNE 21, 1932

On their first morning in Hollywood, Isobel and Will had breakfast in the room.

"Ah had a note from Herbie," Isobel said, breaking off a tiny corner of her toast and chewing it slowly.

"I noticed," Will growled. "What'd he want?"

"He loves Alexine very much," said Isobel, sipping her tea.

"Five of him wouldn't be worth one of her."

"He always put me in mind a George O'Brien," said Isobel. "No spark. He wants me t' look out fer any memento a Leatrice Joy. Alexine dotes on the woman, ya know."

"Do I ever," said Will. "Remember when she bobbed her hair like Leatrice's and wanted to wear Ian's suit jackets all the time?"

"No spark a'tall," Isobel murmured.

"I thought O'Brien was swell in *The*

Iron Horse," said Will.

"Ah wanted t' go back t' see Madge Bellamy again but ah was afraid the man'd make me doze off."

"Herbie's closer to Ed Wynn, as far as I'm concerned. A real schlemiel."

"He loves Alexine very much," said Isobel, closing the subject.

They decided to begin their day with a visit to Pickfair, the palace from which Douglas Fairbanks and Mary Pickford had reigned for more than a decade. Armed with a map of the movie stars' homes and some tips from the man at the Roosevelt's front desk, they set out for Beverly Hills.

It was about ten o'clock, before the California sun had burned all the blue from the sky and thrown a pale wash over everything on the land, when they spotted the tall stone pillars and high iron gate that marked the royal residence. Parked up across the street gazing toward the entrance, they could see a small portion of winding drive, dappled by shadows from the massive trees that obscured all but a speck of the white mansion beyond.

The abbreviated view did not disturb Isobel at all. The night before she had carefully studied several postcard views of Pickfair and could picture now with absolute clarity the sprawling white house with its green roof and trim, the patches of vine that crawled its outer walls, its candy-striped awnings. She knew the rolling lawn was covered with flowering bushes — blue, fuchsia, gold — and that it sloped down gently to the pool, which was emerald and enormous. She knew that on the pool's surface lay a misty reproduction of the house itself. Sitting across the street in the Graham-Paige, hands folded in her lap, eyes trained on the closed iron gate, she lingered over each feature in her mind's eye, her silence distinctly reverential.

The process took about fifteen minutes, this day and every other. It became a daily service of worship whose ritual seldom varied. The black car drew up to the curb and halted. Isobel shifted slightly in her seat so that she could look comfortably past Will toward Pickfair's gate. She folded her hands in her lap and sat absolutely still. What inner obeisances she made, what internal rites she performed in the quiet, were known only to her. But she always signaled their completion by turning to face front and making a small noise, a cross between a throat-clearing and a sigh. Then Will started the motor and they drove off to begin their day.

TUESDAY, JUNE 21

That's some slick cottage Doug and Mary have out in the Hills of Beverly. Course it's gated and fenced and treed against intrusions of the hoi polloi — and rightly so. We think they should have a moat if they want one! But what I saw was swell and Isobel described the rest, in living color yet.

The other star domains we ogled today included Clara Bow's, an unassuming little stucco (you'd never figger this Jazz Baby for something so modest), and Mr. and Mrs. Edmund Lowe's (she's Lilyan Tashman). I don't know where the Captain gets her info but she tells me Lilyan had the first white piano in

Hollywood. A real pacesetter, this ex-Follies gal. We searched high and low for the place where Wally Reid, God bless him, used to hang his *chapeau* but no soap. We'll try again tomorrow.

We also discovered Pig'N Whistle cafes and Isobel tried the John Barrymore Special, a concoction with marshmallow, vanilla and chocolate ice cream, fresh strawberries, whipped cream, pecan halves and Nabisco wafers. Our hero ordered the extravaganza named for Helen Twelvetrees. They have regular food in this jernt too and pastries to go, a different one every day of the week. We've already got our eye on Wednesday's Chocolate Cream Rolls.

Tonight to *Man About Town* with Warner Baxter. Ted Lewis personal appeared. Home immediately afterward, too tired to postcard or to continue scrivening here.

When the Armistice was declared on November 11, 1918, relief suffused places where the Claflins had never even acknowledged there was tension. The War was over and Jamie was still alive. He belonged to them again.

Jamie would never have believed this. As he approached Detroit on the train, just before Christmas, his intention was clear and distinctly limited. He would stay through the holidays and then be off again, this time to study or travel or work. He wasn't sure what he would do; he was certain only that he would do it somewhere else.

At home he found his father wrapped in an air of desolation and drinking half a bottle of whiskey every night. His mother seemed quite cheerful but rather abstracted, her smile slightly out of focus. Will, apparently, was an invalid, emaciated, pale, carried about the vast spaces of the new house by Miss Farnum. Alexine preferred to spend all her spare time with Will, a distinctly unnatural choice for a sixteen-year-old girl, Jamie thought. And Ian had become even more stolid.

Within a few days, Jamie decided to stay. He felt in his family something broken. He could at least, he reasoned, remain with them until it was mended.

To assist Isobel with Christmas shopping and other tasks attendant upon the holidays, Robert loaned her one of his employees named Riley. An enormous, good-natured man, as black as the car in which, as he said, he "carried Mis' Claflin around," Isobel became immediately and wholly dependent on him. After the holidays, she asked so frequently to borrow Riley that Robert finally shifted him to the household payroll on a permanent basis.

Miss Farnum's career also underwent a metamorphosis. In the week between Christmas and New Year's, the doctor directed that Will begin eating regular food and trying to walk on his own, thus removing the functions Miss Farnum had been hired to perform. Isobel, who'd become quite attached to Miss Farnum's generous ministrations, quickly pointed out to Robert that the holidays were no time to let someone go.

When they ended, Isobel expressed concern about the pace of Will's recovery.

"Ah think he'll do better, Bertie, if Nurse Farnum exercises im," she said.

"What's wrong with the lad exercisin' imself?" Robert asked.

"He's noo trained fer it," Isobel pointed out.

"What trainin' does he need t' move is legs?" Robert inquired.

"They're weak as feathers," said Isobel. "They'll blow right out from under im."

Miss Farnum stayed.

By February Will was getting around very well, well enough to accompany Isobel to a matinee at least twice a week. But then his birthday was looming.

"Ah think the lad's heart would break if Nurse Farnum weren't here fer his tenth," said Isobel. "He's very fond a er, ya know."

Later in the spring Miss Farnum herself had a birthday. And it was unthinkable to Isobel that she be let go anywhere near the time of *that* occasion. So, as summer approached, Miss Farnum was still under the Claflin roof. Although Isobel clung stubbornly to the title "Nurse," Miss Farnum had, in fact, left the medical arts far behind. She was now the Claflin housekeeper and absolutely indispensable as such.

"Riley and Farnum . . . Farnum and Riley," Robert would mutter. "Sounds like a bloody vaudeville act."

But he never again raised the question of dismissal.

JUNE 22, 1932

Isobel carried with her to Hollywood a scrapbook bound in brown suede and containing one hundred heavy black pages. The first free moment she had, she cut the top off a Roosevelt Hotel letterhead, that part bearing a picture of the hotel and the legend "Winning the West," and wrote along its edge: My Travels In Hollywood. This she pasted on the scrapbook's first page. She surrounded it with a few pressed sprigs of desert flowers; the first fortune she received from the Roosevelt's lobby scale ("you are very shrewd and thoroughly capable of managing a large enterprise"); two small heads, Doug's and Mary's, lopped from their bodies in a movie magazine; two small color pictures of Old California Missions, a series; and in each corner a sticker commemorating the tenth Olympic Games, being held later that summer in Los Angeles.

Each day she added something to the book: postcards, snapshots, 2″ x 1″ store-bought photos of Los Angeles streets and buildings, theater programs, menus, glossies of the stars, more Olympiad stickers, ticket stubs, cutouts of the stars from tabloids and magazines, Sunday bulletins from local churches, more fortunes from the lobby scale, items from the gossip columns.

Will, well aware how seriously Isobel took this enterprise, referred to the scrapbook as her "work."

WEDNESDAY, JUNE 22

Up at the crack of ten and breakfast in the room (this is some hard life!) before visiting Mecca (Pickfair, to you boneheads). Thence to town for the earlybird matinees. Isobel settled on

Thunder Below with Tallulah, Paul Lukas and Charlie Bickford, La Bankhead playing "the flower of the tropic camp, the only white woman on half a continent." Anyway, that's how the ballyhoo had it. Our hero needed a little more gaiety than that promised so he hied himself down the street to *The Tenderfoot* with Joe Brown. I think I made the right choice cuz all the Captain said afterward was "She's noo Dietrich."

A bit of shopping at Bullock's in midafternoon, Isobel searching for something for Alex's bairn-to-be after putting yours truly on star alert. Slim pickins on both accounts. She ended up with two pair of gloves for herself and I glimpsed a profile I could've sworn was Donald Crisp's until the guy ruined everything by turning around. Some people got no class! Isobel was just as glad since she's never forgiven Donald for what he did to Lillian Gish in *Broken Blossoms*.

In the evening to see *The Dark Horse* with Bette Davis, Warren William, Guy Kibbee and Frank McHugh. Frank was there tonight, in the flesh, and the movie was a fine one. To the Pig'N Whistle afterward, our hero wising-up this time and sticking with their Famous Malted Milk; Capt. Isobel, not so easily discouraged, digging through another John Barrymore Special, plus half-a-dozen Chocolate Cream Rolls to go.

And also in the flesh, exiting the Roosevelt as we entered, was Bette herself. Did Isobel ever fall for her! She'd still be in the lobby in a trance if I hadn't used my magic powers to break the spell (I reminded her of the Chocolate Creams — and she's nibbling one now as she pores over her work). We couldn't place Bette's escort but whoever he is he's one lucky guy. Course, do you hear me complaining? I'll say not!

By the spring of 1919, Will was accompanying Isobel whenever she went to the movies. Robert argued if the boy was well enough to do that, he was well enough to begin making up the lost school year through tutoring. Will wasn't ready for that kind of strain, Isobel insisted. Besides, she pointed out, there were things to be learned from the pictures.

"Well now, what is it the lad's learnin' from *Knickerbocker Buckaroo,*" Robert asked, "or *Trueheart Susie,* ah'd like t' know?"

"Ya wouldna understand, Bertie. But he's too weak t' tutor."

Once Isobel settled something in her mind, it was impossible for anyone else to undo it. Robert knew this and when he heard the edge of intransigence in her voice, he stopped arguing.

One of Isobel's favorite films was *Broken Blossoms,* even though she suffered terribly every time she saw it. Whenever Donald Crisp, the father, brutalized Lillian Gish, his daughter, Isobel shielded her eyes. And when he beat her to death in a drunken rage, Isobel invariably uttered a cry and turned her body away from the screen. But when Richard Barthelmess arrived and meted out justice by killing Crisp, she watched every moment with relish. When Barthelmess then dispatched himself, she fell into a deep sadness, which clung to her long after the picture ended.

"Do you like to be sad?" Will asked, as they rode home after seeing *Broken Blossoms* for the third time.

"A course not, Willie." Her voice was filled with melancholy.

"You're always sad when we see this movie but you always want to see it again," said Will.

"Sadness is part a life, laddie. Ya canna change that."

"*The Miracle Man* was sad when Lon Chaney was crippled and you said you hated it."

"A cripple's noo sad, Willie. It's ugly."

"Aren't ugly things part of life?" he asked.

"No, laddie. They dinna have t' be." Isobel signaled the end of the conversation by patting his cheek.

She began to boycott Chaney's movies because of the threat of ugliness. She also observed rigidly a ban on any picture featuring Marguerite Clark. She felt Marguerite was a blatant and very poor imitation of Little Mary. She loathed

Charles Ray, finding him dull beyond description, and any mention of Nazimova elicited a response that Isobel never varied and never explained: "Ah hate the woman."

She had nothing but admiration, however, for Gloria Swanson, the Talmadges, Betty Compson and Bebe Daniels, whom she'd discovered was part Scotch. She thought Thomas Meighan and George Walsh had potential, though she doubted they'd ever rank as top box office stars. And she was still an ardent fan of Clara Kimball Young, who specialized in playing wronged wives.

JUNE 23, 1932

Isobel and Will focused the following morning on homes of the stars in Hollywood itself. During the excursion, Isobel gave such free rein to her anecdotal sense that Will threatened to hire her out as a tour guide. She said she was afraid she'd freeze up with a large group.

They found first the home of

Norma Talmadge.

"Ah didna know she lived on our street," said Isobel, gazing up the broad stone stairs that reached from the sprawling residence all the way down to Hollywood Boulevard. "Ah think this is the Cudahy mansion where she lived with Mr. Schenck."

"Who was Cudahy?" Will asked.

"A millionaire. He killed himself in the house before Norma and Mr. Schenck bought it. They say it's jinxed now and maybe it's so. After all, Norma and Mr. Schenck're noo together, are they?"

"Not according to Gil Roland they're not," said Will.

"Ah knew in *Camille* they were really in love." Her tone was confidential.

"You sure called that one right," said Will.

"Ah'm surprised Norma'd be right on the road," Isobel remarked as they drove away.

She continued her recitation as they pulled up before Vilma Banky and Rod La Rocque's.

"They called her The Hungarian

Rhapsody, Willie . . . and she was too. The Hungarian made talkies hard fer er but she's happy t' be retired. Ah liked er best with Ronald Colman . . . such a lovely girl she was. At her wedding to Rod, they tore er gown t' shreds."

Isobel found Warren Kerrigan's home "cozy," John Boles's "impressive," and May Allison's "chilly."

Approaching North Stanley Avenue, where the map placed William Haines's mansion, they noticed a woman walking toward them on the opposite side of the street. It was unusual to see anyone on foot in residential Hollywood. Also unusual was the enormous limousine that crept along beside her like a shadow.

"She's familiar, Willie," Isobel said as they passed the woman.

"I couldn't see her face for the hair," he said, turning onto North Stanley.

"It was Tallulah." Isobel's voice was just above a whisper. "Turn around, Willie. That was Tallulah."

"You've been seeing too many movies," Will teased. But he wheeled the car into a sharp turn and headed back the

95

way they'd come.

The Rolls-Royce loomed ahead of them and abreast of it, on the sidewalk, strode a small figure with a mass of hair tumbling around her shoulders.

"Go slow, Willie, but dinna stop." Isobel pulled herself fully erect in the seat, her head facing front. As they passed the Rolls, she snapped her eyes to the right and then back, quickly as a snake's tongue.

"It's er," she whispered. "Slower but dinna stop." Now she shot a glance over her right shoulder. "It's er," she repeated.

As Will tried to take a look himself, he inadvertently brought the car to a complete halt and the woman drew alongside them.

"Start it up," Isobel hissed, eyes straight ahead. "Start it up."

As the car began moving again, both Isobel and Will allowed themselves a final look to the right. Tallulah, her head bent down slightly, was grinning at them and waving.

THURSDAY, JUNE 23

We had some morning, I wanna tell ya. Capt. Isobel decreed we'd scout the Hollywood homes and on our way to Billy Haines's who should we encounter, out for her morning constitutional, but Miss Bankhead herself. I swear! Course it took the Captain's shrewd eye to spot her beneath that golden mane. And when she did, such a case of jitters I've never seen. Our hero, I'm happy to say, maintained his composure. And a good thing too cuz when Tallu gave the Cap'n a tumble and waved at her, I thought I'd have to administer the salts. She didn't catch her breath until we were on our way into *State's Attorney* and even Dear Jack (Mr. Barrymore to you dolts) couldn't break the spell entirely.

What I want to know is this: do Eddie Tolan or any of the other Olympic boys know about Tallulah's system of training with a Rolls? It's a slick way to go, fellas. Try it!

Dinner on the Roof, a brief look-see at the dansant afterward, a walk on le boulevard, complete with postcarding and a raid on the newsstand, and then to work in the room. Cap discovers an item and flashes it to me: Tallulah is renting Bill Haines's place. She also points out that we never did get to the house itself. So North Stanley Avenue goes on the top of mañana's agenda, right after Pickfair.

Ta-ta.

The last days of August that year were unusually hot. The air was oppressive and when Will went outdoors he felt its weight pressing on him. So he began staying inside more often, lying down, holding cold cloths against his head. Even when Riley drove Isobel and him to the pictures, he frequently became short of breath in the automobile itself or while walking from the car into the theater. Isobel thought he ought to see a doctor. Robert said his lungs had probably atrophied from lack of activity and he ought to get out and run around the block.

The night before Will was to return to school, he suffered seizures of terrible wheezing. The rasping noise of his fight for air was awful to hear.

"It's a fit, Bertie," said Isobel, covering her ears. "The lad's taken a fit."

"Aye," Robert muttered, "it's a fit all right . . . a fit sayin' he's noo fit t' go anywhere tomorrow. Get Farnum doon here t' tend im."

Will's wheezing subsided with the dawn but left him much too depleted to go to school that day. The doctor came and confirmed Miss Farnum's diagnosis of asthma. If it didn't recur, he said, Will should be able to attend school as long as he limited his physical activity.

The wheezing began again that night just as Will was falling asleep. And again, it lasted until the first light of morning. The seizures, in fact, continued daily in precisely this pattern until mid-October. By then it was too late for Will to reenter school. Now he would have to wait until midterm, nearly four months away.

Robert argued that the boy should have a tutor. Isobel insisted that would cause great strain.

"A smatter a strain wouldna hurt the

lad," said Robert. "He's noo strained fer years now."

"It's the strain that caused the fits," said Isobel.

"It wasna strain and they werena fits," said Robert.

"Bertie," Isobel said, "a merry heart doeth like good medicine."

"What's a merry heart t' do with the lad's schoolin', ah'd like t' know?"

"He's more chance at merriness without a tutor."

"Aye," said Robert, "ah dinna doubt that. Keep im merry then, however ya will. But this time let me see the medicine work."

FRIDAY, JUNE 24

Pickfair behind us by 9:30 and we make a beeline for the place Mrs. Haines's boy Bill calls home. Sho nuff, the Rolls had Tallulah out for her morning walk but we glide by like we're high-hatting her, even though I can feel Isobel's eyes practically popping out of their sockets sideways.

The Haines home disappoints — too

few windows, the Captain says — but not the reception we get from Tallu on our way out of her neighborhood. Today she blows a kiss and dashes the Captain's pose to smithereens. She waves back and Tallu sends another smacker winging her way. She waves again. Our hero just tries to keep the heap on the road and scrams while Cap still has enough oxygen left to keep her lungs pumping. Her condition's stable by the time we reach Santa Monica for our first view of the Pacific.

We dropped in for luncheon at one of the Brown Derbies and discovered the Marquis de la Falaise had the same idea (he used to belong to Gloria Swanson but now Connie Bennett's got him). He was within spitting distance (no, I did *not* — it's just a guesstimate) so Isobel gave food the go-by and simply drank him in. Since she'd just heard, from a most reliable source, that Connie received 150,000 simoleons for four and a half weeks' work — which has gotta be some kind of record — she wondered, for our hero's ears only, if any part of that might be underwriting the gentleman's lunch. Whether or no, he seems a nice chap.

Passing through the Beverly foothills on our way home for an afternoon siesta, we searched again for Wally Reid's. No dice. We did, however, spy Corinne Griffith's (decided not to go in cuz we were already late for our nap), Colleen Moore's (a Michigander, in case ya forgot) and Buddy Rogers's — there he was, Charles himself, getting into his auto in his drive — and in some slick outfit: boots to the knee, jodhpurs, ascot at the neck. Probably off for an afternoon of polo or some such.

Up refreshed and to dinner on the Roof (they now crack open the Coke when they see the Captain coming). Then to town to see Platinum Jeannie doing her stuff in *Redheaded Woman* — wotta pitcher! — and afterward to the Pig'N Whistle. Isobel's fighting her way through another John Barrymore Special when our hero gets a waitress to swear Jack never touched one of the things in his life. Mr. P'NW just named it for him. And is Isobel ever relieved to put down her spoon and order a Coke and a couple of ladyfingers!

Then home to work on the volume that bids fair to surpass anything you'll find in your neighborhood library and, at last, to bed in the early yawning.

Besides Will's tutoring, other subjects of running disputes between Robert and Isobel that autumn were visits to Alexine's college, Robert's drinking, Jamie's infrequent presence at home and Woodrow Wilson's mental health. Robert could wax long, loud and various on all these topics. Isobel, on the other hand, had concise and immutable positions, which she simply reiterated whenever necessary.

"She's so close," Robert would say, referring to Alexine's presence at a small Presbyterian college nearby. "It canna be more'n two hours. We could go right from church and have Sunday dinner with the lass."

"She'll be home at Thanksgiving," Isobel would say.

"Well, that's noo tomorrow, is it? Let's go see er tomorrow. We'll be home by supper.''

"Thanksgiving," Isobel repeated.

Robert's drinking no longer occurred in spells or in silent, secretive nightly bouts. Now he talked about it.

"Ah believe ah'll have a drink," he'd say, shortly after arriving home for the evening. "And why not? Ah've worked hard. No reason ah canna let doon a bit. There's no one here'll converse with me since ah've noo seen *The Delicious Little Devil* and *Scarlet Days* and whatever else is playin' around town. So ah believe ah'll have a drink."

"It changes ya, Bertie," Isobel would say.

"And what if it does," he'd bluster. "Ah've worked hard. Ah can relax in m' own home, fer God's sake."

After a few drinks, Robert would raise the subject of Jamie.

"If James were here ah could talk t' im," he'd mutter. "Why canna the lad spend an evening at home, ah'd like t' know. Can ya explain that? Does he have t' be out every night of is life?"

"Leave im be," Isobel would say.

"Well, ah dinna have much choice now, do ah? Ah mean, ah pretty much have t' leave im be. After all, ah dinna even know where he is."

And as for Woodrow Wilson, who had collapsed and vanished from sight, Robert maintained he was "stark, ravin' mad and bloody well outta is mind, the lunatic," while Isobel contended the President was "not quite up t' snuff."

When their disagreements spilled over into mealtime, Will found it almost impossible to eat. Surrounded by what his father called "argy-bargy," he had trouble swallowing. Knowing how this would annoy Robert, should he notice it, Will developed a system of concealment. Shortly after placing a piece of food in his mouth, he brought his napkin up to his lips and poked the food into it with his tongue. Then he lowered the napkin, dropping the food into his lap. At the end of the meal, he shuffled all the lightly masticated bits of food into the napkin, shoved it into his pocket and delivered it later to a neighborhood dog.

Robert noticed only that Will

occasionally went outdoors in the evening and expressed himself pleased that his son seemed finally to be recognizing the value of fresh air. Miss Farnum noticed spots on the front of Will's trousers, but when she inquired about them, he became so huffy that she backed off.

The night Robert discovered Will's system ("the lad's supper's in is lap! There's noo a bite of it went into is mouth. It's all lyin' there in is lap!"), Will determined to talk to Jamie. If he were present at meals, Will felt, things would be smoother.

Will struggled to stay awake that night, listening for Jamie's tread on the stairs. When it finally came, Will ran to the bedroom door and tugged at his brother in the darkness.

"Hey, Willie . . ." Jamie began.

"Shh." Will's hiss was vehement and Jamie tiptoed in while Will quietly closed the door.

"What's the secret?" Jamie asked.

"Whisper," Will commanded before scampering back to his bed. "I don't want them to know I'm awake." He motioned

Jamie toward him.

"Must be pretty important," said Jamie, leaning on the foot of the bedstead.

"I wish you could be home for supper every once in a while." Will blurted it out.

"That's why you waylaid me? To tell me that?"

"It would be easier with you there," Will plunged on. "Sometimes it's okay, but sometimes when Isobel and Pop go back and forth I can't eat . . ."

"Hold it," Jamie raised his hands. "You're talking about argy-bargy, right?"

Will nodded.

"And when it happens at supper it makes you sick?"

Will nodded again.

"I know, Willie. It makes me sick too." Jamie started to laugh but Will's face stopped him.

"When you're around it doesn't happen," Will said.

"It just seems that way, Willie. I certainly can't prevent argy-bargy. Nobody can do that. Of course, when I'm there Pop can discuss business and that distracts him."

"It seems easier when you're there," Will said.

Jamie stared at his brother.

"Easier for me." Will's voice was barely a whisper.

"Oh, Willie." For a moment Jamie looked about to cry. Then he gave a couple sharp raps on the bedstead with his knuckles and smiled. "I'll try to be there, Willie. I really will try."

JUNE 25, 1932

Believing age deserved only scorn, Isobel would have preferred that her fiftieth birthday pass unnoticed. When an early morning telegram arrived from Alexine and Herbert, she said to Will:

"Ah dinna see the point a dredgin' it up," as though it were a dark piece of the past.

And a few minutes later, when Will answered a knock and found the entire doorway filled with flowers from Ian and Ethel, Isobel admired them but refused to acknowledge why they were there.

Everyone ignored the fact that Isobel and Robert had been married on this day thirty-three years before.

Will planned to make June 25 special while carefully avoiding any overt birthday references. He'd arranged for breakfast in the room, reserved tables for lunch at the Ambassador Hotel and dinner at the Biltmore, gotten tickets to a matinee of *Whistling in the Dark* with Ernest Truex at the Belasco, and ascertained there was a nine o'clock show that evening of *Thunder Below,* Tallulah's picture, which Isobel had expressed interest in reexamining.

The papers that arrived on the breakfast tray carried the first pictures of John Barrymore, Jr., now three weeks old.

"It's the Barrymore nose," Isobel decided, "but both Jack and Dolores through the eyes."

Isobel also saw in the paper an advertisement for a parasol at Bullock's.

"Ah like it better'n the one ah'm carryin', Willie," she said, showing him the ad.

So after they'd been to Pickfair they headed directly downtown. Isobel bought not only the parasol but a dress as well. Radically different from the rest of her wardrobe, it was a bold floral print with short sleeves. To accompany it, she bought gloves with large fur ruffs at the wrist and an orange turban hat that matched one of the colors in her dress.

Throughout the day she solicited Will's opinion of her outfit.

"Are the colors too bright?" she asked as they strolled toward the Ambassador, having just visited the bungalow on its grounds where John Barrymore lived when he first arrived in Hollywood.

"You're the prettiest flower of them all," Will answered, indicating the blooms lining their path.

At the matinee an enormous woman, dressed in a bright print, sat directly in front of them. When Isobel asked if she in any way resembled the woman, Will assured her she did not.

"Does it suit me, Willie?" she inquired, sitting down to dinner.

"Made to order . . . for Isobel by Adrian."

But when they arrived back at the

Roosevelt that night, Isobel folded up the dress instead of hanging it in the closet. She placed it in a box, setting the hat and gloves inside with it.

"Safekeeping?" Will asked, watching her pack it away.

"It's just a reminder," she said cryptically, putting the box in the closet where it remained.

SATURDAY, JUNE 25

Exercise on the snore shelf interrupted at eight ayem by a telegram from Alex and Herbie. These guys in the sticks don't seem to realize that here in Dreamland we don't get up with the chickens. I mean, a man needs his rest if he's going to keep up the pace.

But since the telegram commemorated the Divine Isobel's birthday, I couldn't be too sore (oh yeah?). Anyway, I would've been awakened moments later by the arrival of Ian's offering, a basket of posies roughly the size of a giant sequoia. Was I glad I'd cancelled my modest corsage? I'll say. Isobel wanted to make

111

like this was just any old day anyhoo (Jamie was a respecter of those wishes, I guess — not a peep from him).

After viewing *Thunder Below,* yours truly must admit a preference for La Bankhead au naturel (didn't know I could speak Continental, did ya?). You know, the way we see her every morning.

Ho-hum.

———————

For a week, Jamie was present at every evening meal. He appeared as Farnum was placing the food on the table and left when she began to clear.

"Well," he'd say, pushing back his chair and rising, "I think I'll get some air."

"Would ya care fer a cigar, James?" Robert would ask.

"No thanks, Pop." Jamie kissed the top of Isobel's head and patted Will.

"Ah'd like t' know the kind a air ya'll be gettin' in Tenny's Saloon," Robert would mutter when Jamie was beyond hearing. Pleased by his son's presence, he didn't want to alienate him but neither did he want to seem a fool.

"Jamie dotes on the night air," Isobel murmured.

"Oh, yeah," said Ian.

Then Jamie missed three nights in a row. Near midnight on the third evening, he knocked at Will's door and whispered into the darkness.

"Willie? Willie? Are you awake?"

Roused from a light sleep, Will turned on his lamp and motioned Jamie in. As he neared the bed, the smell of whiskey floated toward Will.

"Guess you've been down to Tenny's, huh?" said Will as casually as he could manage.

"Tenny's? Good lord, no. I wouldn't go near that dump."

"But Pop said . . ."

"What did Pop say? I'll tell what Pop said: 'The lad's off t' Tenny's t' get sodden with drink.' "

Will giggled at Jamie's imitation.

"Well," Jamie continued, "I don't mind. It's all right with me if that's what he thinks. It's best if that's what he thinks."

"Ian thinks so too," said Will.

"Ian will always think what Pop thinks. And Isobel, I'm sure, thinks I'm out taking the air."

"She does," said Will.

"What about you, Willie? What do you think?"

"I smell whiskey," said Will.

Jamie laughed. "Do I seem sodden with drink?"

"No," Will said.

"Well, what do you think? Yours is the only opinion I care about. Do you think I'd leave you alone with the argy-bargy to go down to the corner and fill myself with whiskey?"

"I wouldn't blame you if you did," said Will. "I know you tried."

"Oh, Willie, I did try. I tried all last week." Jamie paused. "Do you remember Jane Doyle?"

"Sure," said Will. "She's Dylan's wife."

"I love her," Jamie said. "Do you understand, Willie?"

"You drink because you're unhappy," said Will.

"No," said Jamie. "I don't drink at all."

"What's the smell then?" Will asked.

"I mean I don't spend the evening drinking. Sometimes on the way home I stop for a drink. I spend evenings with her. That's when I see her. That's the only time we have."

"She loves you too?"

"She does," said Jamie. "She really does. Only a very good reason would make me desert you, Willie. Do you understand?"

"Yes," said Will.

"You're the only one I'd trust with the truth."

"What about Dylan?" Will asked.

"I want her to divorce him. She wants to wait. As long as Pop's got him running the night shift, I won't push anything."

"I hated him," Will said.

"So does she," said Jamie.

A sharp departure from our usual shed-yule this morn. We substituted the First Methodist Chuch of Hollywood for Mecca (worship is worship, say we), there to hear the pastor sermonize on the topic "Does Religion Make a Difference?" He concluded it did, but whaddya expect?

Figgering Tallulah would be beauty-resting on a Sunday ayem, we scratched North Stanley from the day's itinerary and repaired directly to Chop'N Tweet Tweet after services. Feeling adventurous, our hero tried the Dreamland Special Salad, which turns out to be fresh sliced pineapple, a couple of dollops of chicken salad and assorted finger sandwiches. The Cap'n had a chicken sandwich, minus bread. Trays beans all around, as usual.

Just made it to the matinee of *Strangers of the Evening* — only fair — and a colored revue with Bill Robinson who's the real article, as far as we're concerned. He starts dancing where most folks leave off. I'd suggested *The Man Who Played God* with B. Davis and Mr. Arliss, but

Isobel says George reminds her too much of Aunt Bess.

Inasmuch as Mrs. C. had fallen behind in her work — the high life is time-consuming, fellas, let me tell ya — we went directly home after the show. By dinner she'd added about ten more pages and we took it along to show the waiters, especially Paul, her latest crush (third in line behind Bette and Tallu) and a dead ringer for Phillips Holmes.

Our meal on the Roof was accompanied by the Sunday Evening Dinner Musicale, courtesy of Mr. Joe Rosenfelt and his Trio Ensemble. As strains of Herbert, Friml, et al. (Al who? You figger it out), filled the room, we were joined by Margaret Seddon, Elizabeth Patterson and Will Mahoney (you'll remember his fabulous dance on the xylophone). Will was disguised behind a cigar but he couldn't fool the Captain. In other words, the place was lousy with bit players.

After dinner, across the street to see *Grand Hotel* again, just in case we missed anything, and then home to bed in the wee sma' hours.

Things I never noodle now: Corinne Griffith is one of Hollywood's richest ladies and not repeat not because of her beauty (squawkies hit Corinne as hard as anybody) but through shrewd real estate investments. Good show, C.G.

Will and Ian had never displayed much interest in each other. For the first several years of Will's life, Ian thought of him as "the baby," worthy of only minimal consideration. Will thought of Ian as the least interesting of the "older ones." But by the fall of 1919 their mutual lack of interest had turned to outright hostility. Will was envious of Ian's position as an after-school worker at the foundry; Ian was jealous of the time Will spent with Isobel.

Ian took to writing vicious little notes to his brother and signing them with the names of Will's favorite stars.

"If there's one thing I can't stand, it's a mama's boy. Richard Barthelmess."

"I wouldn't be where I am today if all I did when I was a boy was go to the movies. Doug Fairbanks.''

''I hate sissies more than anything in the world. Mabel Normand.''

Will could never think of a way to retaliate so he endured Ian's missives in silence. Ian, as it turned out, arranged his own comeuppance.

Desperate to break the circle of exclusivity that surrounded Isobel and Will, he wangled two Sunday matinee tickets in advance from the manager of the Broadway Strand and enclosed them in a handwritten invitation to Isobel.

''Mr. Ian Angus Claflin,'' it read, ''requests the honor of the presence of Mrs. Isobel Claflin at a showing of *Her Greatest Performance,* Ellen Terry's only screen presentation.''

Ian had also copied part of Triangle's promotional material and put it in the envelope: ''A triumphant climax to the career of the greatest living actress. A tribute to her artistry that she should select for screen presentation in the sweetness of her maturity a role portraying the greatest of God's gifts, a mother.''

Anxious to play his triumphant scene

before the largest possible audience, Ian presented the invitation to Isobel at dinner.

"Ya're a dear lad," she said, reading it as Ian beamed at her. "Did ya see this, Bertie?" She passed the invitation to Robert.

"I even got tickets," said Ian. "Look in the envelope."

"Aye," said Isobel. "Ah know yer father'd like this one. He once saw Mrs. Terry on the stage, ya know. Could ya get tickets fer him and Willie?"

"Ah've noo time t' be runnin' off t' the movies," said Robert.

"We could go in the evening," Isobel suggested.

"Ian studies in the evening," Robert pointed out, "unlike some others in this house."

"Forget it," said Ian.

"Ya're a dear lad," Isobel repeated, patting Ian's hand.

"Just forget it." He grabbed the envelope holding the tickets and rushed from the room.

Will felt sorry for Ian that night but his

pity quickly evaporated in the face of a renewed barrage of notes.

"You're the kind of person, hiding behind his mother's skirts, who makes me sick. Clarine Seymour."

"I hate your lily-livered guts. J. Warren Kerrigan."

Still Will was bereft of retaliatory ideas. He hesitated to discuss it with Jamie. He had enough on his mind. Also, Will was embarrassed by the content of the notes. He wasn't sure he wanted Jamie to read them.

At Thanksgiving, however, when Alexine came home from college, Will decided to confide in her. Incensed by Ian's cruelty, she wrote a note of her own and left it on his pillow.

"Anyone who needs to pick on someone so much younger and so much weaker than he is," it said, "is the biggest sissy of them all. Mary Pickford."

Will didn't care for the phrase "so much weaker" but he kept quiet and the note did the trick. Ian stopped.

Now, instead of despising Will, he patronized him. And Will suffered Ian's contempt alone and in silence, reasoning that it was better than the notes and a small enough price to pay for going to the movies with Isobel practically every day.

MONDAY, JUNE 27

Late to my scrivening this eve, due to the length of *House Beautiful,* Charley Ray's comeback show. It was very fine but even if it hadn't been, the hand Charley got on his entrance would have made it worth it. Did I say hand? Let's face it: it was an ovation!

Besides Charley, we saw Jolson, Fifi Dorsay and Harry Langdon, who personal appeared in a connecting benefit. And a pulsating package of pulchritude showing what milady will do to be well dressed this season (a fashion show, ya morons). It was all swell.

Spinning around town this afternoon, we saw the bearded man of *What Price Glory?* fame and Isobel almost jumped out of the car. As if that weren't enough, she nearly leapt out of her skin when she found herself elbow-to-elbow with Dottie

Lee in the elevator tonight. Of course, our hero took it all in stride.

P.S. Did I mention we finally found Wally Reid's? Hard to believe he's been gone almost ten years.

At Christmastime, Robert sent baskets of food to the homes of his workers. Will helped Miss Farnum fill them. Jamie and Ian were in charge of delivery. When Will begged, the year he was ten, to be allowed to go along, Robert finally relented, on one condition: they were to set out early and be home by nine.

Ian, at first, was rather stiff, very full of his sense of mission.

"I know this must be a big sacrifice for you," he said to his older brother as Jamie backed the big sedan down the driveway.

"What do you mean?" Jamie asked.

"Well, after all," Ian huffed, "giving up a night at Tenny's can't be all that easy."

"Oh that," said Jamie. "Well, I guess I can stand it for one night."

"Of course, you can always go later since we have to get *him* home for beddy-bye." Ian gestured toward Will.

"Leave him alone," said Jamie. "Look, this got you out of doing homework tonight, didn't it?"

"I'm all caught up," said Ian.

"Isn't it better than being home with Farnum stuffing dates?" Jamie asked.

"I outgrew that years ago," said Ian.

"You did it last year," said Will.

"Only because you were too *sick*. Anyway, I'm much too old for it now."

"You're not too old for me to toss you out of the car if you keep complaining," said Jamie.

"You wouldn't," said Ian.

"Probably not. But do me a favor, Ian, . . . don't take yourself so seriously . . . at least not tonight."

The first house they stopped at was Porter Washington's, one of the molders. Porter's wife met them at the door, two of her six children peeking out from behind her. She invited the boys in, declared the basket was even bigger than last year's, said their father was the most generous man in this or any other world she knew of, and placed in their hands cups of Porter's Christmas Punch, a hot, spicy mixture that burned its way into Will's stomach and made his whole body glow. Then she gathered her children into the living room and forced them to sing two carols for the Claflin boys. Will had to make a big effort not to laugh out loud during the singing, although he wasn't sure what was so funny. By the time they returned to the automobile, the earlier unpleasantness had been drowned by a wave of Christmas cheer and replaced with an almost manic sense of well being. After all, they were the sons of the world's most generous man.

Their spirits rose higher with each stop. When they were offered punch a second time, Jamie suggested Will pass it up. Will said he was just fine and thought he'd better have it. It would warm him up.

To get to the home of Ellis MacDonald, the day foreman, they had to go by Dylan Doyle's. Jamie suggested they stop there and do some caroling themselves.

About halfway through "Hark, The

Herald Angels Sing,'' Jane appeared at a second-floor window. Softened by the frosted glass, circled with light diffused by her breath on the pane, Will thought she looked like an angel. Glancing quickly sideways, Will saw Jamie thought so too.

By the time they began ''Oh Come All Ye Faithful,'' Jane and the children were downstairs, framed in the doorway. Each time a carol ended, Jamie immediately began another. Will didn't even know several of them but he hummed along. Finally, Jamie fell silent. Jane waved and called out Christmas wishes, mimicked by the children. As Will and Ian headed for the car, Jamie hesitated and Will saw him blow Jane a kiss across the white lawn.

Ellis MacDonald insisted the boys join him and Mrs. MacDonald in a cup of grog. Again, Jamie checked with Will.

''I'm fine,'' he maintained. ''I only drank half the last one.''

''We shouldda brought Riley,'' Ian was muttering as they left the MacDonald's. ''Shouldda brought him.''

''What for?'' Jamie asked.

''Get him to drive. Ian's voice was

muffled as he clambered into the back seat. "Gotta have a driver here."

"Speak for yourself," said Jamie. "I'm in fine shape."

Sitting beside Jamie in the front seat, Will knew it was true. He'd never felt safer in his life. The two of them made the last three deliveries while Ian stayed asleep in the car.

As they turned into the driveway at home, Robert shot out the front door, heading for the car.

"Oh, my God," said Jamie, pretending not to see him and continuing up the drive. "I completely forgot. Can you see my watch, Willie?" He pulled on its chain.

"D'ya know what time it is?" Robert's voice thundered from outside the car. "It's after eleven o'clock."

Jamie came to a stop and opened the door slightly. "Actually, Pop, I really didn't . . ."

Robert flung the door wide and pulled Jamie from the automobile.

"Where's Ian?" he asked, his eyes darting wildly into the darkness. "What've ya done with im?"

"Pop," Jamie began to laugh, "I haven't done anything . . . ."

Robert's hand whacked against Jamie's mouth and killed his words. Then he bent down and pulled Will across the driver's seat and into the driveway.

"Are ya all right, lad?" he asked.

"Sure," said Will, as lightly as he could.

"Where's Ian then?" Robert was shouting again.

"In back, Pop," said Will.

"Is he alive?" asked Robert, finally noticing the heap on the back seat. "What've ya done t' im?"

As Robert opened the back door, Ian began to stir.

"Merry Christmas, Pop," he muttered, throwing his arms around his father's neck. "Merry Christmas."

"Ya smell like a still," Robert growled, hauling Ian out into the cold night air. "A bloody brewery. That's what ya smell like. And it's almost midnight. D'ya see this?" He shoved the face of his watch up against Jamie's nose. "D'ya see what it says?"

"Eleven fifteen," said Jamie, taking a step back.

"Almost bloody midnight," Robert roared. "Get inside, all a ya. Ya've worried yer mother sick. Go on, get inside. A fine Christmas ya're givin' er."

Isobel stood near the back door as her sons came in. "Ya must be chilled t' the bone, laddies. There's hot chocolate on the stove."

"Let em be chilled," said Robert. "Why shouldna they be chilled?"

"And Nurse Farnum left dates, too," Isobel added.

"Let me hear how ya staggered from house t' house, disgracin' yerselves . . . and me," Robert said, following them into the kitchen. "Ah may as well hear it now."

"Don't be ridiculous, Pop," said Jamie, taking cups from the cupboard.

"Ridiculous? Ridiculous, am ah? And what're all a ya, fer God's sake . . . crawlin' up t'a house on all fours with a basket in yer teeth like a dog?"

Jamie began to laugh, spilling the

chocolate he was pouring.

"We weren't crawling, Pop," said Will.

"D'ya think ah'm blind or stupid that ah dinna see the condition ya're in?" Robert roared.

"Ah think they're cold, Bertie," said Isobel.

"They're that all right and heartless too t' put ya through the worry they did."

"Ah think they're chilled." Isobel handed a cup of chocolate to Ian who was making a great effort to sit up at the kitchen table.

"They're full t' the snoot, all a em . . . including wee Willie."

"I'm fine, Pop," Will said. "Really I am."

"A course *ya think* ya're fine. That's what whiskey does t' ya. But what would ya know about that, after all? A lad not even ten years old."

"I'm almost eleven," said Will.

"But James here knows enough fer the rest a ya put together. Ah shouldda known better'n t' trust im. Anyone who can sit in the stench a Tenny's night after bloody night, swillin' doon rotten

130

whiskey, is not t' be trusted. Ah shouldda known ya'd be staggerin' about in the streets and yer mother half mad with worry. It's a fine beginnin' fer her Christmas holidays, thank ya very much."

"Oh, Pop. We weren't staggering in the streets," said Jamie. "Ian and I each had a few cups of grog and Willie maybe one and a half and the reason we're so late is that everybody had to sit us down and tell us stories about what a generous man our father is."

"Be that as it may," Robert muttered. "Ah canna believe Ian had only a few cups . . ."

"It doesn't agree with me," said Ian unnecessarily, his blotchy face and puffy eyes evidence enough.

"Well, ah suppose that's a blessin," said Robert.

"And you were the one worried sick," Jamie said.

"And who wouldna be? Ah'd yer solemn oath y'd have the lad back here by nine."

"I'm sorry, Pop. I forgot about the time."

"The snow slows things up," said Isobel. "Ah didna get home from *Till the Clouds Roll By* till nearly eleven."

And as they ate stuffed dates and drank hot chocolate, Isobel described Douglas Fairbanks' most spectacular feats, while Robert roamed around the kitchen, muttering about the disgrace of his drunken sons. This gradually subsided into a series of unintelligible grunts and snorts. Then it stopped altogether.

"So ya had t' suffer through stories about me, did ya?" Robert said, finally pulling a chair up to the table.

"Everybody had one," said Will.

"And ya didna disgrace yerselves?"

"Nor you," said Jamie.

"And they liked the baskets, did they?"

"Mrs. Washington said it was much bigger than last year's," said Will.

"Aye. Well . . . she's right there."

"And we sang carols at the Doyles," Will said.

"Ya're good lads." Isobel extracted the filling from a date and popped it into her mouth, setting the filling aside.

"And ah gave Dylan a Christmas

present of the day shift," said Robert.

"What?" Jamie's voice was sharp.

"Ah know ya'll noo like workin' with im, laddie, but ya may as well begin learnin' t' get on with all kinds."

"Maybe you could switch me to nights?" Jamie didn't sound very hopeful.

"D'ya hate im so much then?"

"I'd just rather not work with im."

"But that's the point, James. He canna do the job imself. He can learn from you . . .if he can learn a'tall. Anyway, we'll try."

"But Pop . . ." Jamie began.

"Ah'll noo hear anymore about it now, laddie. Ah said we'll try it."

JUNE 27, 1932

After a week in Hollywood, Isobel decided it was time to send back home a wave of remembrances. Will dropped her at Bullock's in the early morning and arranged to pick her up there at noon.

A letter from Ian awaited him back at the hotel.

Dear Will,

As much as I hate to intrude on this happy time, I feel I must keep you apprised of developments here. James, I'm afraid, is going downhill fast.

Will hated Ian calling Jamie "James." He'd begun doing it after Robert died, as if patriarchal rights to the name had been willed him.

He no longer confines his drinking to nonworking hours but has taken to keeping a bottle in his desk. Several days recently he has exhibited the distinct effects of overindulgence while on the job. This, need I point out, greatly diminishes his effectiveness and is also, I feel, a dangerous example.

While I realize there is nothing you can do about the situation from such a long distance, I did think you should know. I see, however, no need for you to trouble Isobel with this nor any reason to mention my letter to

James. I think you'll agree it's best that this matter remain between the two of us.

I hope you're having a fine time.

Love,
Ian

Will tore the letter into small pieces. As he sat watching them drift from his hand into the wastebasket, there was a rap on the door and, almost immediately, it flew open.

"Oops, sorry," said the young woman in a maid's uniform. "I didn't see a sign on your door . . ."

"It's all right," said Will. "Please, come in."

"Well, I don't wanna disturb you. I could come back."

"It's really all right," Will assured her. "I know you have work to do."

"If you wanna call it that." She grimaced as she pulled a small cart into the room.

"Would I be in your way if I just sat over there?" Will gestured toward a small writing table.

"Naw," said the young woman. "I'll go right around you."

"Well, you just let me know if I'm in the way," said Will, moving to the table.

He began composing in his head the letter he'd like to write Ian: "I *was* having a fine time, you horse's neck. Probably one of the main reasons Jamie drinks is you. Maybe I'll drink too when I come home and have to spend every day with your pomposity. And maybe I *will* mention your letter to him. I have no desire to sneak around behind his back, even if you do."

But Will put nothing on paper. The phrases simply sputtered in his mind as he watched the maid strip away the bedsheets and replace them with billowing fresh ones.

"Who's the lady you're travelin' with?" she asked, winking at Will as she punched the pillows into new cases.

"We're not exactly traveling," said Will.

"Stayin' awhile?" she asked.

Will nodded.

"Well," she said, "I guess there's a lot to see . . . if you've never seen it."

"Yes," said Will. "There seems to be."

"On the other hand," she said, "if you've seen it, it's not so much."

"I suppose that's true too," Will agreed.

She moved into the bathroom and, as she leaned over the basin, he could see part of her back and the crown of her head reflected in the mirror. Her hair was white blonde and wavy.

"Are you a native?" Will asked, raising his voice slightly.

He could hear her laughing over the running water. "I never met such an animal," she said, "not since I've been here."

"How long have you been here?"

She turned off the water and came to the bathroom doorway. "You really wanna know?" she asked.

Will nodded.

"Two years. I can hardly believe it myself because sometimes it seems like forever. But it's only been two years."

"Where did you come from?" he asked, relieved that she didn't seen to notice how dull his questions were.

"Ohio," she said. "And you wanna know why I came, I suppose?"

"Well . . . not unless you . . ."

"I came to break into the movies." She gave a small, snorting laugh and turned back into the bathroom. "Is there any other reason?"

Will got up from the table and moved about the room, gradually making his way to the bathroom door. She was on her knees beside the tub, scrubbing it.

"Had any luck?" He tried to drape himself casually against the jamb.

"Two days as an extra in *The Sign of the Cross.*"

"De Mille, right?"

"Yeah, that's the S.O.B. He promised me a speakin' part in his next movie."

"Say, that's great," said Will.

"Does this look like a speakin' part to you?" She shut off the water and rose. "Me neither."

Will moved aside as she passed into the bedroom.

"Lemme tell you," she said, running a cloth over the table where he'd been sitting, "this business stinks."

"So why do you stick with it?"

"That's what I came for." She tossed

her cleaning cloths on the pile of linens and rolled them all into a bundle.

"What's your name?" Will asked, not wanting her to go.

"My real name's Frances Linderman," she said, "but I figure it's a little long for a marquee."

"What's the name I should watch for?"

"Rita Raymond," she said. "At least that's it at the moment. I'll let you know if there's any change." She winked again and started toward the door. "Nice talkin' to you."

"Yes, please do. Same here." Will wished he had a better final line but the door closed before he could think of one.

TUESDAY, JUNE 28

Up betimes and to deposit The Great Shopper at Bullock's. By the time I returned at noon, she'd sent a load of cargo Michiganward and gotten a *chapeau* for yours truly, a white straw with polka-dot band, no less. You heard me! I made her promise she'd help fight off the ladies.

This afternoon to some serious

sleuthing. We went by the Doug Jr.'s, Cap making it crystal clear she was there because of young Mr. F. and not the bride. Then to Greta's place on San Vincente (we think it was in there but who could tell for the trees?), Helen Twelvetrees' (is there an echo in here?), Harold Lloyd's, Marion Davies' House in the Hills (a shack compared to the beach palace, I'm told), Bob Young's (do I like him for having a heap in the driveway? I'll say. It's refreshing to see a Hollywoodian with no need to put on the dog), King Vidor's and Uncle Carl Laemmle's. We tried North Stanley Avenue late in the day but not a trace of Tallu. The Captain's really pining now — it's been four days.

A light repast at the Roosevelt — Isobel stuck to Coke and melba, while our hero had two helpings of lettuce and Thousand Island — and then to *Love Is a Racket* with young Douglas. We disagree with the title but the flicker was swell.

A bad day for celebs: our only sighting was Roy D'Arcy and he went out with bustles.

Your scrivener did run into a newcomer though. She was right here in the room disguised as a chambermaid. Known as Rita Raymond to her fans, she's got Harlow's hair and Gaynor's dimple but a charm that's all her own and a speaking part coming up in C. B. De Mille's next pitcher. Keep an eye on this little gal. She's a lulu!

In the winter of 1920, Robert insisted that Will return to school.

"The lad'll dim out his brain if the only thing he knows is *Poor Little Pepina, The Delicious Little Devil . . .*"

"Bertie," Isobel cut in, "he's noo seen *Poor Little Pepina* fer years."

"Ah dinna care when he saw it," Robert retorted. "It's eatin' is mind."

Isobel maintained, just as adamantly, that Will wasn't ready yet. She said that sitting in a small room filled with germ-breathing children would reactivate his asthma, if not something worse. Robert claimed Isobel's main concern was the loss of an escort to the movies. She charged Robert didn't care if Will died. Will wished the whole thing hadn't come up until the fall.

Finally, however, Robert and Isobel reached a compromise. Will was to be allowed to stay home for one more term but during that time he would be tutored and make up the entire fourth grade.

Isobel interviewed the first two prospective tutors and reported to Robert that one looked like Mary Miles Minter and the other like Robert Harron.

"We're noo castin' a photoplay, Is," said Robert. "We're tryin t' find someone who'll teach the lad somethin'."

The next day Robert stayed home and interviewed three prospects, finally settling on a rather severe-looking middle-aged gentleman named Lemuel Cameron.

"Is he a Scot, Bertie?" Isobel asked.

"Ah dinna know if he's a Scot," said Robert. "And ah dinna care if he looks like Farnum. Ah only want someone t' teach the lad somethin'."

"He puts me more in mind a Henry Walthall," said Isobel.

Mr. Cameron arrived five mornings a

week at exactly nine o'clock. He stayed until noon. After Miss Farnum gave Will his lunch, he worked on his lessons for the next day. Usually, he finished about the time Isobel arrived home from the matinee and she gave him a detailed account of whatever she'd seen. He was allowed to go to the movies himself only on Saturday.

JUNE 29, 1932

The day after he met Rita Raymond, Will suggested to Isobel that they have breakfast at a coffee shop down the street.

"It won't do to get into a rut," he said. "You know, adventure and all that."

When his juice arrived, he gulped it.

"Oh, no," he said, ostentatiously patting a couple of his pockets. "I must've left it . . ."

"What is it, Willie?" Isobel asked.

"The night man gave me directions to Toluca Lake Park . . . Dick Arlen, Charlie Farrell, that bunch . . . and I think I left them in the room."

"We'll go back when we've finished."

"No need for you to make the trek,"

Will said. "I'll go get them now. Be back in no time."

Will ran to the hotel and up the back stairs, arriving, breathless and sweating, on the seventh floor. The door to 708 was ajar and the noise of a vacuum spilled into the hall. After hesitating for several long moments, he walked into the room.

"Good morning." He tried to make his voice boom over the vacuum's roar but it came out like a whisper.

"Good morning, Rita." He tried again and she clicked off the machine and turned toward him.

"Hey, it's you," she said, smiling. "Hi there."

"Forgot something," he said, pointing toward the dresser top, chagrined to see it empty.

"Say," said Rita, "what's *your* name?"

"Will Claflin," he said.

"Well, that's real nice," she said.

"Yes." The panic was too great. He grabbed a theater program that lay on the bed, stuffed it into his pocket and started for the door.

"Good to see you," she said, giving

144

him a little salute with her hand.

Out in the hallway, Will got as far as Room 714 before he stopped and went back.

"Say, Rita," he said, reentering 708, "I was wondering if you're ever free?"

She poked her head out of the bathroom.

"I mean, like . . . some evening?" Will felt as though he might choke.

"I know what you mean," said Rita.

"I mean . . . I wondered if you might . . . be available?"

"Name the time."

"What?" Will's voice sounded like a screech in his ears.

"I said name the time."

"Well . . ." He had never expected her to accept. He was completely unprepared. "What about tomorrow night?"

"Swell," she said. "I'll meet you downstairs. Seven-thirty's good for me."

"Seven-thirty would be fine. Seven-thirty. See you then." Will tried to duplicate the salute she'd given him earlier but it came out looking like a rabbit punch. He also, while exiting, knocked his shoulder against the door. But none of that mattered. He was euphoric.

It wasn't until hours later, when he realized he had no idea how to separate himself from Isobel for an evening, that his giddiness gave way to gloom.

WEDNESDAY, JUNE 29

Spent the ayem tracking down real estate in North Hollywood and part of the afternoon at *Is My Face Red?,* accompanied by a so-so Paul Ash stage show. After the matinee we made tracks for North Stanley and finally caught up with Our Gal Tal.

BANKHEAD SPEAKS! You heard me. As we inched past the Rolls and turned to smile, real friendly like, she turns and booms: "Hello, daaaahlings." Isobel managed to flutter a hanky at her. Our hero managed to get the car back on the road after it crawled over the curb. Was my face red?

After dinner to a neighborhood theater to see Carole Lombard in *No Man of Her Own* (even though she knows Carole's got one — Bill Powell, ya dunderheads — the

Captain swears she glimpsed true love between Carole and her costar Mr. Gable) and then to some shopwindowing along Wilshire.

When I told Cap I was feeling a touch of the pip, she prescribed Chocolate Cream Rolls, which I'm nibbling while I scriven here. Wonder what the remedy would've been if it were Thursday?

Well, shuteye beckons and I respond. Oh yes, one last thing: while chewing the rag with Rita this morning, we made a date for tomorrow *soir* (night, ya nitwits, night!).

———————————

Jamie enlisted Will's help with his romance. Occasionally, when it appeared Dylan would have to stay on at the foundry into the evening, Jamie contacted Will during the afternoon, transmitting the message in a simple code they'd devised. When Will finished his studies, he rode his bike to the Doyle house and delivered the message to Jane.

Robert was delighted to hear that Will sometimes went out to exercise in the late afternoons, delighted that Jamie took such an interest in Will's lessons he would phone him during the day to urge him on. That, and the fact that Jamie was present more often at dinner, gave Robert great hope for his eldest son. Finally, he felt Jamie was adjusting to life as it is.

The first time Will took a message to Jane, he simply blurted it at her and left. The second time, she asked him into the house for cookies and milk with her children, Roscoe and Millicent. That was awful.

Roscoe was just like his father, loud and overweight and intolerable. He kept spouting baseball statistics, punching Will on the arm with each new piece of data, saying: "Bet you didn't know that, huh? Huh?" He also bullied his sister. Will left as quickly as he could.

The third time Will delivered a message he'd planned a swift retreat but Jane stopped him as he turned to go.

"Could you come in for a few minutes?" she asked, catching him with her sad eyes. When Will hesitated, she added: "The children are at my mother's."

Their passage into the kitchen was silent and the hush continued while Jane cut a piece of cake for Will and brewed tea for herself. Will had finished the cake and was feeling very uncomfortable by the time Jane sat down at the table with him.

"I want to thank you, Will," she said. "I know this isn't easy for you either."

"Well . . . it's all right . . ." His voice trailed off.

"It's hard to keep a secret. I know that." She looked directly at Will, her hands clasped around the warm cup. "Jamie says you're a big help to him. I'm sure you are. He hasn't got anyone else."

"He says you haven't got anyone at all."

"Does he?" Jane smiled slightly. "Well, maybe I don't need someone so much . . . I don't know. That's just the way it is, isn't it?"

"I guess so." Will felt he might cry if he continued looking in her eyes.

"It's hard for Jamie to accept things as they are. He always thinks he can make things change . . . anything really . . . if he just tries hard enough. I don't know. Sometimes change isn't possible. But he's young. He doesn't know that yet."

"Not that you're so old." Will felt he must defend her from herself.

"No, not that I'm so old." Jane laughed softly and stared down into her cup.

"Well, I guess I'd better get started." He was uneasy in the silence, unable to think of anything else to say.

"I love him, Will." She looked up. "You have my permission to remind him of that. Sometimes he forgets."

Walking to the door, Jane rested her hand on Will's back. When they reached it, she gave him a quick squeeze and kissed the top of his head, not as if he were a child but as if he were a friend.

JUNE 30, 1932

All day Thursday Will planted suggestions of his impending illness. He rose slowly from bed; he experienced some dizziness at lunch; he felt weak and shaky in midafternoon. But when Isobel suggested they stay in that night and have dinner in the room, he minimized his symptoms.

"I'm sure it's nothing," he said. "But maybe we should make it a short evening. All I need is a good night's sleep."

So they had an early dinner at Pig'N Whistle and went to the seven o'clock show of *Westward Passage* with Ann Harding.

Shortly after they settled into their seats, Will gasped and doubled over in pain.

"What is it, Willie?" Isobel asked.

"I don't know," said Will through clenched teeth. "Guess I'm not going to get past this thing as easily as I thought."

"It's noo yer appendix, thank God," said Isobel.

"Look, maybe I'd better go back to the room and lie down."

"Aye," said Isobel. "Ya'd best lie doon."

"But there's no point in you missing the picture. I'll fix it up with the doorman to get you a cab afterward."

"Aye. Now get along, laddie."

"Enjoy the show." Will pushed himself out of his seat with great effort, staying bent in half until he reached the lobby. Then he straightened up and asked the doorman to watch for Isobel when the picture ended.

It was 7:15 by the time he got back to the room. Quickly, he changed into blue slacks, put on his white flannel vest and jacket, grabbed his new hat and ran for the elevator.

Rita was just coming through the revolving door as Will arrived in the lobby. She wore a black dress that came to a V in front, a small black hat tilted slightly down toward one eye and a string of pearls around her neck. Will thought he'd never seen anything quite so spectacular. He wanted to tell her how beautiful she looked.

"Well, that's pretty good timing," he said instead, twirling his hat around and around in his hands.

"I believe in bein' punctual," said Rita.

"Yes . . . well . . ."

"And I guess you do too."

"What's your pleasure?" Will had

152

hoped that might sound smooth. Hearing it aloud, it didn't.

"I'll leave it up to you." Rita didn't seem to notice. He was grateful for that.

"I'll try not to disappoint you. Have you eaten?"

"Not since lunch."

"Well, how about the Ambassador? The food's good and I hear they've got a swell little band." Why had he said that? He didn't even know how to dance.

"Ver-ry swanky," said Rita. "But it's okay by me."

In the car Will felt Rita's physical presence acutely and it made speaking even more difficult. Afraid his voice would emerge in a croak, he held back. The silence didn't seem to bother her. He found it agonizing.

"You're shy, aren't you?" she said, finally breaking it.

"Yes." Will was startled into honesty.

"Well, don't worry about it with me. I used to be that way myself."

"Really?"

"Sure. So don't worry about it, okay?"

"Okay," said Will. "I wanted to tell

you that you look really spiffy."

"Thanks." said Rita. "You're not so bad yourself."

Will felt his face coloring. He changed the subject. "I wondered why you didn't want me to pick you up."

"Cause I live in a dump," Rita said. "You don't get anything very ritzy on a maid's salary."

"I wouldn't mind."

"You might."

"Well, wait till your name's up in lights."

"I'm waitin', all right. What else can I do?"

When Rita went to the powder room after dinner, Will found a telephone and called Isobel but there was no answer. It was 9:30. She should have been home.

"I'm a little rusty," he warned Rita on their way to the dance floor.

"I bet you're just modest," she said.

And once they began moving together, Will's feet indeed seemed quite light. His body felt almost graceful.

"You don't give yourself enough credit," said Rita, resting her cheek on his shoulder. "I've danced with a lot worse."

"I think the credit belongs to you," said Will.

"What kind of malarky is that?" Her body was soft against his.

"All I know is that I wasn't ever any good before."

"I'm your magic, Willie, right?"

"I think maybe you are," he said.

Will excused himself at 10:30 to phone Isobel again but there was still no answer. When he returned to their table, he told Rita they'd better have their last dance.

"After all, you're a working girl," he said. "I don't want you to be sore at me tomorrow."

"If I didn't know better, I'd think you were dumpin' me for someone else . . . a late date."

"Well, you do know better. I figure if I get you home early you'll come out with me again during the week."

"I might." Rita winked at him and Will's heart began racing. "Will you get me a cab?"

"Not on your life," he said. "I'm taking you home."

"That's what you think, bigshot. Just call me a cab."

Will was stung. "All right," he said stiffly. "If that's what you want."

"Look, I told you it's a dump. You're not missin' anything."

When she climbed into the back seat of the taxi, Will wanted very much to lean in and kiss her goodnight. Instead, he closed the door and handed the driver a few bills he'd crumpled in his fist.

"Take care of the little lady," he said gruffly, waving at Rita through the window as the cab pulled away.

When he arrived at the Roosevelt, he went directly to the desk.

"Have you heard from Mrs. Claflin?" he asked. "Room 708?"

"I believe she just came in, sir." The clerk inclined his head slightly toward the elevators.

When Will turned to look, there she was. He loosened his tie, bent over slightly and headed for her.

"Rather late for a girl on her own, isn't it?"

"Oh, Willie. Ya startled me. Why aren't

ya in yer bed?"

"Why aren't you? Did you have trouble getting back here?"

"Ah saw it twice. D'ya think Ann looks a bit like Ethel, Willie?"

"Never thought about it," said Will.

"Well, she's noo fresh in yer mind. I didna think so the first time either."

"But Ethel's dark."

"It's the shape a the face." The elevator doors opened and Isobel stepped into the cage.

'I had to see a doc," Will said, following her.

"D'ya feel better then?"

"Well, not yet. He gave me something that's supposed to be terrific but it doesn't take effect for at least twelve hours. He said I should take it easy until tomorrow afternoon . . . see how I feel then."

"Aye."

"I was already home and in bed when I realized I should have someone take a look-see. The hotel doc was off tonight so they sent me all the way out to Santa Monica . . . Adelaide Drive. I guess it's the closest place with a doc who keeps night hours."

"Ah think Aileen Pringle's near there, Willie."

"I hate to cramp your style," said Will, as they came into the room, "but I guess you'd better plan to go shopping or do something else on your own in the morning and I'll lie low and see if this miracle drug works."

"D'ya remember the bag Mary carried in *Kiki,* Willie? Ah got one the other day fer Alexine but Ethel should have one too. Ah'll get it in the mornin'."

"I'll see that you get a ride," said Will. "I guess it would be silly for me not to give this stuff every chance to work, wouldn't it?"

"If Ethel were fair, she could be Ann's sister," Isobel said. "Ah saw that clearly the second time."

THURSDAY, JUNE 30

Capt. Isobel spent this eve at Ann Harding's flicker *Westward Passage* (twice yet!) while our hero squired Rita Raymond to the Ambassador (if you want to avoid the rabble, this is the place to do it!). There we *mangéed* and performed the Terpsichorean rites (dining and dancing to you boneheads) and a good time was had by all.

On March 28, 1920 Mary Pickford married Douglas Fairbanks. On March 29 Jane Doyle killed herself. Isobel had seen the marriage coming. No one, apparently, had sensed the approaching death.

"She had everything to live for," said Dylan.

"Even livin' with *that* lout canna be that bad," said Robert.

"Such a lovely girl," said Isobel.

"I thought she could hang on," Jamie told Will. "I told her I'd figure something out."

Jamie's grief and his efforts to disguise it turned him even further inward. Robert was baffled by his son's behavior but thought perhaps the strain of working with Dylan was affecting him. He switched Jamie to the night shift. Now Jamie spent the entire day in bed, rising just in time to report for work. Only Will knew the reason for his withdrawal and he couldn't seem to help.

When Jamie announced late in the spring that he was going away, Robert didn't even try to stop him. He seemed finally to realize there was in his son something he could neither comprehend nor alter.

Jamie said he wanted to travel during the summer but promised Robert he would consider enrolling in college in the fall. Jamie told Will he had no idea what he would do. He only knew he couldn't stay. And, once again, Will felt as he had when Jamie enlisted: abandoned, bereft and sure that he'd never see his brother again.

JULY 1, 1932

Friday morning Will saw to it that Isobel was out of the room and en route to Bullock's by nine o'clock. He didn't remove the DO NOT DISTURB sign until he was showered, shaved and dressed. When Rita knocked, he was carefully arranged at the writing table with stationery,

160

newspapers and George Arliss's biography before him.

"Morning," he said as she entered.

"I thought you'd be out sightseeing by now," she said.

"Well, you can get a little tired of that. Anyway, I've got some correspondence to catch up on . . . some reading." he gestured toward his props. "Let me know if I'm in your way."

"You're not." She flashed Will the grin that so disturbed his insides. "I can tell you that right now."

When she vanished into the bathroom, he picked up his pen.

"Dear Ian," he wrote, "Rita Raymond . . . Rita Raymond . . . Rita Raymond . . . Rita Raymond . . ."

He put the pen down and went to the bathroom door. "Guess you got home all right," he said.

"Sure," she said. "It was a swell evening . . . just a little short."

"We'll make it longer next time," said Will.

"Sure."

He felt as awkward and constrained as

he had at the beginning of last evening. He tried to recall how he'd gotten past it then and remembered he'd simply been honest.

"I'd like to kiss you," he said.

Rita looked up from the sink and met his eyes in the mirror. Holding his gaze, she twisted off the faucets. Then she turned toward him.

"So." There wasn't a trace of a question in her voice.

Will walked to her and put his hands on her shoulders. When their mouths came together, she slid her arms up around his neck and he let his hands ride down her back, pulling her in close to him. He felt both her mouth and body softly melting into his.

"You surprise me, Willie," Rita said, pulling back slightly after a few moments.

"Please stay," Will urged, drawing her body against his again.

"You mean now?"

Will nodded.

"You really do surprise me," Rita repeated. "I've gotta do three more rooms."

"Go do them quickly and come back,

. . . please."

"Okay," said Rita, still rather startled. "Sure."

As soon as the door closed behind her, Will was certain she wouldn't return. Why should she? And, if she did, would he know what to do? He tried very hard to concentrate on everything he'd ever heard about the act of sex. Judging by the way his body felt, he didn't think he'd have any trouble becoming erect. Thank God for that! But what about pulling out? Weren't you supposed to do that as insurance against pregnancy? But when? And, for that matter, what about going in? Did girls like to do other things first? Or was it afterward? And what were the things?

By the time Rita returned Will was frenzied with self-doubt, his body numb, his penis apathetic. He wished she hadn't come.

"Change your mind?" she asked, sensing the shift.

"No!" It sounded to Will like a shout. "But if you'd rather not . . ."

"I wouldn't be here if I'd rather

not," said Rita.

"Look," said Will, deciding to try honesty one more time, "I'm not much of a sheik. I haven't really changed my mind. I just . . . oh, to blazes with it! I've never done it before and I'm damned scared."

Rita laughed but it didn't make Will feel foolish. In fact, after a few moments, he joined her.

"But you're forgettin' one thing," she said finally.

"What's that?"

"I'm your magic."

"Oh." It was a sigh of relief and gratitude. "I remember now."

Will pulled her down next to him on the edge of the bed and wrapped his arms around her.

"I won't forget that ever again." His mouth moved against her hair. "Not ever again."

As they made love, Will had the same sense of unexpected grace he'd had the night before when they'd danced. His hands found the proper places on her body. His body wound around hers with

164

easy fluidity. He entered her, when the time came, effortlessly. He felt, all in all, it was the single most felicitous thing he'd ever done in his life. He guessed, when he thought about it afterward, that she'd guided him every step of the way. But if she didn't mind, why should he? And she didn't seem to.

"That was very nice, Willie," she said. "Very nice."

"Can I see you tonight?" he asked, anticipating already his future need for her.

"Weekends aren't so good for me," said Rita.

"You mean I won't see you until Monday?" Will felt demolished at the prospect of two entire days without her.

"Weekends just aren't so good." There was a warning in her voice.

"Whatever you say." He tried to sound casual. "But at least give me your phone number so we can talk."

"I said I'd see you Monday." Now her tone was hard. "Isn't that enough?"

"Sure." Will backed off. "That's fine."

Rita took her clothes into the bathroom to dress and Will hurried into his while she was gone. He was smoothing out the bed when he heard Isobel's key in the lock.

"You're early." He raised his voice, hoping Rita would hear. "I told the maid I'd fix the bed when I got up. She's just finishing the bathroom."

"Dinna holler so, Willie. Has the pip gone t' yer ears?"

"Maybe." Will stuck a finger in his ear and waggled it. "But I feel much better."

"The bags were all gone so ah got Ethel a hat." Isobel was untying the hatbox string when Rita emerged from the bathroom.

"She waited to do our room last since I was trying to sleep," Will explained unnecessarily.

"Ya've probably put the girl out." Isobel fished about in her purse and withdrew some coins. "Give er these."

Will followed Rita to the door, the change jingling in his hands.

"Oh, thank you so much, sir," Rita said as he held it out to her.

166

"Well," said Will, "I hope I wasn't in your way."

"Not at all. Anytime you want to sleep late, you just let me know." She grinned at him and started down the hall.

He watched until she vanished around a corner and then he turned back into the room, the weight of the next seventy-two hours pressing on him like an enormous cold stone.

FRIDAY, JULY 1

Isobel insisted on opening Bullock's herself this yawning. Yours truly stayed behind, crossing paths with Rita Raymond during her rounds and confirming that she's some Sheba — if any confirmation were needed.

Being as how the Captain spent last evening with Ann Harding, she wanted to stop by the house this afternoon. So we ferreted out the Harding Hacienda in the Hollywood Hills (bet ya didn't know I could alliterate!). It's a sprawling stucco jernt with the standard red tile roof and plenty of balconies. Our Mystery Reporter (initials I.C., if that's any help) rumors that there's trouble in this particular paradise between Ann and hubby Harry Bannister. We hope not, but these things happen.

After running by Mecca (I wonder if Doug and Mary noticed we were late), we took in a couple hours of ocean breezes before hieing ourselves to North Stanley. Miss B. was already gliding along the avenue when we arrived and we'd just about decided she was going to high-hat us when she hollered at us to stop. Our hero, who always does what the movie stars tell him, screeched to a halt.

"Good afternoon, daaaahlings," Tallulah said, approaching the car.

"Aaaaaaaarrgghh," we replied.

"I feel like we're old friends," said she. "Introduce yourselves."

Since the Captain couldn't seem to remember her name, and wouldn't have been able to say it if she had, having lost the power of speech, your scrivener gave both monickers. Then handshakes all round, adieus and Tallulah resumed her constitutional. It took us about fifteen minutes to commence breathing again and when we did we repaired directly to our room to recuperate.

Tonight to see *Miss Pinkerton* with Joan Blondell (good show!) and home early.

Re R.R. and the aforementioned encounter: seeing as this is a nice party I'll give a go-by to the blow-by-blow but you may see my secretary for particulars (now wait a minute! How'd she get into this?).

In the summer of 1920, Robert decided his family needed a proper vacation. So, at the end of July, they all left for Poland Springs, Maine, although none of them wanted to go.

Robert himself was always uneasy when he was away from the foundry for more than a day at a time. Isobel disliked the disruption of her strict schedule and especially abhorred being shipped to a place without movie houses. Alexine was enamoured of a young man from college and dreaded putting such distance between them even though she'd only seen him once all summer. Ian, always anxious to prove himself indispensable to his father, would have preferred to continue his training at the foundry. Will had never been away from home before and simply didn't know if he'd like it.

Once they arrived, Robert and Ian adjusted quite quickly to the resort life. They played a minimum of two rounds of golf each day, Robert insisting Will accompany them on at least one. It was good exercise, he said. Feeling anything would be better than just trailing after his father and brother, receiving scornful looks from the caddies, Will suggested he try carrying Robert's and Ian's bags. He lasted only two holes.

"He's noo been well," Robert explained to the young man who replaced Will. "But he'll be carryin' again when he gets is strength back."

Will was grateful to Robert for covering his humiliation but the gratitude didn't diminish his mortification. He'd had no contact with boys his own age for nearly two years. He saw now how far behind he was and the rest of the vacation became, for him, a grueling effort to catch up. He swam twice a day; he played tennis with Alexine; he trotted around the golf course instead of walking; and each night he went to bed exhausted.

"Ah think he's overdoin', Bertie," said Isobel. "He'll be sick again at this rate."

"It's the one way he may get well," Robert replied. "Let im be."

Isobel kept herself aloof from the resort's activities. Her only participation was to stroll beneath her parasol to the golf course to meet Robert and Ian after their last round of the day. And this she did only because Robert insisted. Stripped of her usual avenues of removal, she simply acquiesced.

By citing her age she dismissed, however, Robert's suggestion that she play tennis with Alexine.

"Is, ah didna say ya were Molla Bjurstedt. But ya're no old crone either."

When he pointed out that half the women who used the courts were older than she, she pointed out that it was their right to make spectacles of themselves but it didn't mean she had to.

She spent most of her time on the sprawling veranda of the hotel, watching the other guests come and go, developing a speaking acquaintance with one of them, a rather courtly old gentleman she felt bore a marked resemblance to Sidney Drew. Often he joined her on the porch in the morning and occasionally they took tea together if it didn't interfere with her walk to the golf course.

Alexine made friends with a young woman from Boston named Sophia Moore and together they developed a crush on the tennis instructor, spending the bulk of their time on or near the courts.

"Ah'd no idea ya were so interested in the sport, Alex," Robert teased. "Did ya take it up at school?"

"No," said Alexine, "not really."

"Aaah. Ah see. So it's just here at the Springs ya've begun t' fancy it."

"It's not the tennis," said Ian. "It's the instructor. Personally, I think he's a sap."

"You're just jealous because you wish Sophia would pay some attention to you," said Alexine.

"Aaah . . . the instructor, is

it?'' said Robert.

''It is not,'' Alexine said.

''I heard them giggling about him,'' said Ian. ''You'd think they were high school girls.''

''How was it ya came t' hear em, laddie?''

''Because every minute he's not playing golf, he's sneaking around after Sophia,'' said Alexine.

''That's a lie. I would never *sneak around* after anyone who was interested in that jerk of an instructor.''

But, despite his protestations, Ian was quite taken with Sophia. She, however, had no feeling for him. And the tennis instructor, it seemed, was without interest in either Sophia or Alexine. Will, consumed with his rigorous regimen, made friends with no one. And when the time came to go home, everyone was relieved.

SATURDAY, JULY 2

FLASH!!!FLASH!!!FLASH!!!
Harlow tied the knot today with Paul (Thalberg's-right-hand-man) Bern. Irving

and his Norma stood up for them, we understand, and we hope that's just the beginning of nice things for Jeannie and her new spouse. Life hasn't always been a bed of roses for this sweetheart — she's had tragedy as well as triumph. We say: "Give this little girl a great big hand" and give her a break while you're at it (we hear she's been working awful hard).

Spent the evening viewing *The Man Who Played God*. Cuz Bette D. is in it too, Isobel decided she could ignore the fact that Mr. Arliss and Aunt Bess are look-alikes. Once there, she was so enchanted by Bette she didn't even notice George.

Today's Riddle: what handsome young newcomer to our town wishes he had the phone number of a lovely young newcomer to films?

Tune in tomorrow for more clues.

In the autumn of 1920, after they'd returned from Maine, the Claflins all plunged back into their separate lives.

Isobel had missed the announcement of

John Barrymore's August wedding to poet Michael Strange and now devoured every word she could find about it. Both had had previous marriages and Isobel hoped they might find together the happiness that had eluded them with others. When the news of Olive Thomas's apparent suicide reached Isobel, she was stunned. She'd known her to be a sweet girl, her delicate face framed in curls, her dark eyes sparkling with a zest for life, her young husband, Little Mary's brother Jack, at her side. How was it possible that she'd been found, filled with poison, in a Paris hotel room? When some decidedly seamy answers to that question began to be whispered, Isobel rushed to Olive's defense as swiftly as Little Mary herself. Miss Pickford called the rumors "sickening aspersions." Isobel labeled them "filth."

Robert found that the grumblings of his work force had grown louder during his absence, something he tended to ascribe to Dylan Doyle's temporary stewardship rather than the forces of history. When Ian said the problems were a reflection of the labor movement, not of Dylan's bad management, Robert pointed out that there'd been a labor movement before he went to Maine but only minor dissatisfactions among his employees.

"It's Dylan bloody Doyle, ah tell ya, and no wonder they're grousin'. They dinna like workin' fer a lout with half the wits they've got themselves. And why should they?"

To placate his men, Robert raised wages, slightly shortened working hours and added vacation time, efforts he would have made, in any case, to forestall the possibility of unionization. The thought of his workers being joined to some outside federation was anathema to him, implying, he felt, that he wasn't capable of giving them fair and decent treatment without coercion. He meant to prove otherwise.

Alexine returned to college, eager to resume last year's romance, the tennis instructor a quickly fading memory. Ian was a high school senior, planning a campaign for student government president and working at the foundry on weekends. And Will returned to school, facing a strenuous year.

Robert had been so pleased by Will's progress in the spring that he'd proposed a pact to his youngest son. If Will could cover both the fifth and sixth grades in the coming year, with tutorial help, Robert would let him begin working at the foundry after school the following year. Not only would Will be caught up academically, he would also begin his apprenticeship at the foundry at an earlier age than either Jamie or Ian had. These were powerful incentives and Will agreed to try. Robert noted that this schedule would leave little, if any, time for movie-going. Will was willing to make that sacrifice. He only hoped Isobel would understand. When she didn't even seem to notice, he was surprised and somewhat hurt.

SUNDAY, JULY 3

Early ayem visits this Sabbath to both Immanuel Presbyterian and Mecca. Then a spin by Mr. Harlow's place in Benedict

Canyon — not that we expected to see the newlyweds brunching on the front terrace! We don't even know if they're in town. But we both agreed it would make a swell spot for a honeymoon.

After a light repast at P'NW (gotta save our appetites for dinner tonight with Mr. Rosenfelt), off to a matinee of *The Rich Are Always with Us* (so true, so true, and never more evident than in this burg) with Ruth Chatterton and George Brent. Capt. Isobel is convinced that playing lovers was no act for these two and I accepted a wager based on same. If Ruth and Georgie aren't linked publicly within the next six months, the Cap'n will cease and desist from Coca Cola for a month. If they are, I'll foot the bill for a month's worth of C.C. (Have I got rocks in my head?)

And speaking of our hero, whilst seeking relief this afternoon in the theater's chambre du men (which reminds me: Where did I put *la plume de ma tante?*), who should he find himself shoulder to shoulder with? Only Spencer Tracy, that's who! Only the guy who was so fine in last year's *Up the River!* Only one of the hottest up-and-comers around! And being as how our hero sensed this was no time for handshakes, he just gave Spence a simple, understated nod. Man-to-man, and all that. I wanna tell ya, folks, out here you never know when you're gonna find yourself nose to nose (or whatever) with a star. It can happen anytime, as the above should make clear.

Joe R. and his Trio concentrated on Léhar and Lizst tonight at the Dinner Musicale, which suited us fine, and after listening the while we retired early to our suite (that's "sweet," not "soot," ya dimwits).

Things I Never Noodle Now: Barbara Stanwyck, the little gal who made it *so big* in the film of the same name, was néed Ruby Stevens.

Today's clue to yesterday's riddle to be answered tomorrow (and if you think you're confused, you should see me): One of the parties' initials are R.R. Both hail from the midwest.

In October, Will received his first

letter from Jamie.

Dearest Willie,

I'm sorry I haven't written sooner but I've been on the move, only recently coming to rest (if you can call it that) in Cincinnati. I'm not sure I'll stay here but it's no worse than a lot of places I've been and they do have a university, which may be something to think about in January. At the moment, I'm working as a welder at a place called Union Machine Co, trying to save some money and getting a feel of the place. I can just hear Pop on the subject of my employment in a foundry: if the bloody fool wanted to do that, he could have stayed here to do it! Believe me, it wasn't my first choice but it pays a lot better than waiting on tables.

That was the only work I could find in Boston. And I didn't do much better in Baltimore. And the day I arrived in New York a bomb exploded on Wall Street, killing several people and injuring hundreds of others, and the only job around was running ''errands'' for a bootlegger, who happened to be my landlord. So I decided maybe I wasn't meant to seek my fortune in the East.

Mr. Cox, the Democratic nominee, was in town the other day and I went to hear him speak. Maybe he's no ball of fire but he has to be better than Harding. If I were old enough, though, I think I'd vote for Debs. And I can just hear Pop on that subject also: is the lad daft to be wasting his ballot on a lunatic red jailbird!

I'll try to write more often and maybe you'll write to me now that I have an address. Please don't think a scarcity of letters has meant a scarcity of thoughts.

If I could have stayed, Willie, I would have. I hope you know that.

Love,
Jamie

JULY 4, 1932

Early Monday, after seventy-two hours without Rita, Will began trying to extricate himself from a morning with Isobel.

"I thought I might take a few hours to catch up on some correspondence," he said as they were dressing.

"Ah've noo written a card m'self fer days," said Isobel.

"But I'd be happy to drop you somewhere first."

"Ah'd just as soon write."

"Had enough of Bullock's for a while?"

"Aye."

The last thing Will wanted was to be in the room with Isobel when Rita arrived. At breakfast he tried another tack.

"We can put off letter-writing another day, can't we?" he asked.

"Ah suppose so, Willie."

"I've been thinking I really should have the car looked over. We've covered a lot of territory since it was serviced."

"Aye."

"I spotted a good garage the other day. Maybe I should just run it over there and stick with it . . . make sure they fix it up right."

"Ah'll do m' cards while ya're gone."

"Well, no telling how long I'll be. Maybe you'd like to try the tour they're advertising in the lobby."

"See The Movie Homes?"

"That's the one," said Will. "Of course, you probably know more than they do. But it never hurts to take a look at the competition."

"Aye."

Will went to the front desk, discovered that the tour left in fifteen minutes and bought a ticket.

"She may try to run the whole show," Will warned the guide as he put Isobel aboard the bus.

"Oh, yeah?" said the guide. "So maybe I can rest the voicebox a little."

Will stood on the curb until the bus pulled away. Then he tore back to the hotel and up to the seventh floor. Rita was just finishing the room.

"Well, hi there, breathless," she said as

he flew through the door.

"I didn't want to miss you," he panted.

"So I see," said Rita.

"And I missed you terribly over the weekend," he said.

"I hope that didn't spoil it for you."

"No, no," said Will, beginning to collect himself. "It didn't. I just wished I could see you, that's all."

"Well, now you see me." Rita bent down to pick up a bucket and a bundle of linen. "And now you don't." She started for the door.

"Can't you stay just for a few minutes?" Will asked, catching hold of her arm.

"I really can't," she said.

"Can't you come back then?"

She hesitated. "I don't think so, Will."

"I mean after you're all finished."

"I know what you mean." Her voice was sharp. "Today's pretty busy. I gotta go out to Universal later to see about some extra work."

"Just come back for a few minutes, . . . please."

"All right, all right," said Rita. "But

let me go now. I don't wanna finish late.''

"Look,'' said Will, when she returned, ''I know you're in a hurry and I know you've got a lot on your mind. But just tell me when you're free so we can make a date.''

"Maybe this whole thing isn't such a good idea,'' Rita said.

"What do you mean, *'this whole thing'*? What *whole thing?*'' Will heard his voice rising.

"You and me,'' said Rita. ''That whole thing. Maybe it just isn't such a good idea.''

"Look, I'm not asking you to marry me. I'm just asking you for a date.'' Will was surprised by his own forcefulness.

"You got a point there.'' Rita broke the tension with a laugh. ''Well, like I said, I got a chance at some extra work and that kinda leaves everything up in the air.''

"Tomorrow night?'' His perseverance surprised him also.

"I hate to say yes and hafta break it.''

"Wednesday then.'' It was not a question.

"All right,'' said Rita. ''Same time,

same place, if that's okay with you."

"Suits me," he said rather stiffly.

"Oh, come on, Willie boy." Rita poked him lightly in the ribs. "Forget that other stuff I said."

"It's forgotten." He tried to sound airy but failed.

"So I'll see you Wednesday."

As Rita held up her hand in a farewell gesture, Will grabbed it and pulled her against him, pressing his mouth down against hers, his movements angry. But as their bodies stayed together, the anger was replaced by longing. He felt again the sensation of his flesh melting into hers. When she pulled back, he was startled.

"Wait a minute, wait a minute," she said softly. "This is no time to sweep me off my feet."

"Anytime's a good time for that." He marveled at how smooth he sounded.

"Today could be my big break," Rita said. "Today could be the day I get picked outta a million faces. And you wanna make me late for it?"

"Today could be the day the director spots you in a crowd and says: 'I want you, little lady, to replace our ailing star.' ''

"So I gotta go. You understand, don't you?"

"Would I stand in the way of your career?"

"You tell me."

"Absolutely not."

When Isobel returned from the tour, Will spent a full five minutes displaying his chagrin at not having checked with the garage before making their morning plans. They couldn't service the car after all and the next available time was Wednesday night. So not only had he wasted a morning and missed the tour but now he'd have to throw away an evening as well!

"Ya didna miss much, Willie," Isobel said. "Ah'd seen all but two."

"I had a hunch we probably did better on our own," said Will. "From now on we'll stick with Claflin tours. Right?"

"Aye," said Isobel.

MONDAY, JULY 4

While the rest of the U.S. of A. celebrated independence with picnics and parades, Mrs. R. Claflin and Son did something a little different. We simply took the day off. We declared our independence from the rugged schedule we've been on (it may sound like it's all glamour and glitter, folks, but the place is killing) and locked ourselves in our room from lunchtime on. We needed a break. The Captain had fallen behind in her work. Your scrivener had just plain fallen. Before retiring for the day, however, Isobel checked out the tour given by "The Original Movie Home Guides" and reported back that these guys ain't got nothin' on us.

For the evening's repast, Cap enjoyed wrestling with a chicken, away from the stares of other diners, and yours truly put away four portions of lettuce with Thousand Island.

Riddle Answer: Our mystery couple is Rita Raymond and W.D. Claflin (he belongs to the Motor City Claflins) and you can look for them around town Wednesday night.

Ta-ta.

Isobel had not exhibited any enthusiasm for the suffrage battle. She felt, in fact, that the women were hounding President Wilson unnecessarily and at a time when the poor man had enough on his mind. But when the nineteenth amendment became law, she cast her vote as eagerly as any suffragette. That she cast it for the Democrat Cox left Robert temporarily speechless with dismay.

"He'll stick t' Mr. Wilson's ideas." Isobel thought the gurgling noises from Robert's end of the table were caused by a misdirected swallow, not by her announcement. "Eat a cube a bread, Bertie."

"Ah noo need bread," Robert rasped, shoving the words through his closed throat.

"Try the stout then." Isobel popped a morsel of food into her own mouth and chewed.

"That's just the point," Robert sputtered.

"Aye . . . have some," Isobel urged.

"He'll do exactly the same as that crackbrain Wilson." Robert's partially restored voice began climbing.

Grasping the topic now, Isobel addressed herself to it. "And, Bertie, he's runnin' with a Roosevelt."

"Ah dinna care if he's runnin' with the king! It's no reason t' vote fer im."

"Ah'm free t' exercise m' franchise," Isobel asserted calmly.

"Ah'll say ya are. Ah'll say ya bloody well are."

"Watch yer tongue, Bertie."

"It's the very reason we shoulda kept the vote t' ourselves." Her composure made Robert even more frenzied.

"Ah'm no Suff."

"A course ya're not." His anger cooled quickly before her icy indignation.

"Ah never was."

"Ah know that, Is."

"The Suffs robbed the poor man a the little peace he had."

"Aye, Is. That they did."

And the matter of Mr. Cox was dropped. It turned up, however, in muttered allusions whenever Isobel did something particularly baffling.

"It doesna surprise me," Robert would say. "Ah'm noo surprised by anythin' comin' from someone who voted fer Cox."

Although Dylan Doyle didn't actually cast his ballot for the Democrat, he did flirt with the idea of supporting him and his flirtation was highly public. He seemed to delight in throwing Cox's name around. If his intent was to provoke, he was successful.

"Why ya bloody idiot," Robert would rage, "d'ya want four more years a the same bibble-babble? A vote fer Cox is a vote fer the League and a vote fer more snoopin' into our affairs which is why business is so damn bloody bad as it is, ya bloody idiot."

In the wake of Harding's landslide victory, Robert forgave Dylan and Dylan swore he'd contributed to Harding's sweep. By this time, however, something else had arisen between the two men.

Although Robert had finally accepted Dylan's basic shortcomings, he could not tolerate a new strain of incompetence he felt was caused by whiskey.

"Ah understand that a man likes a good belt now and then," he said to Dylan, finally taking him aside for a talk. "Ah'm noo above it m'self. But not on company time . . . not while there's work t' be done."

"I never brought whiskey onto these premises," Dylan blustered.

"Maybe noo in a bottle," said Robert. "But ya carried in a snootful often enough. Ya reek a the stuff."

Dylan's attempt at bluff collapsed and he seemed almost eager to berate himself.

"I know, Robbie. You're right. I can smell myself. And it's worst in the morning. The kids don't like to come near me."

"Then, fer God's sake, get hold a yerself, man. Ah know it's been rough but consider the wee ones."

"Do you think I don't think of them? Do you think I don't try?"

"Is there aught ah can do t' help?"

Robert asked.

"Buy me out." Dylan blurted the words.

"Are ya daft? It's all ya've got."

"I'm not cut out for this, Robbie. I never will be. I only got into it because of Blackwell . . . and it was a mistake from the beginning."

"Aye. That's the truth. Ah'm glad ya've seen it yerself."

"How could I miss? I get my nose rubbed in it everyday. And now, with Janie gone, I see everyday that I'm no good as a father either."

"Dinna be too hard on yerself," said Robert. "We've all got faults, ya know."

"Anyway, I thought maybe I could start over . . . try something else. My sister's out in California. I thought I might try something out there."

"Ah'd like t' help but it's a bad time fer ready cash . . ."

"I know that." Dylan broke in on him. "And I wouldn't need the whole thing now . . . just enough to get me started. I'm sure we could arrange something."

"Aye, Dylan. Ah'm sure we can. Ah'll speak t' m' bank."

Robert borrowed sufficient cash to send Dylan Doyle heading West with a respectable reserve and an agreement to pay off the remainder in the next three years. With Harding in the White House, things were bound to improve.

TUESDAY, JULY 5

Spent the day at Carl Laemmle's jernt out in North Hollywood (known to you hayseeds as Universal City). Even though we weren't exactly mobbed by bigshots, it was a fascinating excursion.

The place was loaded with signs telling you, and I paraphrase, to SHUT UP when the red light's on. So we whispered and tiptoed from stage to stage until a Mr. Kaufman appeared to take us in hand (the name didn't fool us none — he's gotta be one of the twenty-odd relations Uncle Carl's got on the payroll).

Well, we think Mr. K. should be knighted for the tour he staged. First he got us past one of those red lights to

194

watch John Stahl, master director, at work. And what a whale of a job it is just to get a scene set up for shooting! Mr. K. hustled us away before the players arrived. Temperament, you know — and why not?

After a look-see at the makeup and costume departments and a peek into a few of the eighty dressing rooms, he steered us to one of U. City's restaurants. But could we eat? The Captain managed two Cokes while I struggled to down an éclair. Too busy ogling to bother with food! Isobel immediately spotted Tala Birell and I thought I saw Billy Bakewell across the way (this latter sighting unconfirmed). Most of the diners were extras (no, she was *not* there) or bit players but even so we felt pretty hotsy-totsy. Probably half of them were trying to figure out who we were.

In the afternoon we checked out the lot itself — lot, my eye! Whoever dubbed this place Universal City knew whereof he spoke. The main street is six miles long . . . it's got its own police and fire departments . . . and the damned thing is spread out over hundreds and hundreds of acres. I've got the feet tonight to prove it. After upwards of an hour in the midday heat, Mr. K. and I were flagging but not Cap. Gallant Fox would've blushed with shame to see her pace. I guess the only thing out this way that isn't gargantuan is Uncle Carl himself. This nabob, a giant of the motion picture industry, stands only five feet tall.

Today's Real McCoy award to Ralph Bellamy, who we ran into at the studio and who's just about as nize as they come.

Isobel's only regret is that Uncle Carl let Bette's contract lapse last year. If he hadn't, she's sure we'd have seen Herself at work today. Oh well, ya can't win 'em all.

And did we thank Miss Wittington, social secretary here at the Roosevelt, for arranging it all? Orchids to you, Miss W.

As hopeless as Dylan had been, his absence left a gap in the foundry management. Now sole owner, Robert hated to think of relinquishing any portion of that possession so he set out to replace

Dylan with someone who wouldn't insist on a partnership. The only men willing to forgo this were young and Robert interviewed a score of prospects. He found something wrong with each of them. One was "uppish"; another "naught but a clawback"; another was "the worst sot" he'd ever seen. In fact, the flaw they all shared was that none of them was Jamie. Finally, Robert wrote to his eldest son.

Dear James:

I'll put it to you simply: I've bought Dylan out and I want you to come and help me run the bloody foundry. I know you haven't got my love for it but what I'm offering is a good job with good pay and a job you'd do well.

We've had our difficulties in the past. Maybe at times I've been too harsh. But even if I've been mistaken, my motives have been good, as they are now. This would be a fine opportunity and I hope you'll be able to see it as such.

Please think this over carefully and

let me know as soon as possible.
Love from

Your Father

Despite Robert's plea for a swift decision, Jamie withheld his answer for two months. And when it came it was surrounded by conditions. He agreed to return but only for two-and-a-half years. In the fall of 1923 he planned to attend school full time. Robert, in the meantime, must train someone to replace him. Although he would live at home for financial reasons, he wanted it understood he was a grown man, free to come and go as he pleased, without interrogation. He wished to be regarded as a boarder, even though he would not be paying rent. His father must accept that Jamie had his own opinions, some of them surely at odds with Robert's. Robert was not to challenge these views relentlessly but learn to live with them, as Jamie would try to live with Robert's ideas. Robert was not to refer to Jamie as an anarchist.

Robert meekly accepted his son's terms and Jamie was back in Detroit by the beginning of March, their reunion aided immensely by the fact that Harding's election to the presidency had not caused a miraculous upturn in the fortunes of American business. Depression persisted and Robert and Jamie united against the foe.

Will, of course, was delighted to have Jamie back in the house. Even though they spent little time together, Jamie's proximity took the edge off the loneliness Will had felt during this year of intensive study.

Ian was almost never at home, his afternoons filled with the duties of student government head, evenings consumed with social activities befitting one in his position. Even so, Jamie's return made him somewhat apprehensive. Once again it put him second in line for his father's attention. It also meant he would be taking orders from his brother during weekend stints at the foundry. Ian wasn't sure he'd like that.

Isobel seemed less struck by Jamie's presence than by the growth during his absence of his resemblance to Wallace

Reid. Her first glimpse of Jamie came close on the heels of an afternoon viewing of *The Affairs of Anatol,* featuring Reid and Gloria Swanson. Riley collected her that day from the Michigan Theater and, departing from the usual way home, took a route that led past the railroad terminal. When he drew up alongside Jamie, who was standing in front, Isobel swooned in the back seat. When she revived she confided to her son: "Ah thought ya were Wally himself."

JULY 6, 1932

Although Will had prepared Isobel for his disappearance Wednesday night, it was still difficult to accomplish when the time arrived.

"Canna ya take the car and leave it, Willie?" she asked between tiny bites of the chicken breast that was her early supper.

Will drained the double chocolate malt that was his. "I just don't trust these monkeys," he said. "I figure if I'm there there's less chance they'll bollix it up."

"Ya'll noo regret missin' Mae, Willie?"

"I'll say I will!" He tried to sound fervent. "But if the car's not in good shape tomorrow we'll have to skip North Stanley and it's already been several days. Tallulah probably thinks we've dropped her."

"Ah think she's crude," said Isobel.

"Tallulah?" Will couldn't believe his ears.

"Mae," said Isobel.

"Would you rather go someplace else? There's a Hoot Gibson just down the street."

"Ah dinna care fer is wife."

"Since when? You used to like Sally."

"They're havin' troubles." Isobel dabbed with her napkin at the corners of her mouth. "Ah canna believe Hoot's causin' em."

"I thought you were going to boycott Miss West," said Will, signaling for the check.

"Ah want t' see what all the fuss's about."

"Well, the driver will take you anywhere you want to go if you change your mind." Guilt about his deception had caused Will to hire Isobel a car.

"Dinna ferget the Chocolate Cream Rolls," she said as he handed her into the automobile.

"The Chocolate Cream Rolls?" Will banged his head, straightening up in surprise.

"It's Wednesday, Willie. Ya'll go right by on the way home from the garage."

"It's Wednesday," said Will. "Of course . . . Chocolate Cream."

Isobel fluttered her hand in a gentle farewell wave as Will closed the door. His watch confirmed it would be impossible to make it to the Pig'N Whistle before meeting Rita. Hoping some alternative means of acquiring the Chocolate Cream Rolls would occur to him, he hurried to his room to shave and change clothes.

The only part of the evening he had planned was his opening line.

"As Richard Bennett said to Alison Skipworth in *If I Had a Million,*" he said, wishing the line weren't quite so long. "if you could do anything, have anything, what would it be?"

"See the Mae West picture." Rita's answer was immediate.

"You're on." Will took a masterful hold on her elbow and steered her through the lobby. Only as they emerged into the warm night was he struck by the implications of her request.

"I said anything at all," he reminded her.

"I heard you," she said.

Will considered his options. Isobel always sat on the ground floor in the center. They could sit in back or in the balcony. But perhaps Rita preferred orchestra center. He could suggest they attend the second show but they might very well cross paths with Isobel between shows. He could tell the truth. But Rita might think he was ashamed of her or afraid of his mother.

"I feel like a real schlemiel," he said, finally pulling over to the curb. "I saw the picture last night."

"Well, why didn't you say so?"

"I felt so stupid . . . after playing the bigshot: if you could do anything, have anything . . ."

"It's okay, bigshot. You can tell me all about it."

"I don't want to spoil it for you."

"You couldn't. I got a girlfriend's seen it three times and she says it just keeps gettin' better and better."

"How about *One-Way Passage?*" Will had noticed the marquee a few blocks back.

"Suits me, bigtime."

"Look, I'm sorry. I ought to know better than to come on like a smoothie." Will wasn't comfortable with this line of conversation but it was better than being questioned about the Mae West picture. "It always backfires."

"That's bunk, Willie. I don't believe it."

"You ought to believe it. You've seen me go flat on my puss more than once."

"Don't be so hard on yourself. You've got your own brand of charm."

During the love scenes between William Powell and Kay Francis Will could feel his whole body humming. When Bill kissed Kay, Will's mouth burned. When Bill took Kay in a crushing embrace, Will's arms ached. He felt certain Rita must be aware of the currents running through him but sidelong glances at her revealed nothing. She appeared to be completely absorbed in the movie.

Wanting desperately to touch her but wanting also to accomplish this with some delicacy, Will waited for a few minutes after one of the love scenes and then, casually he hoped, threw an arm across the back of Rita's seat. A few minutes after that he let his hand flop onto her shoulder. During the next love scene he could not resist squeezing that shoulder and pulling the upper half of Rita's body toward him.

"I hate to cramp your style," she whispered, drawing away slightly, "but do you want to get me all in a dither? In here?"

Will grinned at her in the darkness and relaxed his grip, satisfied to know that the throbbing he felt was mutual.

After the movie, at Rita's suggestion, they went to the Club Elysée, a low-ceilinged, dimly lit speakeasy that was a short drive from the theater and around the corner from a Pig'N Whistle. Will remembered the Chocolate Cream Rolls as they passed by but felt that stopping to get them might damage the evening's mood.

When Rita ordered a drink, Will joined her in what he hoped was a natural manner. "Likewise," he said, holding up two fingers.

Halfway through their drinks, they took to the dance floor, a surface the shape and approximately the size of a large hatbox, and danced several numbers. Each time Will moved into a position facing the long bar running across the back of the club, he felt he was being watched. Finally, he focused on a pair of eyes belonging to a dark-haired man who leaned against the bar. Will was not mistaken. The man was looking directly at him.

"You," said Rita, when they arrived back at their table, "are just a natural-born hoofer."

"Do you think so?" he was delighted by her praise. "Maybe I should give up the easy life and try for my big break."

"Don't talk to me about big breaks!"

Rita's voice hardened.

"No dice at Universal?"

"No dice, he asks. I'll say no dice. And you oughta see the girls they picked. You'd think they're doin' *Frankenstein's Daughters*. I mean, I may not be so spiffy . . ."

"But you are." Will's interruption was passionate. "That's exactly what you are." He raised his glass in salute to her, then drained it.

"You're sweet, Willie boy." Rita put her hand on his arm.

"I think I'd rather be spiffy," said Will.

"Naw. Sweet is better."

He leaned across the table toward her. "You said I was a pretty swell dancer, right? Well, don't laugh but there's a guy at the bar who's been eying me. Do you promise not to laugh?"

"I'll try."

"Well . . . do you suppose he could be a talent scout?"

Rita broke into immediate laughter.

"Thanks a lot," said Will. "Thanks very much. Some promise."

He signaled the waiter for two more drinks while Rita struggled to control herself.

"Look, I know it's a goofy idea," said Will, "and I only thought of it because this guy started staring at me while we were dancing."

"What makes you think he was starin' at you and not me?" Rita asked.

"He was looking straight at me. I could tell. And he's still doing it. Don't turn around."

The waiter placed their drinks before them and Will took a large gulp of his.

"Well, if you think it's talent he's after, let's show him some." Rita rose and headed for the dance floor.

Will took another generous swallow and, getting up to follow her, felt it hit his head and legs simultaneously. The only thing in his stomach was a four-hour-old malted milk, not enough to impede the whiskey's action.

The band played a slow, velvet version of "Bidin' My Time" and Will felt that he and Rita were wrapped around and gently carried by the musical line. But when the music changed to an upbeat rendition of "Soon," the floating sensation ceased. Will felt precarious. His legs became so elastic he couldn't control them. He wasn't always certain he felt the floor beneath his feet. When the band began punching out a reprise of the refrain in double-time staccato beats, Will excused himself and went to the men's room.

Staring into the mirror after splashing cold water on his face, he saw a door reflected in it. The door opened onto a back alley and Will paced up and down, gulping in the night air. Steadying a bit, he realized that the lights he saw at the end of the alleyway belonged to the Pig'N Whistle. He ran toward them, rushed in to the bakery counter, ordered a double portion of Chocolate Cream Rolls, gobbled two on his way back to the Elysée, quickly checked his appearance in the men's room mirror and emerged into the club ten minutes after he'd left the dance floor.

About halfway to the table, he realized he was carrying the Pig'N Whistle box and looked to see if Rita was watching him.

The table was empty. Relieved, Will hurried toward it, shoving the Chocolate Creams under his chair as he sat down. Then he noticed Rita talking to the man at the bar.

They appeared to be quite engrossed. Will turned away quickly, trying to strike a casual pose, wondering how many people had noticed that the young woman who'd come in with him was now absorbed in conversation with another man.

"Long time no see." Rita slid onto her chair, grinning at him. "I was beginnin' to think you dumped me."

"I wasn't gone that long." Will protested.

"How 'bout another drink?"

"Sure." Will swiveled around to look for the waiter, determined not to ask about the man at the bar but to wait and see if Rita mentioned him.

Two drinks and several dances later, she still hadn't. Fortified by the whiskey, Will inquired.

"Okay, Rita. Let's have it."

"What're you talkin' about, Willie boy?"

"Don't play dumb with me, kiddo. Who's the mug at the bar?"

"The mug at the . . . oh, him?" Rita gave a shriek of laughter. "So you did see me talkin' to him."

"I'll say I did . . . and there'd better be an explanation."

"Do you know what you sound like?" Rita asked.

"No, I do not."

"You sound just like the movies." She howled again.

"*Is* there an explanation?"

"Oh, yeah. There definitely is . . . but it's one I was hopin' to keep from you."

"I'll bet," Will muttered darkly.

"You were absolutely right," said Rita. "The guy's a scout."

"No kidding!" The delicate shell of Will's hauteur cracked and shattered.

"But he's not interested in you. That's why I decided not to tell you."

"Oh, I get it." Will's twinge lasted only a moment.

"He's interested in me."

"Hey, that's great! Just swell. Tell me

211

what he said."

"I never know whether to trust these guys, you know. But he did give me a name at Paramount . . . said to call tomorrow for an appointment."

"Hey, just think! Twenty-four hours from now you could be sitting across the desk from Zukor himself."

"That would make it tomorrow night and if I'm in Zukor's office tomorrow night the furniture in question won't be a desk."

"You mean you really believe those casting couch stories?"

"Do I believe them? Willie boy, I've lived them!"

"You mean you've gone to see some high-muck-a-muck about a job and he . . ." Will was unable to complete the question.

"I didn't say I ever went through with it."

"No, of course not." His relief was evident.

"Do you want to know something?" Rita's mouth curved into a flirtatious smile.

"Sure." Will hoped his pounding heart didn't echo in his voice.

"I think you were jealous." Now Rita's eyes teased him as well.

"What do you mean?"

"The guy at the bar . . . when I was talkin' to him."

"You think I was jealous of him?"

"Before you knew he was a scout, I mean."

Will wasn't sure whether an admission of jealousy would please Rita or offend her. And he wanted very much, at this moment, to please her.

"Weren't you?" she prompted.

"Well, maybe just a little."

"I thought so." Her tone indicated nothing.

"But it didn't last."

"I thought so." This time she leaned over and whispered the phrase against Will's cheek. Waves of desire radiated throughout his body from the spot she'd brushed with her lips.

"Let's get out of here." His voice was hoarse, his breathing rapid.

"Okay by me," said Rita, running a

finger across his chin.

Will shoved back his chair and, as he rose to help Rita up, pushed his foot through the lid of the Pig'N Whistle box and into the Chocolate Cream Rolls up to his ankle. He shook his foot sharply but the box clung to it like a dog clamped on a bone. Moving Rita's chair, he jiggled his foot a few more times but still it hung on. As she got up, he placed his free foot on the box and pulled upward with his imprisoned one, finally wrenching it free. Then he followed her toward the exit, leaving behind the mashed box, its contents oozing onto the carpet, and a trail of Chocolate Cream footprints.

As they headed for the car, Will realized he had no idea where to take Rita to make love to her. He didn't want to annoy her by suggesting her place. She'd been so vehement the other night. Isobel would be back in the hotel room by now so that was out. And Rita might be insulted if he offered to rent a room.

"Why don't we drive out to the ocean?" she said as they climbed into the car.

Will was filled with gratitude for her sensitivity. "You won't be sore tomorrow that I kept you out so late?"

"I'm off tomorrow."

"You're off?" Already he felt destitute, knowing he wouldn't see her the next day.

"My girlfriend's workin' for me and I'm workin' for her Saturday and Sunday."

The prospect of Rita's presence over the weekend assuaged him somewhat.

"The ocean sounds great," he said, realizing he had pulled into traffic only when he heard the horns that sounded at his abrupt entrance.

"You okay to drive?" Rita asked.

"Sure." Will gripped the wheel a little tighter and tried to concentrate. Focusing on the car ahead, he managed to follow it in a fairly straight line. But when the traffic became sparse and Sunset Boulevard began to twist into continuous curves, it was more difficult.

"I've had a few trips in my life I've enjoyed more," said Rita when they finally pulled up alongside the wide, empty beach.

"If I were really stewed, I couldn't have gotten us here," Will insisted.

"My hero." Rita gave the words a dramatic reading and threw open her arms. Will began sliding along the seat, then suddenly pitched forward into Rita's embrace. It was the last moment of the evening that he remembered.

WEDNESDAY, JULY 6

A riddle: Who's got pie in his eye, who's got his sheets to the wind, whose gills are fried, whose bun is on . . . who's got a . . . ?

Isobel saw *The Four Horsemen of the Apocalypse* on the second day of its run at the Palms State. And on the third, fourth, fifth and sixth. When she glimpsed the eyes of Rudolph Valentino gazing from beneath the tilt of his gaucho hat, when she watched his perfectly sculpted lips whispering love beside the cheek of Alice Terry, when she saw his body move sinuously through a tango in an

Argentinian cafe, she was committed. She didn't need *The Conquering Power, Camille* or *The Sheik* to clinch her ardor. It flamed, full and fervent, at first sight.

She never used the diminutive "Rudy" when referring to the smoldering Latin. She never called him Rudolph. She always used his entire name, Rudolph Valentino, perhaps as a gesture of respect for his magnificence, perhaps to separate her passion from that of the hordes who spoke of him with such familiarity. Or perhaps she observed this formality as a means of keeping Valentino somewhat at bay. Without some insulation, however slight, the feelings he unleashed could incinerate her.

There was nothing decorous about these sentiments. They bore no relation to her admiration for Fairbanks, her worship of Barrymore, her respect for Bushman. These were emotions that surged through her body and made her somewhat desperate. Valentino was also distinguished from the other deities in Isobel's pantheon by the fact that she never believed genuine the love she witnessed between him and his leading ladies. On the contrary, she was given to reviling his costars with a particular viciousness.

"It's a nasty little mouth she's got," she said of Alice Terry after her second viewing of *The Four Horsemen*.

"Ah thought ya liked her, Is," Robert responded, pleased to hear his wife initiating conversation.

"Never," said Isobel with some vehemence.

"Ah recall her in a picture with Bessie Barriscale. Ya were fond a that."

"Ah'd noo be fond a anything with such shifty eyes."

"Ah dinna recall that. And what's wrong with the mouth then?"

"Pinched and mean," said Isobel. "As nasty as they come."

When Valentino played Armand to Nazimova's Camille, Isobel's old loathing of the Russian actress was rekindled. She pronounced her a "third-rate Theda Bara," noting that "Theda erself's bad enough."

She had nothing but scorn for Agnes

Ayres, the object of Valentino's fiery lovemaking in *The Sheik*. The only thing that saved Agnes from being wholly ordinary was her "horrible bulbous nose." Even with it, said Isobel, "ah wouldna know the woman if she walked in m' front door."

But the insults she heaped on Valentino's leading ladies were mild compared with the abuse she directed at one of the ladies in his off-screen life. Natacha Rambova, the second Mrs. Valentino, was, according to Isobel, a "foul demon," "black fiend," or "vile beast."

Pressed to explain the harshness of these judgments, she presented a case resting on four key points: Natacha was Nazimova's protégé (that alone, Isobel implied, was sufficient to condemn her but there was more, much more); she was an impostor (if she was indeed the stepdaughter of cosmetics manufacturer Richard Hudnut, why didn't she say so? And why didn't she use the name, her name, Winifred Hudnut, which would make that clear?); she tricked Valentino into bigamy (surely *she* knew that an interlocutory decree of divorce meant he wasn't truly severed from his first wife for one year, something he, a man of another culture, could hardly be expected to understand); and most damaging and despicable of all, she did not love Valentino (hadn't she said, after all, in the black-and-white print of *Movie Weekly,* that she was entering the union for "congeniality," not romance?).

And if this evidence did not conclusively prove how truly odious Natacha Rambova was, Isobel indicated there was still more where it came from, if one just cared to look. That Valentino himself had, quite clearly, failed to do so bothered Isobel not at all. He rose, above his loathsome liaison, an innocent victim, a stainless martyr. Natacha Rambova was a "scurvy spirit." Rudolph Valentino was "nobility itself" to be able to endure life with her.

JULY 7, 1932

Will felt the room's emptiness when he awakened Thursday morning. Nevertheless, he sat up and called Isobel's name. When

220

there was no reply he fell back against the pillows in relief.

A glimpse of his trousers, one cuff a mosaic of brown and yellow streaks, initiated recollections of the previous evening. When he realized they stopped abruptly at the ocean's edge, he began to panic. He grabbed for his journal and read the abortive, obviously drunken, entry. No help there. What had happened? What hadn't? How had he gotten home? Where was the car? And Rita? What about Rita?

A look at the clock told him she should be arriving soon. She would banish the mysteries. Hopefully, that wouldn't be too embarrassing. Then he remembered her day off and felt doomed. How could he endure these questions for twenty-four hours?

A key rattled in the lock.

"Ah thought ah'd let ya sleep since ya got in late," said Isobel, setting a stack of magazines on the dresser.

"New issues?" Will inquired.

"Aye . . . and Mae on the front a half a em."

"Did you like the picture?" He was relieved they'd hit on a topic that would buy him time.

"She's so *big,* Willie."

"Yes, I guess she is."

"Ah canna find the Chocolate Creams."

It hadn't bought much and Will uttered a moan that brought Isobel to his bedside. What was the use? He may just as well tell the truth.

"Look at my pants," He gestured toward the floor where he'd flung them. "Just look at them."

Isobel stared for a moment at Will's trousers, then crossed the room and looked beneath them.

"Ah dinna see the Creams, Willie."

"I said *look* at them."

"Ya got em a mite spotty at the garage."

"Is that what you see? Is that it?" The edge of hysteria in Will's voice sharpened.

"What is it, Willie? Ya seem delirious."

The word sank slowly into his consciousness. "Delirious? Oh . . . yes . . . I probably am. Excuse me, please."

He ran to the bathroom, neglecting to shut the door, and vomited long and loud.

"I think it's a relapse," he said afterward, shuffling to the bathroom door and propping himself up there.

Seeing Isobel in the farthest corner of the room, drained of color and frantically working a fan in front of her face, Will realized the open door had been a stroke of genius. It had exposed her to the full violence of his retching, a powerful diversionary device. There would be no further mention of Chocolate Creams, no inquiries about the previous night. She would wish only to exit.

"Ah thought ah might do some shoppin', Willie." Already she was gathering up her purse and parasol.

"I guess I'd better lay low," said Will. "I feel rotten about this."

"Aye," she murmured. "Lay low."

"How will you get around?" he asked.

"A cab'll do nicely." She passed Will on her way to the door. "Take care then."

He watched her move down the hallway, relief and remorse contending for supremacy. Remorse held a slight edge until her small figure vanished. Then relief shoved it aside as he closed the door and got back into bed.

Vomiting, Will thought, had really been quite reassuring. Given the contents of his stomach, wasn't it unlikely he'd also vomited last night? And wasn't it also likely that if something dreadful had happened to the car he'd have heard about it this morning? Wouldn't there be some sign of disaster? Trembling, he crept across the room to his suit jacket. The car keys were in the pocket. Thank God for that! Now if only he had the Chocolate Cream Rolls everything would probably be fine. Chances were, presented with them on her return to the hotel, Isobel wouldn't even remember to reopen the subject of last evening.

Will began pulling on his clothes as he completed the thought. Deciding a cab would be quicker than taking the car from the garage, he grabbed one outside the Roosevelt and urged the driver to race up Hollywood Boulevard. It didn't strike him, until he was sailing through Pig'N

Whistle's doors, that today, of course, was Thursday.

"I can't believe it," he squawked, staring at the bakery case filled with angelfood cakes.

"Whatsa matta, bud. You got somethin' against angelfood?" The woman behind the counter spoke and cracked her gum simultaneously.

"I can't believe it's Thursday," Will wailed.

"The calendar don't lie." She jerked her head toward a large square on the wall reading: Thursday July 7.

"I know, I know." Will felt despair replacing his hysteria. "You see, I have to have Chocolate Cream Rolls."

"They're Wednesday."

"I know that."

"Whatta you mean, you hafta have 'em?" Suspicion flared in the woman's narrowed eyes.

"I mean I always get them on Wednesday but yesterday I didn't so I need them today."

"Oh yeah? How come you didn't get 'em?"

"It's a long story." He felt weariness settle on his shoulders like two oversized birds. "Anyway, they're not really for me. They're for my mother."

"Oh yeah? Well, that's kinda sweet."

Will looked to see if the woman was ridiculing him but couldn't find a trace of mockery in her face. "She sort of counts on them," he said.

"The angelfood's better, you know. You oughta get her started on that."

"She hates angelfood." Will felt as though he might cry. He also felt he wouldn't care if he did.

"Well," her gum gave three sharp explosions, "tell you what. Sometimes some of the stores has stuff leftover. We ain't supposed to sell it cause it ain't a hundred percent fresh."

"What happens to it?" Will was slightly invigorated by the beginnings of hope.

"Well, Mr. Pig or Mr. Whistle, one of them guys, sends it all off to a soup kitchen downtown. But it usually don't get picked up till later in the day."

"You wouldn't have any here, would you?" Will hoped he sounded plaintive, not wheedling.

The woman stared at him, silent except for her snapping gum. "We ain't supposed to sell it," she said finally.

"Who would know?" Will whispered, glancing about to confirm that the shop was quite empty. "I can't tell you what it would mean to me."

After a moment's hestitation, she wheeled around and disappeared into a back room, emerging shortly with a small package, her eyes darting from side to side, head jerking repeatedly in the direction of a cash register at the end of the counter, looking as though she'd contracted a nervous disorder during her absence.

Will followed her spasms, meeting her at the register where she pressed the package on him, then set her hands dancing over the keys. She let him take out his money but after pretending to receive it, she shoved it back at him and began hissing: "Get outta here! Get outta here!"

"Thank you." Will hissed back at her, grabbed his package and moved swiftly toward the street.

Back in the room, he placed the box on the dresser, stripped off his clothes and returned to bed. Within a few moments he was asleep.

THURSDAY, JULY 7

A lazy day today for your scrivener while the Captain went off on her own to do you-know-what. And to mark the end of a big shopping day, or to celebrate the end of my slight relapse (it was nothing, really nothing), or to commemorate the reunion of the Cap'n and her mate after a night and day apart, or all of the above, we decided to dine at the Biltmore. And you can have it, as far as we're concerned. It's a lot of boiled shirts and some very swanky prices — you could last a week at P'NW on the lagniappe alone — and just not our sort of place. We like a jernt where you can let your hair down a mite and not feel you have to pass inspection everytime the waiter brings another spoon.

And lower our tresses we did, after taking in *One-Way Passage* (just as good the second time around — a real tribute to Bill and Kay). We repaired to the porker's place immediatement (that's parley-voo for right now) and dug into, respectively and ladies first: a Chocolate Drop (straight chocolate — ice cream and syrup — with whipped cream and cherry garnishee, a Nabisco wafer and a banana that Cap cut dead) and a Cupid's Delight (hang onto your hats! this one's got vanilla and strawberry I.C., strawberries crushed, peaches and pineapple sliced, sweet wafers and ditto the above garnishee). And now we're singin': We got those eleven P.M. bellyache-because-we-ate-our-sundaes-late-lyin'-in-bed-Pig'N Whistle blues (see my agent for performance rights).

Today's Riddle: As we write here, what new star may be ascending in the Paramount firmament?

Today's Clue: Roosevelt Hotel patrons were among the first in town to become acquainted with her charms.

———————

Autumn 1921, was a cloudless season

229

for Will. He was beginning the seventh grade with his own class. Robert kept his promise and put Will to work at the foundry after school. He had a standing date with Jamie each Sunday afternoon. And Ian had gone off to college.

The Arbuckle case broke just as Will began work at the foundry. So engrossed was Isobel with the horror of Fatty's predicament — quite clearly, she believed, he was the victim of a fiendish frameup — that she didn't even seem to notice Will's employment. When he arrived home for supper at six o'clock, she greeted him just as though he were coming in after school at three. But gradually, as her outrage was replaced by the somewhat less potent emotion of admiration — this for Minta Durfee, the comedian's estranged wife who stood by him throughout the ordeal — the change in Will's schedule began to register.

"Isn't it late, Willie?" she asked one night.

"I don't finish till five-thirty," he said. "I came right home."

"What is it ya're doin', laddie?"

"Pop told you, Isobel. I'm working at the foundry . . . odd jobs, sweeping up, stuff like that."

"Aye," Isobel murmured. "Ya look a mite sooty."

"I haven't cleaned up yet."

"Did they tell ya it was filthy work?"

"I like it." Will felt challenged and rose to defend his new profession against *their* slurs, whoever "they" were.

"Willie tells me he's at the foundry now," Isobel said at supper.

"Aye." Robert finished chewing a mouthful of food. "It canna come as a big surprise, Is. Ah told ya the plans a month ago."

"Ah dinna know if the lad's strong enough, Bertie."

"He is." Robert cut a large piece of meat and put it into his mouth.

"Ah dinna know if he's got time for is schoolwork."

"He has." Robert continued chewing.

"Did ya tell im it was filthy?" Isobel asked.

"The lad's seen the place before . . . and seen how *filthy* is father is when he

231

comes home from it.'' Robert's grip on his silverware whitened his knuckles.

''Did ya tell im he'd come home lookin' like a sweep?''

''Did ya ask him if he minded?'' There was no mistaking Robert's anger now as he laid down his knife and fork and leaned forward. ''It may be he likes the dirt, like is father and brothers before im.''

''He's noo as strong as the other lads.''

''Ah've noo got im carryin' castings on is back, fer God's sake. He's hearty enough t' lift a bucket and broom.''

''He was never as strong.''

''And what would ya have im do, ah'd like t' know? Come home from school and crawl t' is bed? Meet ya at the pictures and take lessons in bein' a man from yer darlin' Rudy? What, fer God's sake, would ya have the lad do?''

''Rudolph Valentino's a fine man.'' Isobel's voice was quiet but firm.

''He may very well be. Ah dinna know. But he's noo yer son . . . and he's noo yer husband.'' Robert blurted out this last phrase surprising, and embarrassing,

232

himself. Wadding up his napkin, he threw it on the table and quickly left the room. In a few moments he returned.

"Ah'll noo be driven from m' own table," he said, going directly to the decanter on the sideboard and pouring himself a drink.

"That's noo the table, Bertie."

"Dinna twit me in front a the lad," Robert thundered. "Or any other time, fer that matter." He took a large swallow of whiskey, planted the glass on the sideboard and began pacing up and down before it.

"There's a thing or two ah'd like t' point out. It's because a the filthy bloody foundry that we're sittin' in this house." Robert's rage poked holes in the reasonable facade he was trying to construct. "And it's because a the filthy bloody foundry that there's food on the table and clothes on our backs."

"The drink makes ya flushed, Bertie."

He took another enormous swallow. "The filthy bloody foundry allows ya t' go off t' the bloody movies everyday a yer life and gives ya a car and driver t' carry ya there. It sends yer children t' college, it keeps a servant in yer house . . .''

"Who's that, Bertie?"

"That's Farnum, fer God's sake. That's who it is."

"Ah dinna think a Nurse Farnum as a servant." Isobel seemed genuinely surprised.

"Well, she is, whether or noo ya think it . . . and it's all thanks t' the filthy bloody foundry!" Robert emptied his glass and refilled it. "Now considerin' these benefits, considerin' the things ah've named, is it really too much t' ask that ya keep yer distress t' yerself when yer darlin' bairn comes home with a smudge on is cheek?"

Isobel looked prepared to answer. Robert held up one hand to silence her and, with the other, brought his glass to his mouth.

"And . . ." He drank and waited for the whiskey to travel downward. "And, ah'd like t' know, what good did it do the lad when ya were keepin' im here with ya all sweet and clean? Ah'd like t' know what that did fer im. And ah'll tell ya. It made im a puny little minikin too weak t' make is own lungs work and too feeble t' carry a schoolbag.''

''Ya're answerin' yer own questions, Bertie.''

''Aye,'' said Robert, ''ah am. That ah am. And one a m' answers is t' let the lad get a little snuffy, thank ya very much. A man may not get all mucked up in the photoplays but he bloody well does in life and the lad may as well learn it. Ya had yer chance, Is. Now it's mine.''

And Will felt that he was now, quite clearly, in his father's custody. He worked very hard to please him, an effort that left Will neither time nor energy to mourn the passing of his leisure days with Isobel. If she noticed this, she gave no sign. She found companionship at the Adams, the Capitol, the Broadway Strand. She gave her dreams to Rudolph Valentino. It seemed to Will her world was quite full without him.

JULY 8, 1932

Part of Will's penance for his delinquent night and day was to forgo even trying to contact Rita on Friday morning. He and Isobel breakfasted and left the hotel by nine.

As they sat outside Pickfair's closed iron gate, sunlight cut through the morning haze. Golden streaks drove into the earth before them, the light ricocheting up into the car, washing Isobel and Will with its glow. The radiance complemented perfectly their reverent silence.

"Now that you're a pro," said Will when the rites ended, "why don't you take me on the tour?"

She directed him first to Charlie Chaplin's hilltop home, visible only as a strip of red-tiled roof through the surrounding trees.

"The roof'll give ya an idea of the size," Isobel pointed out. "And Charlie built it in is bachelor days."

"I'd like to see his idea of a family joint," said Will.

"Ah believe wee Charles and Sydney

236

were born here.''

''You mean he squeezed in room for a nursery? Must've been tight.''

''The poor lads,'' Isobel murmured, ''havin' t' live with that baggage.'' Her loathing of Lita Grey, Chaplin's ex-wife, had abated little since its birth at their messy divorce trial.

Again, at Barrymore's house, they gazed at a portion of sienna roof.

''Ah hope the wee bairn's well,'' said Isobel. ''Dear Jack's startin' a picture soon.''

''With his new gal Katharine Hepburn,'' said Will.

''Ah've heard she wears overalls.''

When they pulled up in front of Constance Bennett's, Will coaxed Isobel out of the car and took a snapshot of her with the large white house in the background.

''Ah wonder why Connie's right on the street?'' Isobel mused.

''Maybe she likes mingling with the little people,'' suggested Will.

''Not Connie,'' said Isobel. ''Ah wonder why she's noo in the hills?''

Finding Eddie Cantor's house "on the street," however, seemed to Isobel quite proper.

"He was always a mite common," she confided to Will. "At least Connie had some trees in front."

Since they were in Beverly Hills, Will suggested the nearby Brown Derby for lunch. They were settled at a table, Isobel with a Coke, Will with soda water, reading their menus, when Will noticed Isobel raising her eyes to shoot brief but piercing glances past him.

"What is it?" he asked finally.

"Ah think Mary Astor's over yer shoulder, Willie," she whispered. "Dinna look."

"Are you sure?"

After two more furtive glances, Isobel nodded.

"How can you tell?" Will asked.

"She's got the look of a new mum."

"This must be one of her first times out."

"Aye." Isobel sipped her Coke, staring now toward the Astor table. "The lassie was born just three weeks ago."

"Who's Mary with?" Will asked.

"Ah canna see the face . . . but ah think it's business."

"Probably."

"Ah'm noo surprised she and dear Jack had bairns at the same time."

Isobel saw a Lobster Newburg going by on its way to Mary's table and ordered the same. Will had fruit salad and a basket of hot rolls.

"Ah dinna think she ever got over im."

"Barrymore? You think she's still carrying a torch?"

"Ah knew in *Beau Brummel* they were really in love."

"But still . . . after all they've both been through?"

"It's hard t' ferget a first love, Willie."

"Yes, I can imagine . . ." His voice trailed off as his mind veered to a reverie of Rita. After luxuriating in his fantasies for a few moments, he realized that if he wanted to reach her today, he'd better try now.

"Don't let Mary get away," he said to Isobel. "I'll be right back."

"Miss Raymond, please." There was a

long silence from the Roosevelt's operator. "She's on the housekeeping staff."

"I'm sorry sir. I don't see . . ."

"How about Linderman?" Will asked.

"Yes. We have a Frances Linderman."

"Is she in the hotel?"

"I'll try to locate her, sir."

Will was just about to give up when Rita's voice came over the line. He cleared his throat noisily and deepened his voice.

"Is this the young lady who called Mr. Zukor's office and got an appointment?"

"It's the young lady all right but she didn't get any appointment."

"You didn't?" Will asked the question in his own voice. "What's the matter with those monkeys?"

"Hey, what is this?"

"It's me."

"Thanks for all the help."

"Me. Will."

"Oh, Willie boy. I shoulda known."

"What do you mean you didn't get the appointment?"

"I'm gonna let you in on a little secret . . . life doesn't always turn out like the movies."

"Well, I thought at least they'd let you test . . ."

"Test?" Rita's snort of derisive laughter cut him off. "They never even heard of me."

"You mean that guy didn't tell them . . ."

"I mean they never even heard of *him*."

"He was a phony?" Will was dumbfounded.

"I think you're finally beginnin' to get the picture."

"Why I'd like to take a swipe at that so-and-so . . ."

Rita interrupted. "Okay, tough guy. Simmer down. I'm no farther behind than I already was."

"You're a lot more disappointed."

"So . . . it's happened before, it'll happen again. That's life."

"Not in my book, it's not."

"Well, I guess we're readin' different books. Listen, I gotta get back to work."

"I just wanted to say I was sorry about the other night," said Will.

"Nothin' to be sorry for."

"No?" Will's voice squeaked with

hope. "Are you sure?"

"What's that supposed to mean?"

"Well, I felt a little down the next day and I just hoped you hadn't noticed . . ."

"You seemed fine to me." He thought he heard a compliment in her voice but he couldn't be sure.

"I guess it wasn't exactly Powell and Francis." He wanted to pin this thing down if he could.

"Close enough for my money," said Rita.

"Really?" Now his voice cracked. "Well, I'm glad you thought so."

"You didn't? I get the feelin' you got some doubts."

"Oh, no. Absolutely not. I thought it was . . . I thought it was just swell. I really did."

"I gotta go. I can feel Mr. Big Eyes starin' at me."

"Could I see you tonight?"

"I told you about weekends. Gotta go. Bye."

When he returned, Isobel was gazing dispiritedly at Mary Astor's now empty table.

"Shucks!" He snapped his fingers in mock dejection. "I was sure she'd wait to say goodbye to me."

"It wasna Mary after all." Isobel's sense of betrayal crept into her voice. "It was an impostor."

"Well, of all the lousy stunts to pull!"

"Ah canna eat, Willie." Isobel's food lay rearranged, but unconsumed, on her plate.

Will motioned for the waiter. "Could you please clear this and bring us a dish of chocolate ice cream and some sweet wafers?"

"Yes, of course, sir. The Newburg was not satisfactory?"

"Oh, yes. I'm sure it was. I'm sure it was excellent. It was just a mistake . . . not yours though . . . our mistake. We just shouldn't have ordered it in the first place."

Will was relieved when the waiter finally vanished and he could stop trying to explain.

FRIDAY, JULY 8

Signed up early this ayem for Capt. Claflin's Tours of the Movie Homes and recommend it highly to any other stargazers. One very classy note: this tour ends up at the Derby for lunch. Unfortunately, today there was a cruel sham perpetrated on that hotspot's patrons by a young woman pretending to be Mary Astor.

I guess these bogus articles don't realize that sooner or later they'll be found out. And I also guess that this town is full of such shysters. Like the jackanapes who represented himself to a certain party as a talent scout the other night at the Elysée. We think that playing on other people's hopes and dreams is about as shabby a trick as we've come across in a long time and if we ever come across the mountebank himself, we intend to tell him so — right in the kisser. I'se regusted by the whole thing!

An afternoon at Forest Lawn's Wee Kirk O' the Heather was soothing and restorative. This is a replica of the spot where Mrs. Laurie's gal Annie used to worship on the auld sod. It's surrounded by an abundance of lush flora (they ain't tellin' where they keep the fauna) and we strolled the paths that wind throughout extensive grounds, quite forgetting it was a "memorial park" (see my secretary for the Michiganese translation).

Home to a light supper and thence to the early show of *Wayward* with Pauline Frederick, Dick Arlen and Nancy Carroll. Isobel fears Nancy isn't getting the treatment she deserves from the Paramount bigshots. But let's hope Cap is wrong about that. This is one star we'd hate to see waning.

Tattlers are tattling about: The new sheik in town whom an up-and-comer of the gentler sex swears *does* hold a candle to William Powell. Haw!!

When Isobel relinquished all claim to Will, Robert was both pleased and distressed. He was delighted by his son's absence from the movie theaters, disturbed by this sign of his wife's increasing distance from the rest of the household.

Remoteness shrouded Isobel during the long winter of 1922 and into the spring, lifting only for Fatty Arbuckle's acquittal, descending again immediately thereafter. She was elusive, drifting in and out of household activities, a fugitive from her family. Robert suffered greatly from this state of affairs and sought more frequently than ever to assuage his pain with alcohol. Many spring evenings he never even appeared for dinner but made noisy entrances late at night. Once before breakfast, Will saw him standing at the sideboard pouring a drink.

But as summer approached Robert seemed to take himself in hand. He regularly attended the evening meal and seldom had more than a single whiskey before sitting down to it. One night, taking Will and Jamie aside, he explained the reversal in his behavior.

"Yer mother's noo been happy, lads, as ya've no doubt observed. It's difficult fer er t' see all a ya growin' up." Robert walked back and forth before the sofa where he'd placed his sons. "And ya may also've noticed that ah've noo been a picture a merriment m' self. Ah canna deny it."

"You had a rough year with the business, Pop," said Jamie.

"Aye, it's true. But that's in the past and there're other things ah'm puttin' in the past as well." Robert sat now in a chair facing the sofa and leaned forward. "Yer mother's birthday's comin' up, lads, and ah think we should give er the grandest party she's ever seen."

"Maybe it would just remind her," said Jamie, "remind her that we're all growing up."

"Ah'll noo write er age on the banners, James." Robert was hurt that his idea hadn't received an immediate endorsement.

"Who'll come?" Will asked.

"Ah haven't a guest list yet. There's plenty a time fer that."

"I think it's a great idea, Pop." Jamie was eager to dispel any doubts about his support. "Don't you, Willie?"

"Sure," said Will.

"We'll do anything we can to

help," said Jamie.

"That's m' lads," said Robert. "Ah knew ah could count on ya."

As it turned out, Robert handled all the arrangements himself. He had a room set aside at the Statler Hotel for luncheon on June 25, his wife's fortieth birthday. He directed the chef to prepare ham-and-spinach pie in puff pastry, mile-high ice cream pie and petit-fours. He bought a block of matinee tickets at the Broadway Strand for Fairbanks' *Robin Hood*. He chartered a Bob-Lo Island excursion boat to make a dinner cruise on the Detroit River. And he hired the Statler's chef to prepare the dinner on board: sliced breast of chicken, baby asparagus and chocolate éclairs.

The guest list did pose a problem since Isobel had no friends, as such. The yardstick Robert finally used was to invite only those people Isobel would not find offensive: several neighbors, three couples from the church, a few of Alexine's chums who'd spent some time at the house over the years, a former associate of Blackwell's who was now a judge, and his wife, a floorwalker at Hudson's Department Store of whom Isobel was quite fond and, of course, Farnum and Riley.

Alexine had arrived home from college two days earlier and she and Isobel were scheduled to lunch on the twenty-fifth at the Statler and attend a matinee of *Beyond the Rocks* with Valentino and Gloria Swanson. When they entered the hotel, Alexine steered Isobel toward the special dining room where some twenty-five people were gathered in her honor.

As the doors swung open, Isobel's eye fell on Mr. and Mrs. Fitch from the church and her hand shot out to impede Alexine's forward progress.

"If we're caught by the Fitches we'll noo make the show," she whispered. "He's windy."

Before Isobel could begin to execute her retreat, the sound of the crowd singing "Happy Birthday" froze her in the doorway. When her own name boomed at her from the song's third line, she looked about frantically as though trying to escape.

"It's for you," Alexine said.

"Ah realize that," Isobel hissed.

Robert separated himself from the crowd as the song ended and approached his wife.

"Happy birthday, Is." He placed his hands on her shoulders and bent to kiss her cheek.

"Ah'd no idea, Bertie. We're on our way t' *Beyond the Rocks.*"

"Ya're goin' ferther'n that," he said.

"What d'ya mean?" There was a trace of panic in her voice.

"Ya'll see, Is. Ya'll see." Robert patted her hand as he placed it on his arm and led her toward the guests. Even though she was acquainted with all of them, Robert presented her as though she were a new and most noteworthy arrival in their midst. His pride in the elegance of the occasion, his delight at being able to share it with his wife, were evident as they circled the room.

"I never saw Pop look so happy." Will stood with his brothers and sister near the table where their parents would eventually arrive. Its center held a silver bowl swollen with brilliantly colored summer flowers. The edges sparkled with crystal and gold-ringed china.

"What about Isobel?" Alexine stretched onto her toes, trying to locate her mother's tiny figure in the crowd. "How does she seem?"

"Much better than I expected," said Jamie. "She may even be enjoying herself."

"Well, of course she's enjoying herself," said Ian. "It's a perfectly swell party."

"Well, of course it's a perfectly swell party, Ian," Alexine snapped back at her brother, "but that doesn't necessarily mean she's enjoying herself."

"Why wouldn't she be?" Ian asked.

"Oh, Ian." Jamie's sigh held more sorrow than rebuke.

"Well, why wouldn't she?" Ian looked from one to another, challenging each.

"Because she's different," said Will.

"Oh, what do you know?" Now Ian was exasperated.

"Willie's right," said Jamie.

"You always back him up, don't you? It's very touching."

"Please don't fight," Alexine begged.

"Who's fighting?" Ian spit the words at her before moving toward his parents who were nearing the table.

"She swears it was a great surprise," Robert announced to his children. "Ya all did a fine job."

And as the day unfolded, it was evident that Isobel began to enjoy her position as the centerpiece of this magnificent pageant. By dinner time she had relaxed into the role fully, relishing a stroll around the deck on Robert's arm, chatting with her guests. They spoke of Fairbanks' derring-do, the splendid Claflin children, how Isobel looked like a woman half her age, and the gentle night air that wrapped the entire occasion in benevolence.

Late in the evening with the river carrying them home, Isobel voiced her only regret.

"Ah wish ah'd worn m' new silk," she told Robert.

"If ya've no complaint beyond that ya'll make me a happy man."

"Just the new silk," said Isobel. "That's all."

JULY 9, 1932

Isobel indicated Saturday morning that she'd like to see *Wayward* again at the early matinee. Will begged off easily, citing a backlog of correspondence, and during breakfast he managed to escape long enough to leave a scribbled note to Rita in the room.

"Please, *please* try to be here at 1:10 this afternoon," it read. "I'll be desolate if you're not. Love, Will"

All during the morning rounds with Isobel Will fretted that the note sounded too desperate. He worried that it would put Rita off. And when he burst into the room that afternoon and found it empty, his fears were confirmed. Then he saw her note to him.

"I will try, Willy boy," she had written, "but I can't promise. You must not be desalate tho if I don't come. I would hate to think of that. If I am not here by two I am not coming. Rita."

Will wondered if her abrupt sign-off indicated that his note had irritated her. He knew he must make every effort to keep his ardor in check. Rita, obviously, was the sort who needed breathing room. He must be careful not to push her. He must strive for an air of nonchalance.

But when he heard her at the door fifteen minutes before two, he flew toward the sound and drew her into a crushing embrace before she'd even had time to remove her key from the lock.

"I was so afraid you wouldn't come," he murmured. "My God, I'm glad to see you."

"Hold on a minute, lover boy." Rita tried to pull back. "Would you mind if I at least closed the door?"

"I don't care," Will muttered. "Who cares?"

"I care!" Rita extricated herself and closed the door. "You wanna get me fired?"

"No, of course not. I'm sorry. I'm just so glad you came."

"I got that message, Willie boy." Rita walked into the room. "But I can't stay."

"What do you mean you can't stay?" Will's voice was shrill.

"Aren't I speakin' plain English?" Rita asked. "I thought I was."

"I mean, why can't you?" Will tried to soften his vehemence.

"Have I missed somethin'?" Rita addressed the room at large, her face filled with exaggerated confusion. "Did I get married or engaged or somethin'? Did I say I'd punch a clock when I wasn't workin'? Did I sign away my life and not even remember I did it?"

"I'm sorry. I really am." Will's struggle for control was evident in his voice. "I don't know what got into me. I just hoped you could stay. That's all."

"Well, I hoped so too." Rita now turned to look at him. "You oughta know that."

"Sure," said Will. "I do. Just forget it, will you?"

"It's forgotten." Rita broke into a grin and threw open her arms.

"What about tomorrow?" Will felt a tingling spread through his limbs as Rita's body came up against his.

"What about now?" Rita's hand slid down from Will's shoulder to between his legs.

"I thought you couldn't stay." He had trouble breathing as he felt himself swell in Rita's hand.

"I can't, for long." Now her hand reached inside his trousers.

"Oh." It was the only syllable he could manage.

"But some things don't take long." Keeping her hand in motion, she fastened her mouth on his and guided him backward until he felt the edge of the bed against his legs. Then, with her free hand, she shoved his upper body gently back onto the bed. His feet stayed on the floor. Kneeling between his legs, she removed her hand from his penis and slipped her mouth around it. Will's cries were a mixture of enormous surprise and intense pleasure. And his last chance at sangfroid disappeared definitively in the cataclysm of his climax.

When Rita raised her head, Will, wide-eyed and slack-jawed, gazed at her. As she pulled up his torso by the shoulders, he left his arms hanging limp at his sides. When she leaned forward to kiss him, he could not tighten his lips.

"Why did you do that?" he asked finally, his voice just above a whisper.

"Give you somethin' to remember me by." She chucked him under the chin and rose.

"What do you mean?"

"I gotta go away." Rita looked in the mirror and smoothed her hair. "For a week."

"A week?" If Will had been less stunned, he would have been hysterical. As it was, he just seemed stupid. "A week?" he repeated.

"My little visit to Universal paid off after all." Rita moved into the bathroom and turned on the water. "But wouldn't you know it's some location thing? And in the desert in the middle of summer?"

"I thought Laemmle shot everything on the lot."

"Yeah, me too. But I guess not." Rita appeared now in the bathroom doorway, patting her face with a towel. "That's show biz, huh?"

"I guess so." Will stared at her bleakly.

"I wanted to make sure you didn't forget me." Rita grinned at him.

"Could I forget you in a week?" Will moved toward her. "A month? A year?"

"Yeah," she wrapped her arms around him, "I know you feel that way now . . ."

"I swear it," Will broke in fervently. "I swear."

"You promise?" Her voice was small and soft.

"With all my heart." He clutched her tighter still.

"You'll think of me all week long?"

"I'll never forget you," Will pledged, "not for a minute."

SATURDAY, JULY 9

Robbie Burns knew whereof he spoke when he said:

> The best laid schemes o' mice
> and men
> Gang aft a-gley;

An' lea'e us nought but grief an'
   pain
For promised joy!

———————————

The Claflins behaved like a honeymoon couple during the summer's weekends. Their sons were occupied at the foundry. Alexine was in the east with her friend Sophia. They had few family responsibilities. And Robert now had both time and money to lavish on his wife and he did so with great generosity and delight. Isobel appeared to receive his offerings with equal pleasure.

Early on Saturdays he took her shopping at Hudson's so that when they strolled Sundays on Belle Isle or motored into the country, she was nearly always in a new gown or new hat. They lunched at the most fashionable places before attending Saturday matinees and at equally elegant spots before seeing a movie or going to the theater at night.

They saw Elsie Janis (Isobel admired especially her imitation of Will Rogers' rope act), Gallagher and Shean, Sir Harry

Lauder (Robert invariably met his rendition of "Roamin' in the Gloamin' " with a great deal of snuffling into his handkerchief), Eva Tanguay.

Robert sat twice through *Blood and Sand,* allowing, after the second viewing, that "perhaps Rudy's got somethin' after all."

"Aye, Bertie," Isobel agreed. "But ah dinna know how he can touch that woman."

"Naldi, is it?"

"Aye. She's naught but a tub of lard."

Robert himself was quite taken with Barbara La Marr, "The Girl Who Is Too Beautiful," when he saw her in *The Prisoner of Zenda* and both he and Isobel thought the new young man playing opposite her was promising. His name was Ramon Novarro and Robert predicted that within a year he would replace Valentino in the heart of American womanhood.

"He'll be breathin' doon Rudy's neck, Is. Wait and see."

Isobel was not prepared to go that far. "He's agreeable, Bertie," she said, "but he'll noo breathe on Rudolph Valentino."

Distinct changes in the way Robert and Isobel treated each other were also evident on weekdays. When Robert arrived home in the evening, they sat alone in the parlor until dinner was served. At dinner, Robert frequently prompted her to repeat for the boys something she'd already reported to him. And she quite obviously, had received news of the day at the foundry before coming to the table.

Robert never went out alone in the evenings. Sometimes he and Isobel walked around the block, savoring the breezes that diminished the day's heat, stopping occasionally to visit a neighbor. Sometimes they sat, side by side, in the backyard until the last light disappeared. Always, they retired at the same time.

Among themselves, the boys took to calling their parents "the bride and groom." Jamie was puzzled but pleased by their new rapport. Will considered it miraculous that both his parents seemed to be happy at the same time and with each other. Ian felt a bit left out.

"It seems like Pop never has a minute anymore," he grumbled. "Or Isobel either, for that matter."

"Count your blessings," said Jamie.

"What's that supposed to mean?" Ian asked sarcastically.

"Never mind, Ian."

"What's it supposed to mean?"

"It means it's better this way."

"What do you mean *this way?*"

"Ah think they're really in love." Jamie mimicked Isobel, dissolving Will in giggles.

"Well, of course they are," Ian huffed. "What's that got to do with anything?"

In the middle of August, in a new maroon Chrysler, Robert and Isobel traveled to northern Michigan, the only journey they had ever taken alone together in their twenty-three-year marriage. They went first to the summer home of a business acquaintance of Robert's that sprawled along two hundred yards of Lake Michigan shoreline near Petoskey. The owner was not in residence but his entire staff was — chef, chauffeur, upstairs and downstairs maids, valet, groom, gardener. After several days of this abundance, they went on to a week of equally impressive, though less personal, opulence at Mackinac Island's Grand Hotel.

The boys and Alexine, who'd just arrived from Boston, arranged a homecoming celebration for their parents. But from the moment the car pulled up in front of the house, it was clear neither Isobel nor Robert felt festive. Their children hoped travel fatigue was what they saw imprinted on their parents' faces and went ahead with their plans.

While Alexine escorted them along the streamer-strewn hallway and out into the backyard, Jamie brought in their luggage, Ian put the car away and Will collected the enormous tray of shrimp, lobster and crabmeat waiting in the kitchen. When they'd all gathered under the bright yellow canopy Jamie and Ian had built, Riley poured champagne and passed it around. Sitting in the late summer air, heavy with honeysuckle and cricket whine, the strain seemed to ebb. Alexine chronicled her summer, Jamie gave a rundown of the last two weeks at the foundry, Robert described the places he and Isobel had visited.

At dinner, however, the tension surfaced

again. Isobel seemed quite vacant, picking at her food, throwing an occasional misty smile at no one in particular. All Robert's efforts toward joviality could not disguise his peevishness. Alexine, in particular, made a great show of conviviality but her charade had an increasingly desperate cast to it. Midway through the meal, the veneer cracked.

"Aw, fer God's sake." Robert spit out the words, pushing himself back from the table. "It's noo a reunion we're havin' here . . . it's a bloody wake."

He wrenched his body out of his chair and poured a large glass of whiskey at the sideboard. Before drinking, he glanced back over his shoulder at his family.

"It's a wake," he repeated, the anguish in his voice mirrored in his eyes, "a bloody goddamn wake." Then he quickly emptied his glass and left the room.

"What does he mean?" Alexine asked, looking around the table, about to cry.

"How should we know?" said Ian.

"Isobel," said Alexine, "do you know what he means?"

"Ya'd have t' ask im yerself," said Isobel.

Alexine was willing, but when she rushed through the house calling for Robert, there was no answer. He did not, in fact, make an appearance for two days. And then it was very late at night and he was very drunk, unable to speak to anyone.

Robert never explained his remark, his behavior that evening, nor the abrupt extinction of the glow that lit that summer's days and nights. Only once, sitting in a speak with Jamie, enormously drunk, did he even allude to it.

"Ah woo'd er all summer," he said. "Ah woo'd er . . . ah courted er . . . and then she'd noo have me."

JULY 12 - 13, 1932

Will's vow to Rita proved absolutely accurate during the first days of her absence. She haunted his thoughts. All his internal space was allotted to her. He had no room for anything else. He went through the motions of attending to life but responded only to the dreams of Rita humming beneath his actions.

Isobel appeared oblivious to Will's torment until, on Tuesday morning, he failed to notice Mary Pickford herself gliding through Pickfair's gates in a long, dark automobile. His glassy gaze fixed straight ahead, only his inner eye was registering sight: Rita entering his room, Rita in his arms on the dance floor, Rita kneeling between his legs. The sudden jerking about of Isobel's body interrupted his trance.

"What is it?" he asked.

Her body fell back into a position facing front, her breath emerging in small rasps.

"Ah think it was er." She fanned herself furiously with her hand. "It was . . . it was er."

"Who?"

"Mary," she panted.

"Where?" he asked, stilling her hand and fanning her himself.

"In the car . . ."

"What car?"

"The one with Mary in it."

"I didn't see a car."

"Ya didna see it?" Isobel's disbelief shocked her system into stability like a splash of icy water in the face. She was, suddenly, completely calm. "Ya didna see the car carryin' Mary?"

"No." Will felt ashamed of his lapse. "At least I don't think so."

"Dinna ya know if ya saw Mary or not?"

"I didn't." It was better to be firm, Will decided. "I know I didn't."

"And the car?"

"No."

"It's a relapse, Willie. Ya'll have t' see the doctor again."

After this, Will tried harder to concentrate on the day's affairs. He was successful during Isobel's recitation of the splendors of Marion Davies' beach palace. He failed utterly when they pulled away from Miss Davies' and went onto the beach itself. The heat of the afternoon sun melted Will's resolve and he sank back into reverie. When Isobel spoke from under her nearby umbrella, he heard nothing. To get his attention she had to poke him with the end of her parasol.

"It's gone into yer ears, Willie," she said, as he raised himself onto his elbow.

"What do you mean?"

"Ya didna hear a word ah said."

"What did you say?" Will asked.

"They play charades at Marion's parties."

"It must be the wind," said Will.

"It's blowin' right at ya, laddie." Isobel slipped the scarf from her neck and offered it to the breeze for demonstration. It extended directly out from her fingertips toward Will. "Ya had an uncle who was deaf."

"I'm not deaf," he protested. "I can hear every word you're saying."

"She can have at least fifty fer dinner."

"Who?"

"Dinna ya hear me, Willie?"

"Of course I do."

"And the guest rooms sleep twenty."

"Oh, Marion," said Will.

"Ah dinna think anyone else has such space."

That evening they rode out to the Pasadena Community Playhouse to attend the premiere of *A Plain Man and His Wife,* a domestic comedy starring Louise Dresser. Will did quite well until the beginning of the second act when an ingenue appeared whose smile was reminiscent of Rita's. As it broke across her face, he went spinning out of focus and stayed that way until the play's end.

On the drive back to town he forced himself to stay alert and at the Pig'N Whistle he quickly ordered a malted milk, his first nourishment that day.

"Ah dinna care fer Mr. Freud," said Isobel, nibbling at an Olympic Parfait.

"Oh?" Will tried to make his voice neutral, wondering what he'd missed. He wanted to avoid giving Isobel reasons to urge the doctor on him again.

"He's noo up t' Louise."

"Where'd you get the scoop?" Will asked.

"It's noo a scoop when ya've got eyes in yer head."

"Louise is being analyzed? I thought she looked happy."

"Ya canna be happy t' be on stage with a lout, Willie."

"Of course not." Will caught on and glanced at his program to confirm that a Mr. Ralph Freud had been the leading man. "Louise deserves better."

"Ah'd like t' see er in *Steppin' Sisters*," said Isobel. "Ah think it's downtown."

"Matinee tomorrow, if you like."

"She got er name from Paul."

"Paul Dresser? You mean they were married?"

"He gave er the name," said Isobel. "They werena married."

Will just hadn't the strength to pursue this. The malt in his stomach made him drowsy for the first time in days and that night he slept through until morning. Wednesday he felt slightly less spectral.

In one of the myriad periodicals she bought daily, Isobel read there was a break this week in the shooting of Tallulah's current film. Directly after the Wednesday matinee, she and Will headed for North Stanley Avenue. The street was empty as they approached the Haines mansion.

"I guess she's not on our schedule anymore," said Will.

"She's probably lyin' doon, Willie. She needs the rest."

They passed the house, went to the end of the block and turned around.

"She needs er rest," Isobel repeated as they came back toward the house. "She canna be walkin' around when she's worn out."

Just then the door flew open and Tallulah bounded through it. Simultaneously, the Rolls-Royce slid down the drive and met up with its mistress. When she made a right turn onto the sidewalk, it copied her move on the street.

"Stay back, Willie," Isobel hissed. "Stay back."

"Now she's here and you don't even want to say hello?" Will teased.

"Ah dinna want t' intrude," Isobel murmured.

"Since when is waving to an old friend an intrusion?" Will began easing the car forward. "She'd be hurt if we avoided her."

"Dinna stop when we get t' er, Willie. Keep the car movin'."

They were several yards behind the

Rolls when Tallulah spotted them over her shoulder.

"There you are, dahlings," she boomed, waving as she spoke and starting for the car.

"She's comin' over, Willie." Isobel was panting. "She's comin' here."

Will's foot rammed down on the brake and they shuddered to a stop as she came alongside.

"My God, dahling, be careful," she said to Will. "You'll rattle your brains."

"They already are," he blurted.

"Well, then you must be specially kind to them. Where have you been, dahlings?"

"Steppin' Sisters," Isobel whispered, unable to get the breath for full speech.

"But I haven't seen you for days and I'd grown rather attached to our bizarre little meetings."

"We knew ya were workin'." Isobel's voice was still faint.

"Well, that's the bloody truth, dahlings. I'm working my goddamn ass off."

"We'll sure be looking forward to it," said Will. "The picture."

"Aye," said Isobel.

"Aren't you sweet? But, Jesus Christ, I hope it's better than the last one!"

"You were swell," said Will. "The best thing in it."

"I can use fans like you. Don't stay away so long next time." Tallulah blew them a series of kisses as she backed away toward the sidewalk, giving one final wave over her shoulder before she resumed walking.

"Go fast, Willie." Isobel dabbed at her face with a handkerchief.

Will floored the accelerator and they lurched forward. As they sped past Tallulah, Isobel fluttered her hanky out the window, Will gave what he hoped was a snappy little salute. Back on the main thoroughfare they rode some distance in silence.

"Ah canna believe," Isobel said finally, "that Mr. Zukor knows Tallulah's workin' so hard."

"Why that so-and-so," said Will with some heat, "it wouldn't surprise me if it was on his orders."

"What d'ya mean?" She was surprised

by his vehemence.

"They're pretty tough customers over at Paramount, if you ask me."

"Mr. Zukor's a fine man, Willie." There was a hint of rebuke in Isobel's voice. "Very doon t' earth."

"Well, some of his cronies might not be quite so fine."

"Ah canna believe," said Isobel, "that he knows she's workin' er ass off."

WEDNESDAY, JULY 13

This is Bankhead's Buddy coming to you from 708 at the Roosevelt. Have you missed me? Well, I've missed you too and you're not the only one I've missed. Figger that out!

We climbed off the merry-go-round for a few hours tonight and Isobel's devoting the hiatus (no, that is not first cousin to a hernia!) to creating a special Bankhead section in The Book — at least a dozen pages so far and she's still going strong. All this apropos (check your *Larousse*, ya churls) of some time we spent with Tallu this afternoon. You heard me. We just happened to be cruising along North Stanley when she just happened to be taking her afternoon constitutional and of such coincidences are great events born.

She tells us they've got her slaving away at Paramount and we wonder: Don't you have any rights when you get to the top? It seems to us the bigwigs forget pretty darn fast that they'd be nowhere without their players. Who'd pay a penny to see Zukor's puss plastered across the screen?

Skipped dinner tonight in favor of a double order of Chocolate Cream Rolls. Actually, the Captain ate the lion's share while our hero supplemented his portion with Uneeda biscuits and cherry jelly, bootlegged up from the kitchen by Isobel's latest conquest, a busboy named Ernest. He slips her extra Coke and she lets him look at The Book anytime he wants.

Today's Riddle: What lover-boy from out of town is pining for a local gal who's out of town?

Today's Unanswered Question: What Hollywood visitor can't think about ending his visit?

———————————

After the rupture between his parents, Will felt like an orphan. Isobel reverted to her status of household alien, a condition heightened by her grief for Wallace Reid, who succumbed that winter, at age thirty, to the cumulative effects of morphine addiction. Robert was hidden behind the mists of whiskey. Jamie gave Will what attention he could but the responsibilities of an increasingly prosperous business, responsibilities sharpened by Robert's haziness, consumed him almost entirely.

Will didn't have a lot of spare time to dwell on his isolation. He'd been charged with all tasks relating to the Claflin furnace, which meant rising earlier than ever in the morning to see that it was properly stoked and making certain it was banked before he retired at night. After school he went directly to the foundry, remaining there until six in the evening. By the time he got home, ate supper and prepared his lessons for the next day, it was usually time to check on the furnace and go to bed. He worked at the foundry all day Saturday and Robert insisted he attend church with him and Isobel on Sunday.

The latter activity, the only joint one still practiced by the Claflins, was torture for Will. Wedged in a pew between this man and woman who met once a week to walk through a familial scene, he found it difficult to breathe. The air between them was as dead as the ritual they observed and it stifled him.

On Sunday Robert postponed his first drink of the day until church services were concluded, an agony testified to by the hymnal's quivering movement in his hands. Will often wondered if he was the only one who noticed the tremor. Robert wouldn't have cared if they had. He clung to this weekly observance, not for the congregation's benefit, but for his own. It was his shield against total erosion, his essential illusion. That his wife's participation never moved beyond courteous formality didn't matter. Nor did the fact that he drank limitless quantities of whiskey the rest of the day. His abstinence before services, her consent to be physically present, were enough.

When Will's breathing difficulties finally turned into outright asthma attacks, Robert excused him from the masquerade. Then Will watched from an upstairs window as his parents departed for church. From that distance, observing only their backs, he could almost believe they shared a relationship. They moved in concert, Robert abbreviating his strides to match Isobel's, her hand resting easily on his arm. When he helped her into the car, he was gentle, even courtly. If Will hadn't known better, he would have sworn this Sunday minuet was genuine.

Presented with a free day, Will chose to spend it in the movies. He liked especially spectacular epics such as *The Covered Wagon* and *The Ten Commandments*. When the dust of hundreds of pioneer wagons billowed up from the Western plains, when the Red Sea parted, engulfing thousands in its mammoth waves, nothing else could possibly matter. He also admired greatly Harold Lloyd's unquenchable optimism and thrilled to Ramon Novarro's swordplay in

Scaramouche. He felt Lillian Gish was at her best in *The White Sister* and he wished he looked like Ronald Colman. When Chaney, as the piteous Quasimodo, rode through the Parisian streets to his whipping, Will wept for his ugliness. But it was Pola Negri who caused his sexual awakening.

Just past his fourteenth birthday, Will was wholly untutored in amatory matters. But when Pola walked onto the screen in *Bella Donna,* she set him aflame. Turbaned, bare at the shoulders and midriff, wrapped in the arms of Conway Tearle, she caused tingling sensations along Will's nerves. Skulking about in a sheer black dress, she heated his groin and made it twitch. Clad in high boots, jodhpurs, jacket and tie, she turned his entire body feverish and he feared he would melt.

Startled and confused, Will submitted utterly to the holocaust while in the darkened theater. But outside, sensing his feelings were somewhat unseemly, he tried to abandon them. It was impossible. He moved through his days and nights,

279

lost in a dream of Pola's dark eyes, wholly at the mercy of the new passions so unexpectedly inhabiting his body. Whenever he could, he fueled the fires by watching his temptress on the screen. The rest of the time he tried, without much success, to dampen them. It was exhausting and distracting and he hoped, if this was love, that he'd never feel it again.

JULY 14, 1932

On Thursday, Will received another letter from Ian.

Dear Will,

We're glad to receive Isobel's cards and hear that you're having such a fine time.

Things are just about the same here, which isn't good, as I reported in my last letter. Thank goodness business is light because James appears less and less interested in pulling his share of the load. Light business, however, creates other problems on the financial side of things.

Anyway, I'm glad to know you'll be back in a month and eager to pitch in and do your share, I'm sure.

Love,
Ian

On Thursday Will also received a postcard from Rita. The front bore a tinted rendering of Bridal Veil Falls at Yosemite National Park. On the back she had written: "I am not here but I thought this was pretty. A week seems like a long time in more ways than one! I wonder if you miss me at all? Well I sure will find out as soon as I get back. Love, Rita."

The commotion these few sentences caused in Will was enormous. Quite clearly, Rita felt exactly as he did. She'd practically said it in so many words: "in more ways than one." Surely that referred to him. When Rita returned he would have to be free to see her whenever he wished. He must tell Isobel the truth.

"Do you remember the girl you met in the room one morning?" he asked at dinner, between fruit cocktail and the main course.

"Who was she, Willie?"

"Well, her name is Rita Raymond and . . ."

"Ah mean," Isobel cut in, "what was she doin' in the room?"

Will had hoped to avoid this but saw how foolish his hope had been. "She was working there," he said.

"D'ya mean the maid, Willie?"

"She's really an actress but you've got to live while you wait for a break, you know." He heard the note of apology in his voice and hated it.

"Ah dinna remember," said Isobel.

"It was the day you bought Ethel a hat."

"Aye. The bags were all gone."

"That's the day."

"Ah dinna recall the maid." The waiter set her plate before her. "Paul, ah'll noo have the crabapple t' night."

"Very good, Mrs. Claflin." He removed the two red rings, leaving a solitary chicken breast.

"I'll take them," said Will.

"Yes, sir." Paul set them next to Will's minute steak.

"She was just finishing up the bathroom when you came in," said Will, as the waiter moved away. It was suddenly more important that Isobel remember Rita than that he avoid stressing the menial nature of her present work.

"Aye." Isobel was absorbed by the exacting task of cutting the chicken into tiny pieces.

"You remember?"

"Ah remember the hat. Ah hope Ethel likes it."

"You can't miss her," Will persisted. "She's got Harlow's hair and Gaynor's dimple."

"She doesna sound like a maid, Willie."

"She isn't. She's an actress. I've seen her a few times."

"What're er pictures?"

"Well, *Sign of the Cross,* for one. But that's not what I meant."

"Willie!" The sound of Isobel's voice caused the knot in Will's stomach to tighten. She had guessed all and was angry at his deception. "Dinna look now. Dinna turn around. Ah know the man who just came in."

"Who is it?" Eager as he was to discuss Rita, Will felt reprieved.

"Ah canna place im. Maybe it was *Steppin' Sisters*. Dinna turn or ya'll be starin' right at im."

"Describe him," said Will.

"He's huge, with flat hair and a red face."

"Sounds like Arbuckle," said Will.

"Dinna ya think ah'd know Fatty if ah saw im. It could a been *Miss Pinkerton*. Willie. He's lookin' here now. Ah swear he is."

"Well, it's high time they started recognizing you around town," Will teased.

"He's gettin' up, Willie. He's gettin' up. He's comin' here."

"Can I believe my eyes?" Will recognized the voice before he saw the face. "It is Mrs. Claflin, isn't it?"

"Aye." Isobel's confusion was clear as she extended her hand to meet his.

"It's Mrs. Claflin and . . ." He turned

expectantly toward Will.

"And Will."

"No! I don't believe it. Little Will?"

"Yes," said Will. "Isobel, you remember Dylan? Dylan Doyle?"

She began to crumple as she realized that this was not a face from pictures but from life, and a despised one at that. But by the time Dylan had pulled out a chair and lowered himself into it, unbidden, she had recovered enough to smile tentatively at him.

"Well, well, well." He shook his massive head, causing his jowls to flap. "Isn't this something? Isn't it? How long has it been? Must be ten, twelve years. At least that long. I can't believe my eyes! After all this time. It must be at least ten, twelve years. You know, I never even thought of you folks coming to California. I always wondered if I'd get back to Michigan someday and if I did I always said the first thing I'd do would be to look up Robbie. And now here you are. Isn't this something? Where is he? Where's Rob?"

"He died last year," said Will, hoping

to stop Dylan cold.

"No!" The shock brought only a moment's respite. "No, not Rob. Why I can't believe it. I'm so sorry, Mrs. Claflin. And Will. My sympathies to you both. Why, it's hard to believe. I was sure when I saw you that Rob must be with you. But isn't it something that *you're* here? The two of you. Why, I can hardly believe this is little Will. And that reminds me . . . this'll interest you, Will, . . . I just married off my little Millie last week. Sent her off on a fancy honeymoon only a couple days ago. Now what about you, Will? Any plans in that direction? If I recall you're about that age. Well, I guess it's a good thing you waited to tie the knot or you and your mom wouldn't be here now!"

Isobel winced at the designation Dylan gave her and Will leapt in to change the subject.

"What are you doing these days?" he asked.

"I'm at RKO at the moment . . . ."

Isobel's small gasp stopped him. "In the movies?" she asked.

"That's right, Mrs. Claflin. And I'm a darn sight happier and a lot better at it than I was at trying to run a foundry, I can tell you that." Dylan's laugh exploded from his huge red mouth and Will felt their fellow diners swiveling toward the sound. He wished Dylan would go away. Isobel, however, looked suddenly attentive.

"When I first landed out here I signed with Paramount," Dylan continued. "Started as an extra and then . . ."

"With Fatty?" Isobel asked.

"Sure, I worked with Fatty, Buster, all the greats . . . but, say, you don't want to hear my life story and besides, I don't want to leave that little lady at my table alone too long." Dylan leaned in toward the center of the table and assumed a confidential tone. "These Hollywood wolves would snatch her right up, believe you me. But it would be my great pleasure, Mrs. Claflin, if I could call on you sometime during your visit, maybe show you around the town. You might like to see the way we do things at the studio."

"Aye." Isobel assented quickly.

"Maybe some time next week. You could pick a date and let me know."

"That would be swell," said Will, as Dylan paused to refill his lungs. While Isobel toured the studio, he could see Rita.

"I'll expect to hear from you." Dylan pulled a card from his wallet and handed it to Will. "Well, this has really been something. I still can hardly believe it. Now you just let me know when you'd like the grand tour and I'm at your service."

Heaving himself out of the chair, Dylan shook hands with them both and headed back to his table. Isobel and Will were silent, breathless from the battering waves of Dylan's words.

"Well," Will said finally, "he hasn't changed much."

"Ya dinna know that, Willie."

"We used to think he looked like Mack Swain, remember?"

"Ah wonder if he worked with Mack too?" Isobel gazed toward Dylan's table, struggling to harmonize the memory of old dislike with present knowledge.

"Well, he's still a churl," said Will, "no matter who he worked with."

"Judge not that ya be not judged, Willie."

"Of course, I suppose even a churl could give a pretty slick tour if he's on the inside of things."

"A lotta time's gone by," said Isobel.

"We'll set it up for next week." Will could, he decided, simulate his malaise one final time. Isobel would take her tour; he'd have a day with Rita to make some decisions about the future; afterward, he'd tell Isobel everything. There was really no need to mention it now.

"What about the maid, Willie?"

"The maid?"

"Is she leavin' the room soiled?"

"No, no. Nothing like that."

"Is she stealin'?"

"Oh, no!" Will was horrified.

"They do, ya know."

"Well, certainly not this one."

"Ah've noo noticed anythin' missin'."

"Oh, she'd never do something like that."

"Ah'm glad ya'll vouch fer er, Willie."

"Oh, I will," he said fervently. "I absolutely will."

THURSDAY, JULY 14

Small World Department: Who did we run into at dinner tonight? Dylan Doyle, that's who, and sporting more avoirdupois than ever, if you can believe it. He's in the movies now (we wouldn't have called that one) and offered a look-see at his studio anytime we liked. We'll check it out next week.

Another thing he hasn't lost is the gift of blab so we unwound afterward by watching Mr. Menjou in *Bachelor's Affairs* (we bet Adolphe has plenty of those offscreen too!).

Wouldn't you like to know what Hollywood insider is postcarding a visitor to our town while she's on location? Stay tuned and maybe you'll find out.

———————

In the spring of 1923 Robert hired Herbert Bonine, grooming him as a replacement for Jamie when he entered college in the fall. Herbert was thirty years old, had several years' experience as foreman in a Toledo plant and was an industrious, if not inspired, foundryman. He also possessed an excessive amount of solemnity.

"He's noo got a gift fer drollery," Robert noted when Herbert had been at the foundry a month. "That's certain."

"There were worse things to be without," said Jamie.

"Aye," Robert agreed. "Ah've always Dylan bloody Doyle t' remind me a that."

"Herbie works very hard," Jamie said.

"Aye," said Robert. "Ya can rely on im and ah dinna have t' live with im, after all."

In the autumn, however, that began to change. Alexine, after graduation in June and another summer in the East, was living at home, teaching history at Western High School. Herbert, smitten from the moment he'd met her, called at the house at every possible opportunity.

Although Will hadn't exactly liked Herbert during the months he'd worked with him, they'd gotten along. When Herbert began coming to the house, however, Will's indifference turned to animosity. Herbert's arrival, coinciding as it did with Jamie's departure, seemed to Will the act of a usurper. Even when he realized that Shmerbie, as he derisively called him, was seeking Alexine's affection and not Jamie's place in the family, his enmity remained. Will felt Shmerbie was no more worthy as a suitor for Alexine than he was as a substitute for Jamie.

Robert didn't relish seeing Herbert outside of working hours but he didn't attempt to discourage him either. Herbert's visits gave him a legitimate excuse for a drink at home and he didn't take Herbert's pursuit of Alexine very seriously. Isobel, at first, seemed oblivious to this stranger in the house. More often than not, she was either at the pictures or retired for the night by the time Herbert arrived. On those occasions when their paths did cross, she gave a slight curtsy and a meager tilt of her head in his direction but never actually spoke. When Herbert turned up at Sunday dinner, however — Alexine had insisted that the Claflins revive this occasion; it was barbaric not to — Isobel had to acknowledge him. She did so with great politeness and a minimum of words.

"I'm so pleased to be here, Mrs. Claflin," said Herbert, rushing to pull out her chair.

"Aye."

"It's a great treat for me," he said, seating himself at Isobel's right and receiving a gentle nod of her head. "Knowing so few people here, I'm often alone."

"Ya're noo now," said Isobel, tinkling the bell to summon Miss Farnum.

"Thank you for including me," said Herbert.

"Ya're welcome," said Isobel.

Alexine herself enjoyed Herbert in a perverse sort of way. He was so stolid he made her feel wanton by comparison, something she'd always secretly desired but despaired of achieving. Next to Herbert, she felt downright madcap and she liked the feeling. Also, she was genuinely impressed by the forward thrust

293

of his life, his absolute dedication to making good, a natural bent that he'd bolstered recently by attending the lectures of Émile Coué. He, along with millions of other Americans, had taken up the Frenchman's chant: "Day by day in every way I am getting better and better." When Robert treated Herbert's autosuggestive efforts with scorn ("he seems the same t' me, ah'm afraid t' say"), Alexine defended them.

"I think it's a fine thing that he wants to be the best he can possibly be," she said with some fervor.

"Well, it's still noo good enough fer ya," said Robert. "Dinna ferget that, lassie."

And Alexine didn't. She was keenly aware that there were many things Herbert *didn't* make her feel. But until she met up with someone who could fill in the gaps, he would certainly do.

FRIDAY, JULY 15

Good evening, America. We're coming to you from the heart of Hollywood where it's a great night tonight. The sky's filled with stars and there are even a few (a few? just try and count 'em) here in the theater where we are shortly to witness the world permeer of *Strange Interlude*. The opening's already been delayed an hour cuz even some of the bigshots can't get through the crowd. Some put it at 100,000; we say it's more like double that. But now more luminaries are beginning to enter, announced by Schnozzle Durante.

There's Spencer Tracy, accompanied by a gent of Oriental persuasion; friend, valet or visitor, we can't say . . . Here's Joe E. Brown, swallowtails and all; he's getting a big reception too . . . Ralph Bellamy just came in with Mr. and Mrs. Marion Nixon . . . Ernie Truex, the stager, is sitting right behind them . . . Here's Colleen Moore and her broker fella . . . Anita Page just entered, hooked to a male who's no one as far as we're concerned . . . ditto Fifi Dorsay . . . Greta Nissen and Weldon

Heyburn, still very much the newly-weds . . . There's Charlie Ruggles getting a first-hand report from Roland Young on his trip to the old sod; he just returned Monday week, you know . . . Robert Young aisling it with goodness knows who; we hope this newcomer acquits himself well in tonight's pitcher . . . Eddie Robinson and the Mrs. gliding in . . . Novarro is causing panic in the center section . . . Ethel Barrymore just entered with a brood of Colts . . . Here's marvelous May Robson (she's in the flicker too) with a fella who probably doesn't deserve her . . . We understand the Marxmen are here but can't find them . . . Pauline Frederick just came in, looking devastating in gold-and-brocade with shoes to match . . . Ralph Morgan's here, oozing urbanity, to watch himself on the silver screen . . . Finally, the lady everyone's been waiting for, Norma Shearer, on her Irving's arm, gowned by Letty Lynton (Mrs. I. Claflin has some eye, I wanna tell ya), and looking absolutely radiant . . . And as the lights dim for the overture, here's Clark himself hurrying to his seat; only the star of the whole shebang, that's all!

So enough of the ballyhoo, you say? What of the flicker itself? We think it took a lot of nerve just to attempt it. Figger the play it's based on runs roughly five hours, add to that the fact that we hear the characters' *thoughts,* as well as their speech, and it's one heck of a big order. But we think M-G-M filled it quite nicely. Bouquets to Norma, who's never been better, and special applause for this Gable fella. He's got his own brand of charm and we like it. We also want to single out Mr. Morgan, saddled with the role of Charlie the Chump, a flat tire if ever there was one. Ralph played it to a fare-thee-well. All in all, a whale of a picture.

And might we add a final observation (as if ya had a choice): we've ogled quite a few of the bigshots first-hand, close-up, etcetera, and we feel sorry for them — no irony intended. They've got about as much privacy as a bunch of goldfish!

Set up the grand tour with Dylan for Monday ayem (and I'll be with Rita, my darling Rita). He promises to be here at nine sharp (will she be in the room when I return from breakfast? Will she spend the day with me? I won't let her say no), and says by the end of the day we'll know everything there is to know about a Hollywood studio (I must know if she loves me. I know I love her. There is no longer any doubt).

For those of youse who're wondering about the above style of scribbling, see Eugene O'Neill. He's the guy what invented it.

And now, as Ned said to Nina (known to you numbskulls as Gable and Shearer), let's write finis to this chapter.

———————————

Jamie had completed just one semester when Robert began beseeching him to return to the foundry instead, and to continue his studies at night. Although sensing his request might be unfair, still Robert made it, repeatedly. He needed Jamie. And not only as a business partner. It baffled Robert that this child, of all his children, had acquired such consequence in his life. But he knew it was so. When

Jamie left, some piece of Robert was set adrift. He needed his son as ballast.

Jamie resisted with letters full of strong arguments. He knew for a fact that Herbert was competent, no matter how unpalatable his personality. He could do the job. Also, Jamie pointed out, he would be even more valuable to his father with his metallurgical engineering degree and he'd have it a lot sooner if he stayed in school full time. Finally, he noted that Ian had only a year-and-a-half of college left. Then he would be available.

Robert refuted him point by point. Herbert was a plodder, incapable of the daring and imagination needed to catch the crest of the wave of booming business and ride it. Jamie was brilliant without his degree so the matter of when he received it was hardly crucial. And as for Ian, yes, he would be a great asset. He would court customers, flatter their wives, burnish the foundry's public image. But as for being a true foundryman, he was no substitute for Jamie and they both knew it.

When Jamie came home for spring vacation, he found it was far more difficult to withstand his father's entreaties face to face. Still, he held out.

Home again at the end of the spring semester, he saw that Robert's distraction had intensified. He drank more than ever although he rarely seemed drunk. His performance of the actions that constituted living was unconvincing. Something inside him had slackened. His impersonation of himself was hollow. Jamie, feeling somewhat blackmailed but resigned, finally relented.

Robert insisted they mark the occasion and arranged to do so in the private dining room of an inn several miles outside the city. On a Sunday in July the entire family, and Herbert Bonine, rode into the country as they had so often years before. Alexine, whose attachment to Herbert grew in constancy if not in depth, had requested that he be allowed to come along. And none of the Claflins seemed to mind. Robert's sense of good will extended easily to Herbert. Will only cared that Jamie was present too. Ian thought Herbert actually wasn't a bad sort. Isobel would not have thought of objecting.

Anyway, she had discovered, through trial and error, the exact nod and smile that neutralized Herbert's conversational efforts vis-à-vis her.

Throughout the meal, Alexine, her hair newly bobbed, was sparkling, spilling enough of her light onto Herbert to make him seen almost charming, in a minor way. Jamie, perhaps despite himself, enjoyed the spotlight and Robert's obvious joy at placing him there. If Isobel's participation was less than total, still she and Robert exchanged warm words several times during the meal and she said she thought the celebration was a lovely idea. Even Ian's slightly sour toast to "the conquering hero," its envy thinly disguised, didn't seem discordant but, rather, warmly familiar. During those hours at the inn, Will could almost believe that his family was intact.

JULY 16, 1932

Rare California clouds covered the Saturday sun, causing Isobel and Will to cancel their plans for the beach. They devoted the day instead to viewing Los Angeles architecture, beginning at Pickfair and ending up at the Angelus Temple, seat of Sister Aimee's Foursquare Evangelism. Isobel refused, however, to time their visit to coincide with a worship service.

"Ah dinna care t' see the woman erself," she said.

"I hear it's one of the best shows in town," said Will.

"She's a fraud, Willie."

"Well, you don't have to believe to enjoy the show."

"Ah canna bear er," said Isobel, closing the matter.

Aimiee Semple McPherson Hutton, who billed herself as "The World's Most Pulchritudinous Evangelist," had relinquished any claim she might have had on Isobel's affection or attention several years earlier when she'd spent a month of illicit days and nights with the married operator of her radio station instead of drowning in the Pacific Ocean.

One summer day in 1926, Sister Aimee dropped from sight. Last seen on the beach, her followers mourned what they assumed to be her briny demise while the police searched for clues. It turned out, however, that the Sister had been nowhere near a watery grave but, rather, hotel-hopping with her bald and one-legged Mr. Ormiston. It also turned out that she, quite clearly, had knowledge of the ransom note demanding $500,000 for her release, if indeed the idea wasn't hers in the first place.

Although Isobel was not always able to spot fraudulence, she had a fierce intolerance of it when she did. Any public personage who attempted deliberately to deceive the people was, to her mind, of a lower order, undeserving of normal human consideration. The moment Sister Aimee turned up alive and well and linked with Mr. Ormiston, she fell into this category and with a particularly heavy thud.

Her fall from Isobel's grace did not, however, in any way diminish Isobel's interest in the Temple. Buildings with long statistical pedigrees fascinated her, like Marion Davies' beach house or Grauman's

Chinese Theater. That it took a million and a half dollars to construct this home of Foursquare Evangelism, that five thousand of the faithful could be present in it at one time, that the lighted cross atop it cast a beam visible for fifty miles — these facts gave the Temple a special stature in Isobel's eyes, one having nothing to do with its proprietor.

As they rode toward the Temple, Isobel shared with Will her data on the building. Once inside, she gave him additional figures indicating what it might have been like if they'd been present for a service.

"No less than thirty in the orchestra, Willie."

He gave a low whistle.

"And at least two hundred in the choir."

"That must be really something."

"Aye," she said, "but ah wouldna stay t' save my soul."

At the Temple Will planted the first hint of his impending relapse.

"I'm feeling a little wobbly," he said, after they'd inspected the main hall. "Why don't I just wait here while you explore the rest?"

That, it turned out, took nearly two hours. Isobel visited the Miracle Room, which displayed crutches, braces, wheelchairs, the detritus of the healed. She received a tour of the radio station that sent the Foursquare Gospel around the globe. And when she wandered by mistake into the Foursquare Conservatory of Music, she met Mr. Douglas Dundas Wheatley, who had a brogue, taught voice and invited Isobel to sit in on his class.

"Was ah gone long, Willie?" she inquired when she returned.

"The rest was good for me."

"They sang like angels." A look of transport lingered on Isobel's face.

"I've been thinking maybe I should stay and be healed," Will joked, hoping to highlight the suggestion of illness.

"She couldna heal a mite," Isobel snapped and marched off toward the car.

To make certain his frailty was firmly planted in Isobel's mind, Will complained of dizziness during dinner and suggested they bypass the Pig'N Whistle on the way home from the movies on the grounds that he was too tired even to sip a malted milk. If, Isobel said, he was still as sick as that tomorrow, he ought to see a doctor. Will agreed.

SATURDAY, JULY 16

A jaunt today to Aimee's little jernt on Glendale Blvd. Tonight to dinner and a show. Forgive my brevity, but being as how I'm somewhat under the weather, I just ain't got the steam for details. You understand.

The illusion of family union that flickered on Jamie's return sputtered out very quickly. Each of the Claflins traveled on a separate road and they seldom intersected. Alexine and Will saw most of each other because he was now a student in her tenth-grade history class. He thought she was a fine teacher and this pride, coupled with sudden exposure to what he saw as a host of alternatives, confirmed for Will that Herbert was an unsatisfactory suitor for his sister.

He first tried to sell Alexine on Mr. Boardman, the math teacher.

"Did you know he isn't married?" Will asked.

"Of course I know that," she snapped.

"Well, what's wrong with him?"

"Nothing's *wrong* with him."

"He reminds me a little of John Gilbert."

"Well, exactly. That's exactly it." There was slightly wild note in Alexine's voice.

"I don't understand," said Will.

"Of course you don't. How could you?" Now she sounded as though she might cry.

"Could you try to tell me?"

"He's *so* handsome and *so* charming and *so* smooth . . ." She broke off and paused a moment. "I'm just not in his league," she said finally.

"That's bunk!"

"No it's not, Willie. It's the truth."

Despite his outrage, Will knew that arguing would only exacerbate the pain he'd seen flash in Alexine's eyes.

His next suggestion, a few weeks later, was Mr. Slidecki, a fortyish Pole who also taught history. Will thought he had a very appealing accent.

"He looks just like John Gilbert too . . . when his back's turned." Alexine's scorn was evident but Will persisted.

"He's very intelligent."

"He's old," Alexine shrieked.

"Well, so's Shmerbie."

"His name is Herbie and he's not old. Also, Slidecki smells of vinegar."

When Will tried again, his candidate this time the assistant football coach, Alexine met him head-on.

"You hate Herbie so much you'd rather see me with a huge ox who can't put three words together in a sentence."

"He's not so huge," Will protested.

"His neck is the size of that tree stump in the backyard."

"What tree stump?"

"And his face is flat." Alexine grimaced. "You hate Herbie so much you'd rather see me with a huge flat stump. And he's dumb, Willie. He's really dumb."

"Well, Herbie's no prize either."

"Herbie has many fine qualities and

you're just too young and too shallow to see them. And I suggest you stop presenting me with substitutes and start getting used to him."

"What's that supposed to mean?"

"Just what I said." Alexine, quite clearly, was closing the subject.

Will himself remained faithful to Pola, making no connection between her and the girls he encountered in school. They seemed an entirely different species, a powerless, lackluster one. Pola bewitched him. He sat through her movies twice, sometimes three times, enchanted by the curve of her small mouth, charmed by the tilt of her chin, enamored always of the promises hidden in her deep eyes. He wished to be Rod La Rocque in *Forbidden Paradise,* Ben Lyon in *Lily of the Dust,* Robert Frazer in *Men.* As his infatuation aged, as he surrendered to it utterly, it ceased to alarm him. His fear now was that it would vanish. He could not imagine life without it. Like any zealous lover, his sole concern was that he be allowed to go on feeling his mania. When Isobel asked Will to accompany her to Miss Negri's *Shadows of Paris,* he made an excuse. Pola could not be shared.

Isobel scarcely noticed his refusal, haunted as she was by Rudolph Valentino. His snow-white wig in *Monsieur Beaucaire,* a sharp frame for his penetrating black eyes, the elegant garments of gilded brocade that accentuated his lithe form — these had only served to deepen the spell. George O'Brien was not the only one she now found pallid. Fairbanks, never more engaging than when scaling the palace walls or flying through its windows in *The Thief of Bagdad,* seemed to Isobel slightly off his stride. Thomas Meighan, whom she'd always admired, became an annoyance. She even wondered if dear Jack should have chosen to make *Beau Brummel,* his first film in some time, although it was clear he was deeply in love with costar Mary Astor, and she with him. When the news reached her that thirty-five-year-old Charlie Chaplin had married a sixteen-year-old-girl, it barely caused a ripple. "Ah wonder if they're suited" was all she said.

Jamie's presence did seem to restore Robert's vitality although they hadn't much time together. In the evenings Jamie was in school. Robert spent many of his alone in a speak. But even after his long nights out he arrived home sharp and vigorous. Only when Will stumbled onto his father in an embrace with Miss Katherine Saltonstall, the foundry's secretary, was the source of Robert's new verve fully revealed.

Robert was as surprised to see his son in the huge storeroom closet as Will was to find his father's arms around Miss Saltonstall.

"John Q. asked me to bring him some lading forms," Will's voice croaked at his father down the length of the closet.

"Did he? Ah see." Robert seemed very calm as he lifted several tablets off one of the highest shelves and carried them toward Will. "It's a good thing ah was here, laddie. Ya couldna reach em."

Will stared, still frozen in the doorway, as his father smiled and winked at him.

"Get along now, Willie. Ah'll speak with ya later."

When he did, Robert minimized the importance of what Will had seen.

"Dinna misunderstand, laddie. Katy Saltonstall's a good woman. We're friendly, it's true, but ah'd noo compromise er fer anythin' on earth. That kiss ya saw today . . . sometimes these things happen between a man and woman. But it's noo the end a the world . . . nor the end a anythin' else fer that matter."

"Do you see her besides in the office?" Will blurted it out even though Robert hadn't intended to throw the meeting open for questions.

"Trust me when ah say ah'd noo compromise er, Willie. She's too fine fer that."

Will asked nothing else and when Robert suggested that the matter "best be left between the two of us," Will's pride at the shared trust allayed his lingering doubts.

SUNDAY, JULY 17

Coming to you from the snore shelf, the Roosevelt's saw-bones having just confirmed that your scrivener suffers from a touch of the pip. Bed rest prescribed.

The Captain diagnosed herself as suffering from a lack of *Grand Hotel* (it's been a coupla weeks now) so she ducked across the street to take her fourth crack at it.

T.R. (and if ya don't know what that means by now don't bother reading further): Who's on the edge of his seat waiting for a lady to return from the edge of his life?

_____

When Alexine announced on New Year's Day of 1925 that she planned to marry Herbert Bonine in the spring, no one was surprised. As her resolve to make do with him had strengthened, so had her family's acceptance of him as her prospective mate. Robert was consulted beforehand, of course. And even he, when Herbert requested his daughter's hand, had been able to relinquish it somewhat graciously.

"Ah guess ya are gettin' better 'n better, Herbie," Robert said, patting the shoulder of his future son-in-law. "Ya must be if Alex thinks so."

"Thank you for your confidence, sir." Herbert's beaming face reflected the glow of Robert's blessing.

"Call me Bob, fer God's sake. Ya're practically one of the family."

"Thank you . . . Bob. That's very kind of you."

"It's noo kind." He poured two drinks and placed one in Herbert's hand.

"Yes, sir, . . . Bob."

"And let me tell ya just one thing. Ah care only fer m' lassie's happiness. Just make er happy."

"That's certainly my primary concern," Herbert said.

"Primary or no, just do it." Robert took a gulp of his drink.

"I'll certainly try."

"Sometimes it takes more'n tryin', laddie."

"Well, I'll do all I can. I'll . . ."

"Ah know ya will . . . and here's to ya." Robert poured the rest of the whiskey down his throat and clapped Herbert on the shoulder again.

Isobel urged setting the wedding for March 28, Mary and Doug's anniversary, but Alexine said the weather was too unreliable that early in the year and settled instead on the last Saturday in April, quitting her job at the end of the winter term. Once she'd decided, she said, she thought she might as well do it as soon as possible.

And she needed every moment of the available three months to make the necessary arrangements. Aside from suggesting the Pickford-Fairbanks date, Isobel's part in the planning consisted mostly of meeting Alexine for lunch on those days when she was downtown shopping. Although they discussed the wedding over lunch, Isobel's contributions tended to be heavily influenced by whatever picture she'd just seen. As a result, they were rather inconsistent.

She'd begun by proposing a gown like the one Madge Evans wore when she married Richard Barthelmess in *Classmates:* a simple, light tulle over satin, moderately scooped at the neck, reaching to midcalf and set off by a bouquet burgeoning with ankle-length streamers of white velvet, each dotted with blossoms. However, after seeing *Don Q., Son of Zorro,* she found this rather tame and thought perhaps something with period flavor might be advisable. She'd heard this was not uncommon in Hollywood weddings and hinted that Mary Astor's gown in *Don Q.* might serve as a model. Still later, she advocated the tailored look of Lois Moran's *Stella Dallas* wedding dress.

Alexine listened patiently and then followed her own, quite definite, ideas. Robert had insisted that she spare no expense, and on the day of the wedding it was clear she had taken him at his word.

The church was filled with a profusion of white flowers, a rose-covered arbor running the length of the center aisle, canopies of palest baby's breath covering the side passages, sprays of lilies surrounding the altar. Alexine's attendants, carrying spring flowers, dressed in the green of soft spring buds, were brilliantly colored splashes against the snowy backdrop. Alexine herself was shining. The cap of lace on her dark hair was ringed by a garland of tiny white roses. From it a veil flowed down her back to the floor where it met the train of her ivory satin gown. Her hands held a cluster of white heather and stephanotis, the latter trailing along the panel of antique lace set into the front of her gown. Robert, resplendent in a cutaway he'd had specially made, carried her on his arm with a dignity matching hers. And in this splendor Alexine had created, even Herbert assumed a new aspect. Standing by the altar, waiting for his bride, he looked appealing, tender and almost elegant.

Isobel had chosen to wear a long-sleeved, high-necked lavender silk. When she turned to watch her daughter's procession glide toward her beneath the bower, the tears rising in her blue eyes turned them the same lilac color as her dress. Quickly, she faced front again. By the time Alexine and Robert brushed past her pew, her eyes were dry.

The magnificence of the wedding was repeated at the reception, held in the ballroom of the august Detroit Athletic Club. Alexine waited until she was certain all the guests were gathered there and had champagne-filled goblets in their hands. Then she and Herbert made their entrance.

If C.B. De Mille himself had directed it, the scene could not have played more smoothly. Alexine and Herbert appeared in the doorway, the orchestra fell to humming strings and rolling drums, the room quieted, the goblets rose. As one, it seemed, the guests drank their toast, the musicians launched into a silvery waltz and Alexine and her groom glided to the middle of the room, circling there as the music bid. Slowly, they were joined by other couples: Ian and Miss Sophia Moore of Boston, Alexine's maid of honor, Jamie and one of the bridesmaids, Herbert's parents, Mr. and Mrs. Horace Bonine, Robert and Isobel, his face a study of surprise and delight at finding his tiny wife in his arms, hers hidden against his gray cashmere waistcoat.

The cake of a dozen tiers stood in the center of a table that ran the length of the room and held an assortment of delicacies from Russian caviar and cold roast pheasant to tiny red raspberries and marrons glacés. The champagne was endless and the music never stopped.

From the moment of their arrival until they departed in the new Oldsmobile sedan that was Robert's wedding gift to them, Alexine and Herbert were the centerpiece of a flawless extravaganza. As though she knew the spotlight would never again catch her so fully, Alexine determined to play every moment in its beam to perfection. And she succeeded very well. "The Claflin girl's" wedding stood for a time as the standard of taste and sumptuousness by which other nuptials were judged.

JULY 18, 1932

A phone call at nine o'clock Monday morning summoned Isobel downstairs where Dylan and his car were waiting. The moment she left, Will flew from bed into the shower, quickly shaved and dressed in his favorite shirt and tie, dark jacket and vest, and white flannel trousers. Rita's knock sounded on the door soon after he was ready.

He rushed toward the noise, then caught himself. The intensity of his ardor might be frightening. He didn't want to overwhelm her. Slow down, he told himself, taking several deep breaths before opening the door.

"Hi, Willie boy. You expectin' someone?" She flashed a dazzling grin at him. If he hadn't been clinging to the doorknob, he might have swooned.

"Rita." His voice was barely audible. "Come in."

The smell of her hair, her skin, flowed over him as she passed into the room, weakening him further.

"Did you miss me?" She turned to face

320

him as she asked the question.

Will forced himself forward on wobbly legs. "Oh, Rita, if you knew how I missed you . . ." He reached her and wrapped his arms around her body, pulling it close to his.

"I guess you did," she whispered against his shoulder.

"There's no guessing. I missed you terribly. It was unbearable." The words spilled into Rita's ear. "I couldn't eat or sleep. All I thought of was you. I saw you everywhere. You never left me . . . not for a moment."

"I thought of you, too. Willie boy." She pulled back and looked up into his face.

"Oh, thank God." He bent and covered her mouth with a flurry of small kisses before crushing her against him again. "Thank God . . . thank God."

"There's somethin' we've gotta talk about," Rita said after several moments passed. She untangled herself from Will's embrace and perched on the edge of the bed.

"I'll say there is." He followed her.

"And don't think I didn't think about it all the time you were gone. I know it's impossible for me to live without you. I know that."

"Hey, hold on a minute," Rita said.

"Maybe it seems sudden . . . maybe it is sudden . . . but I've never been more sure of anything in my life."

"Willie boy." Rita placed a finger on his lips to silence him. "My period's late."

"Your period's late?"

"That's what I said."

"Your period's late."

"You got it."

He stared at her, his face expressionless. She gazed steadily back at him.

"You heard me, didn't you?" she asked finally.

"I did," Will affirmed, his look unwavering.

"You know what it means, don't you?"

"I've heard the expression." Will was huffy, realizing she mistook his silence for ignorance.

"Are you upset?" Her voice quavered and Will thought he saw tears glint in her eyes before she lowered them.

"Oh, Rita, no." He broke from his trance. "No, I'm not and you mustn't be. Are you?"

"Well . . ."

"You mustn't be. I'm not upset. I'm thrilled. I am." He reached his hand under her chin and raised her head. "Oh, Rita . . ." He held her face in both hands and gently kissed her mouth.

"You're not upset?" She looked up from beneath her lashes, still uncertain.

"What's the difference?" His hands slid down to her shoulders. "We'd be getting married anyway. Oh, Rita. I'm so happy." He pressed her against him.

It took some time for Will to feel the weight of Rita's stillness. Finally, he couldn't ignore it.

"Rita?" His inquiry didn't budge her. "Rita?" he repeated.

She rose and moved across the room, her silence now terrifying. "We can't get married," she said at last.

"Of course we can." Will bolted from the bed to her side. "What's to stop us?"

"My career, for one thing." She kept

her back to him.

"I wouldn't interfere with your career," Will protested.

"A baby would." Rita's tone was matter-of-fact but Will gasped slightly when she actually said the word. "I can't afford time off just when I'm gettin' started."

"Well, I know it's rough to get a foothold . . ." Will began.

"And besides," she turned toward him now, cutting him off, "What kind of start would that be? You'd feel trapped . . ."

"I wouldn't!"

"I'd feel I forced you into something."

"You didn't!"

"It's just no way to begin, Willie boy. It wouldn't work."

"But, Rita . . ." He felt confused and a little desperate. "What will happen?"

"An abortion." She turned away again. "It's the only way."

"No!" The word exploded from Will's throat. "I couldn't let you. It's dangerous. People die from them."

"Not if it's a good doctor . . . and I know about one."

"You already found one?" Will was horrified.

"A girlfriend went to him last year."

"I don't care who went to him." His voice grew harsh as it rose. "You're not going."

"I thought I could count on you to help me," she rasped back, facing him. "After all, I didn't get into this all by myself, did I? Some gentleman you turned out to be."

"Oh, Rita." Will melted before her fury. "Of course you can count on me. Of course you can."

"You'll help?"

"I'd do anything for you." He reached out to stroke her hair.

"It costs five hundred bucks."

"I'm not sure it's the answer, Rita."

"You haven't got it?" her panic was undisguised.

"It's not the money." Will brushed the question aside. "It's the idea of . . . the thing."

"Then you have got it?"

"I could get it . . . that's not the problem, Rita. Don't you see?"

"Oh, Willie boy." Rita collapsed onto

the bed. "I guess I've been pretty rough on you, comin' in here, makin' my big announcement, not even givin' you time to think. You're awful sweet to worry about me."

"I love you," Will declared, kneeling on the floor beside her, clasping her hands in his.

"I know you do," she crooned, petting his head as he lowered it into her lap. "I know you do. And, Willie, believe me, if there were any other way . . ."

He raised his head to resume the argument. She guided it back to her lap.

"Don't say anymore now. Just think about things. You'll see I'm makin' sense."

Will clasped his arms around her waist. She continued stroking his head.

"You'll see, Willie boy. You'll see." She leaned down and brushed his hair with her lips. "And we'll straighten it all out tomorrow. Now I gotta go or I'll be in double trouble."

Will's head snapped up. "What do you mean?"

"Do you think they're not makin' me

pay for my week off? I work two shifts today.''

''I thought we'd have the afternoon at least.''

''We'll have plenty of time tomorrow.'' She patted his cheek. ''Now I really gotta go. Noon tomorrow here?''

''Fine,'' he answered mechanically.

''And don't look so desperate, Willie boy. Time'll go fast.'' She pressed her lips briefly on his and moved quickly toward the door. Before closing it behind her, she blew him another kiss from the tips of her fingers.

Will remained, inert, on the end of the bed for some time. When he finally rose, he slowly unknotted his striped tie, corroborating his motions by watching them in the mirror above the dresser. He unbuttoned his vest, then his shirt and, with one motion, slid them and his jacket down his arm onto the floor. He undid his belt, unbuttoned his pants and let them fall. Now he stared at the reflection of his almost naked body in the glass, scrutinizing it carefully though he had no idea what he was looking for. Eventually, he stepped out of the circle of his trousers, bent over and picked up his clothing from the floor, and hung each piece in its proper place in the closet. Then he got back into bed.

When Isobel returned in the late afternoon, she awakened him from a light sleep.

"Ah'm glad ya're restin', Willie," she whispered.

He gave a muffled grunt and tossed about a few times to suggest feverishness. He had to make sure he would be free the following afternoon.

Isobel raised a shade, spilling light across her unmade bed and the used towels on the bathroom door.

"Ya know the maid ya mentioned, Willie?"

"Yes." Will sat straight up in bed, his voice sharp. "What about her?"

"She doesna do much of a job."

Will fell back on his pillows. "I told her not to bother today. I told her I was sick."

Isobel hummed as she stood at the dresser, removing her hat and gloves.

"How was the tour?" Will asked.

"Ah'm goin' back tomorrow."

"Tomorrow?' Will's body flew again into a sitting position. "Oh, that's wonderful."

"There's a great deal t' see, Willie. Maybe ya can come along."

"No!" It was almost a shout but Isobel didn't seem to notice. "I mean, I think I need one more day in bed."

"Ya probably do," she agreed.

"But it's wonderful that you're going," Will repeated, "just wonderful."

MONDAY, JULY 18

"It's hardly in a body's pow'r, to keep, at times, frae being sour."

Hear, hear, say we. And more anon.

When Ian graduated from college, he became Vice President for Sales of the Acme Foundry Company.

"Ah know who ya are and what ya do, fer God's sake," Robert fumed when Ian suggested the title.

329

"But Pop," Ian insisted, "other people have to know who's who."

"And who're these other people, if ah may ask?" said Robert.

"Well, certainly customers."

"Ah've done perfectly well sellin' t' people who thought they were buyin' from Bob Claflin. D'ya think they'd have bought more from *President* Claflin?"

"Any proper business has officers, Pop." Ian's pomposity wilted slightly.

"Ah canna think how we've got on without em . . . or without ya, fer that matter." Robert's disdain was unmistakable.

"But it's standard procedure," Ian whined.

"Ah dinna care." Robert dismissed the matter. "Call yerself king, if ya bloody well like."

So Ian assumed the Vice Presidency for Sales, Robert became the President, Jamie the Vice President for Operations and Herbert the General Manager.

Along with his new title and new job, Ian acquired a steady girlfriend. He met her at the Detroit Golf Club, membership in which he judged essential to his work. Almost immediately she became a fixture at Sunday dinner, an occasion Alexine had refused to let lapse even after her marriage. She and Herbert appeared at the Claflin house promptly at noon each Sunday.

Ian's young woman was named Ethel McInnis. This appellation caused Isobel not only to notice, but to esteem her, containing as it did the name of a Barrymore and proof of Scotch ancestry. Ian, of course, was terribly pleased that Isobel approved his choice.

And he relished every detail of the Sunday ritual. He enlisted Will's services as a chauffeur, although Will thought it odd that Ian didn't want to spend these trips alone with Ethel. Apparently, Ian was willing to sacrifice privacy for the grandeur of being driven. And Will was willing to subject himself to Ian's loftiness in return for having the car to himself for an hour or two between delivering the couple back to Ethel's house after dinner and picking Ian up to take him home.

There were times, however, when Will

wondered if possession of the car was sufficient recompense. The moment he slid behind the wheel of the automobile on Sunday morning, Ian treated him as a servant. This was not, of course, radically different from Ian's attitude toward Will at other times; Will was used to it. Besides, Ethel, quite obviously, didn't take it seriously. Once, when Ian was being especially haughty, she actually winked at Will.

This aspect of Ethel made Will wonder how she could endure his brother. If she could see through his pretensions — and they were marched before her in full dress parade every Sunday — how could she bear him? Will watched carefully as Ian led her through the rites: small glasses of sherry poured in the parlor from a rose and gold decanter Will had never seen before; two extra courses added to the meal at Ian's request; decorous conversation, directed by Ian toward current events and the arts.

This last affectation was the most difficult to sustain, requiring as it did the cooperation of the entire family. Ian could usually count on Herbert's compliance, Will's abstention, Jamie's air of amused disinterest. He was less certain of his sister and his parents. Alexine, stung perhaps by her family's quick, warm acceptance of Ethel, something she felt they still withheld from Herbert, used these occasions to jab at Ian, sometimes rather savagely. Robert and Isobel never attacked. They were simply unreliable. Ian never knew what might cause Isobel to veer off into fond musings on a photoplayer or Robert to cast a scornful eye in his direction. But these uncertainties kept him on his toes and when the tone of the conversation fell below what Ian considered a respectable level, Will delighted in seeing him squirm.

Ethel herself treated Ian's shortcomings with a sort of fondness. Far from ignoring them, she called attention to them, but always with a gentle humor that handed Ian a way to save face.

"Ian, you are pigheaded; you really are," she would say, smiling warmly at him. Or: "I wish I knew who you were trying to impress." Or: "If you're not the best, it won't be because you're not trying."

And when Ian smiled back at her, it was possible to believe, for that instant, that his insufferable qualities were just minor quirks, and probably passing ones. She made him look so much better than he was. As for the matter of what he did for her, Will never figured it out.

JULY 19, 1932

Dylan sent his car for Isobel at nine Tuesday morning.

"My best to Mr. Selznick," said Will, his voice as feeble as the wave with which he sent her out the door.

He had three hours before Rita arrived and spent two of them in bed, stiffening his resolve and rehearsing his speech. The last hour he devoted to grooming himself meticulously for the encounter. By the time Rita appeared, Will felt very much in charge of himself and his thoughts.

He led her immediately, in what he felt was masterly fashion, to the deep armchair near the window and seated her in it. Then, standing before her, he began his speech.

"Rita, I've thought things over very carefully." His hands began to quiver and he clasped them behind his back. "I certainly understand your concern about your career and I would never want to stand in your way. However, having a baby would just be a matter of a few months off while . . . the other way could mean your life. I just don't think you should risk that and I know I could never permit it. Besides that, and most important of all, I want you to be my wife."

Will endured her silence as long as he could before asking the question directly. "Rita, will you marry me?"

"Willie boy," she said, "I didn't wanna do it this way but you're not leavin' me any choice."

"Please answer the question." Will tried to regain the initiative he felt slipping away.

"You just don't get it, do you?" What began as a rueful smile hardened on Rita's mouth into something rather unsavory.

"That's no answer." He felt alarm

spreading through him but he couldn't locate the source.

"I'm not about to marry you." Rita rose and brushed past him.

"Maybe there's something you don't understand." He spun around and followed her. "I'd stay here with you. I'm not asking you to go back home."

"There's no misunderstanding, Willie boy." She moved away again. "Look," she turned to face him from across the room, "can't we just treat this thing like a straight business proposition?"

"Business?" Will croaked.

"I'm pregnant, you're responsible, I wanna get rid of it, you help me out . . . straight business."

"But I told you how I felt about that . . ." Will's voice faded. A fierce undertow was carrying him and he hadn't the strength to resist any longer.

"I don't care what you feel, Willie boy. That's the point you're failin' to see here."

"I don't understand." The dark current tumbled Will about, making his voice quaver.

"I see that," said Rita. "Let me try it one more time."

"Yes," Will mumbled, as though she'd asked his permission.

"I need five hundred bucks and if you don't come up with it, I'll see if the old lady'd be willin' to pay."

"The old lady?" Will surprised himself by giggling at this description of Isobel.

"I'm glad you got your sense of humor back, Willie boy, but this ain't exactly a laughin' matter. I gotta have it by this time tomorrow."

Will nodded his head, solemn now, and made a noise of acquiescence.

"So you agree?" Rita had expected more of a fight.

When Will nodded again, she grinned and moved toward him. "Look," she put her hand on his arm, "I'm sorry it worked out this way. I'm sorry I'm not the marryin' kind."

"We could still see each other?" Will found his voice but it was faint.

"Well . . . that would kinda depend on you." She reached up and patted his cheek. "We had some good times, Willie boy, didn't we?''

"Oh, Rita." He grasped her raised hand and pressed its palm against his lips. "We'll work all this out. And I do want to see you. I do . . . no matter what."

"Well, the first thing to work out is the money."

"Yes, of course," Will murmured, now filling her hand with kisses.

"These things are only dangerous if you wait."

"Don't worry. I'll take care of it."

"You're all right, Willie boy. I thought I could count on you."

"I wouldn't let you down."

"Of course you wouldn't. I knew that." Rita lifted her mouth to be kissed and Will bent to it eagerly. "Same time, same place tomorrow?" she asked when they finally broke apart.

"What about this afternoon?" Will felt the eddy of confusion tugging at him again.

"Oh . . . didn't I tell you?" Rita moved to the dresser, checking her reflection in the mirror. "They doubled me up again. And listen, I'd really be outta luck without this job so I better move. After all, these aren't exactly the best of times. A girl's gotta live."

Her pluck made Will want to cry. "I wish I could pay your salary and you could dump this lousy job," he said fervently.

"Don't tempt me, Willie boy. Don't tempt me." Rita turned, winked at him and headed for the door.

Frozen in the center of the room, Will whispered after her: "Goodbye, Rita darling."

TUESDAY, JULY 19

The Captain up at the crack of dawn and off to RKO to watch dear Jack filming *Bill of Divorcement,* all this courtesy of Mr. Dylan Doyle whom Cap declares she finds "a perfect gentleman." This only proves that change is always possible (change your mind, Rita, and marry me, marry me).

After a noontime tête-à-tête — the lady requests we keep her name to ourselves and who're we to argue — I saw to some pressing financial business, then took in an afternoon showing of *The Bird of Paradise* (you are my Paradise, Rita, only you), a South Seas love match between Joel McCrea and Dolores Del Rio (please love me, Rita, as I love you). Thence to a stroll on the streets of Hollywood (and every footstep echoes your name: Rita . . . Rita . . . Rita), running into young Dick Powell at Hollywood and Vine, revolving in the same door as Aline MacMahon when we returned to the hotel at day's end (my days are empty without you, Rita; my nights long, lonely stretches).

Tonight to see *Crooner* (Rita, I am the singer of your name, your troubador, your balladeer), starring the same David Manners Isobel spent the day with on the *B of D* set, and then to P'NW where the Captain attacked a Little Pig Parfait while I sipped Ovaltine. Thence home early and to bed (but not to sleep without you, Rita. Only with you can I find rest. Please try to love me. It's the only thing I'll ever ask).

Rudolph Valentino was cut down by an inflamed appendix on a steamy August day in 1926. Upon receiving the news, Isobel took to her room where she awaited bedside bulletins issued from New York: the discovery of perforated ulcers, the onslaught of peritonitis, the hope when he rallied, the despair when he did not. Her vigil was solitary and unbroken. Only Miss Farnum, who delivered tea and toast twice a day, was allowed to enter the room. The constant low hum of a radio set was the only sound that seeped out from beneath the closed door.

On the day when The Great Director called The Great Lover off the Screen of Life, as some newspapers had it, the hum of the radio ended and silence shrouded the room. Isobel did not emerge until Valentino's body was transported westward and placed, temporarily, in the vault of a friend while employers, ex-wives, alleged lovers, family, managers, strangers squabbled over what to do with the Sheik's earthly shell. This was some two weeks after the death itself and Isobel's appearance was decidedly wraithlike. The pallor of her gaunt cheeks, accentuated by mourning black, was itself reminiscent of death. Her tiny frame, scantily fleshed at the heartiest of times, now had the fragility of a handle on a fine old china cup. The lament in her eyes muted their brilliant blue, covering them with a gray film of grief.

Robert attempted to disguise his shock at this apparition with a somewhat hysterical tirade about the current heat wave.

"It's like bein' blasted by the fires a hell t' be in the bloody shop," he sputtered, trying not to stare at the opposite end of the table. "Ah canna ask the men t' work overtime. Ah canna stand it m'self, fer God's sake. The air's still as a stone, pressin' on ya till ya canna breathe. Ah'll have t' close up if it doesna break."

"McGinty almost fainted when they poured this afternoon," said Will, eager to join the conspiracy of normality. "And my shirt was so wet I had to wring it out."

"Would ya like a fan then, Is?" Robert asked.

Isobel turned her eyes in his direction but they remained unfocused.

"It would give ya a cross breeze." He hoped the concentration of his gaze would dispel the blur of hers. "It would move the air around a mite." He couldn't pierce the screen. It was inviolable.

"You should eat, Isobel," said Ian, missing the point of the charade. "You're too thin."

"Leave er be," Robert hissed, ignoring the fact that Isobel speared a small piece of meat and placed it in her mouth. "Ah dinna know if ah'll have t' close up or noo but if they canna breathe they canna work."

"It can't be that bad, Pop," said Ian.

"And how would ya know, ah wonder? No doubt ya get a breeze or two out on the links. They've probably got the air stirrin' over at the club all right."

"How many times do I have to explain?" Ian whined. "I do business when I'm there."

"Dinna bawl about it and dinna explain

343

it again, if ya please."

Isobel's dim eyes shifted back and forth between her husband and her middle son, her mouth still working over the same piece of meat.

"Haven't sales gone up in the last year?" Ian asked this question of his father at least once a week.

"Aye . . . aye . . . praise be to the Vice President of Sales." Robert uttered his customary response, clasping his hands before him in a prayerful attitude, shooting his eyes heavenward.

"Willie." Absolute stillness fell on the room at the sound of Isobel's voice. "D'ya remember *A Sainted Devil?*"

"Sure." Will's voice shook with surprise at having been singled out. "That was one of his pictures with Nita Naldi."

Isobel fluttered her hand, as if erasing the thought of the overweight villainess. "Ah think that's what he was . . . a sainted devil." She impaled another shred of meat on her fork and raised it to her mouth.

"Yes," said Will, eager to encourage further conversation, "I guess he was."

Everyone remained suspended, watching Isobel's silent chewing, waiting to see if she would interrupt it with further speech. She did not.

Robert eventually returned to his denunciation of the oppressive heat and, somewhat earlier than usual, signaled Will that he was ready for their evening excursion to Ella Finnerty's Blind Pig, a barroom in the far reaches of a building that housed a trunk shop on its street side. They'd begun this habit at the start of Will's summer vacation and followed it with regularity and precision.

After dinner Will brought the car around to the front of the house. Robert, his hat tilted slightly over one eye, strolled down the walk and climbed in beside his son. At Finnerty's, Robert drank several whiskeys during his hour-long stay while Will waited outside in the car. Going home, Robert rode in the back seat in silence. Will deposited him at the front walk before putting the car into the garage and by the time Will entered the house Robert had vanished into his room.

Tonight, however, it was different.

Robert remained inside for almost two hours, and when he emerged his usually steady gait was ragged around the edges. He wrenched open the right-hand passenger door and clambered in beside Will, his hat pushed to the back of his head, a pale straw ring around the bright red circle of his face.

"Carry me off, laddie." He swung his arm in an arc that ran into Will's shoulder. "Take me away."

"Any place in particular?" Will asked.

"Any place but home."

As the car started up, Robert's body jostled about loosely with its motion. "Drive on," he muttered, flinging out his other hand, this time hitting the window. "Drive on."

"I am, Pop." Will realized his father was quite drunk and hoped to soothe him.

"Ah'll noo go home yet. Dinna take me home."

"I won't," Will promised.

Just as he became convinced that his father had fallen asleep, Robert spoke. "Do as ah say, laddie, not as ah do. That way ya'll noo make m' mistakes."

Will hadn't any idea what Robert meant but was reluctant to question him. As it turned out, there was no need. Robert made the queries for him.

"What mistakes, ya may ask?" He rested his hand on Will's arm. "Ah've noo an idea m' dad made mistakes, ya may say."

"Pop . . ." Will jiggled his arm, trying to dislodge the terribly heavy weight Robert's hand had become.

"Drive on!" He withdrew his hand in a reverse circle until it landed in his lap. "Well, there're many, believe it or not. Yer dad's made many, many mistakes."

"Oh, come on, Pop . . ."

"Many." Robert's tone closed the issue. "But ya can spare yerself if ya do as ah say, not as ah do."

Will had nearly decided that he was to be left with only this cryptic admonition when Robert leaned his upper body across the seat.

"Did ya see er eyes, laddie? Did ya see how they were all locked up?" Robert again hung on Will's arm but only briefly this time, falling back against the seat as the car turned a corner.

"Isobel?"

"Yer mother, fer the love a God. Who else? Did ya look in er eyes?"

"Well, not exactly . . ."

"Like an abandoned house with only a ghost livin' in it." Robert's head lolled from side to side. The small sounds he emitted could have been cries or snores. Will couldn't tell as he steered the car along unfamiliar roads.

Suddenly, Robert pulled himself erect.

"Ya must be careful with em, laddie. Ya must be mild."

"Who?"

"The women," Robert said finally. "The girls. Ya must be gentle and dinna make em afraid. If ya frighten em, laddie, ya're lost . . . ya're lost. Do as ah say, not as ah do."

Exhausted by the effort of delivering his message, Robert drooped again in the seat, his head pitched forward, the unmistakable rasps of sleep issuing from his slack mouth. Will continued his aimless movement through the streets for another hour but Robert didn't awaken. When they arrived home, and Robert's eyes finally popped open, fastening on the face of his youngest son, he looked surprised.

"What is it, laddie?" he asked with some alarm.

"We're home."

"We're home," Robert repeated, his voice flat, uncomprehending.

"I brought you home, Pop."

"Aye . . . we're home." Robert patted one of Will's hands, signaling understanding, and began smoothing out his jacket, straightening his hat. When he climbed from the car and started up the walk to the house, he looked to Will as he had every other night for the past few months. And by the time Will arrived in the house after putting away the car, his father had disappeared.

Robert did not speak again of the phantom he found residing in his wife's eyes; nor advise Will further on the conduct of his relations with young ladies. Isobel, though she refused to see *The Son of the Sheik,* Valentino's final film, wore mourning for a year and carried every day of that year a shadow across her face. And Will never felt quite the same about Pola Negri after she dashed to Valentino's bier, collapsed upon it, sobbed inconsolably for the loss of their true love. Will's ardor was not annihilated but it was definitely altered. He had survived his first grand passion.

JULY 20, 1932

"Ah'd like t' go by David's this mornin'." Isobel removed the excess cinnamon dust from her toast by tapping it on the edge of her plate. "Ah think he's in one a the canyons."

"David's?"

"David Manners, Willie. Ah told ya about im last night."

"Of course, of course. I keep forgetting you're on a first name basis with all these big cheeses."

"Maybe Benedict . . ."

"Who's he?"

"Benedict Canyon, Willie. He could be there."

"How do you suggest we find out?"

"Whipple'll know."

"Whipple? Who's Whipple?"

"The driver, Willie."

"The driver? Did I miss something?" Will's threadbare nerves were reflected in his voice.

"Ya still seem a mite feverish, laddie." Isobel dabbed her napkin in the two corners and the center of her mouth although they were spotless.

"I've gotta see the doc at noon."

"Perhaps ya'd better rest till then."

"What driver?" Will asked.

"He belongs t' Dylan."

"Are you seeing him again?"

"Ah'm noo *seein'* Whipple, Willie."

"No, I realize that." Will forced a small laugh. "I meant Dylan. I just wondered if you were seeing him again today."

"He gave me the car . . . and Whipple."

"For the day?"

"Fer as long as ah'd like. It's noo is only one, Willie."

Will gave a long, low whistle of astonishment.

"Ya look a wee bit flushed."

"Yes . . . well . . . I'll just rest this morning. I'll just rest until I see what the doc has to say."

Depositing Isobel in Dylan's car outside the hotel, Will asked when she'd be back.

"Mr. Doyle suggested that Mrs. Claflin might like to join him for lunch at the Beverly Hills Hotel," said Whipple from his post at the open rear door. "He also said Mr. Claflin was welcome to join them."

"Well . . ." said Will, "please tell him Mr. Claflin can't . . . today. But thank you . . . thank him."

"Very good, sir."

As Will watched Isobel disappearing down Hollywood Boulevard, he felt his legs might give out. Perhaps he did have a fever. Maybe he'd better lie down.

Once upstairs, he flung himself on the freshly made bed. Had Rita come in to clean while he was at breakfast? He looked about, seeking her imprint somewhere in the room. Had she touched this pillow? This spread? He could not lie still. He wandered into the bathroom, fingering the clean towels, staring into the immaculate mirror. Then, urged by some inner whisper, he raced to the drawer where he'd put the money and counted it, several times. Satisfied it was the right amount, he resumed ambling.

When Rita arrived at noon, he opened the door with the sheaf of bills in his hand. She grinned at the sight.

"Oh Willie, Willie, Willie boy." She moved in, closing the door and pressing Will against the wall with her body. "I knew I could count on you."

"Rita," he whispered. "Oh, Rita."

She rubbed herself up and down on the swelling between his legs. She clapped her hands on his thighs and then ran them up his body, slowly. When she reached his shoulders she drew her hands along the length of his arms. The heat in his groin was almost unbearable as she continued moving against him. She wound the fingers of one hand around the bills in Will's fist. She lowered the other hand to his crotch.

"Oh, Willie boy, you give me so much."

"There's so much more, Rita." His

voice sounded very far away. "I want to give you so much more."

"I know, I know . . . and you can start tomorrow, right here, nine sharp."

"Yes, Rita. Oh, yes." Will's eyes were closed, his head tilted back against the wall.

"Don't forget now." She stood on tiptoe to kiss the underside of his chin. She gave his groin a final squeeze.

"Oh, Rita, yes . . ."

The sound of the closing door snapped Will's head forward.

"Rita?"

He stared at the wooden panel as if it might answer.

"Rita?" he asked again, his voice bouncing off the walls of the narrow hallway, driving his head back to the wall. As his eyelids fell shut again, his hands found the buttons on his pants.

"Oh, Rita," he groaned, placing himself in the sheath of his hands, sliding them back and forth, back and forth. "Oh, Rita . . . Rita . . . Rita . . ."

He chanted her name all the way to his climax, which sprayed against the opposite wall and rebounded onto his navy slacks. The latter he sent out to be cleaned. The former he attempted to scrub himself. The resultant spot was far more noticeable than the original stain would have been, and Isobel never failed to remark on it.

"That maid should stick t' pictures, Willie," she'd say. "She canna clean."

WEDNESDAY, JULY 20

A tiring day for Cap at various watering holes; a rough go for our hero just staying at home. So tonight we're doing what's best for body and soul: rest in the room and Chocolate Creams. And if you think we're nertz, let's see how you'd withstand the rigors of the high life!

When Ian and Ethel announced their engagement at Christmastime, Isobel urged them, as she had Alexine, to marry on March 28.

Ethel was inclined to acquiesce. "It seems as good a time as any," she said.

Her mother was not. "We want a spring

wedding, dear. March twenty-eighth isn't really spring."

This was only the beginning of divergence between Isobel's and Mrs. McInnis's opinions.

"We two gals have to get together and discuss certain things," said Mrs. McInnis.

"Ah haven't aught t' say," said Isobel.

"She'll do all the talking," Ethel assured her.

"Then there's no need fer me t' be there," Isobel pointed out.

"Would you do it for me?" Ethel asked.

"If ya put it that way . . . aye."

The date was set for a Wednesday afternoon, Isobel to be delivered by Riley to the McInnis's at four o'clock. When she hadn't arrived by five, Mrs. McInnis called Ian at the foundry. When Isobel arrived home shortly after six, Ian was there waiting for her.

"Where have you been?" he demanded, his voice trembling.

"Flesh and the Devil." Isobel, oblivious to his anger, removed her hat and patted her hair into place in the hallway mirror.

"How could you?" he asked.

"Ah've noo seen the Swede before."

"The Swede? Who's the Swede?"

"Greta Garbo. She's new." Isobel's voice was patient. "It's the first chance ah've had t' see er."

"Well, it may be the last chance you'll ever have to see Mrs. McInnis," Ian sputtered.

"She's playin' with Jack Gilbert." Isobel moved toward the parlor. "Ah think they're really in love."

"Did you hear me?" he asked, trailing after her.

Isobel gazed up at her son from the depths of her armchair.

"I said you were supposed to see Mrs. McInnis . . . at four . . . today."

"Was it t'day?"

"It was." Ian, positioned now to tower over Isobel, tried to assume an air of dignified firmness.

"Ah must a fergot." She appeared genuinely puzzled but not in the least intimidated.

"I should say you did. And what about Riley? Why didn't he remind you?"

"Ah told im not t' disturb me till after the second show."

"You saw it twice?" Ian's voice rose again and shattered his pose. He collapsed onto the sofa in defeat, remaining there until a phone call from Ethel roused him.

Yes, he told her, Isobel was fine. Just a silly mix-up. Of course they could arrange another meeting. He thought a luncheon date might be best. Isobel was terribly sorry. Please apologize and say a week from Friday, at noon, would be fine.

Ian made sure Isobel was deposited on the McInnis doorstep at precisely twelve o'clock.

"I didn't realize . . ." Mrs. McInnis began as she led Isobel into the house. "I mean, I had no idea . . . that is, Ian never mentioned . . . I didn't know there'd been a death."

By this time they had arrived in the larger of the two first-floor parlors.

"Aye," said Isobel, as Mrs. McInnis cupped her hand solicitously under her guest's rustling back silk elbow and led her to a chair.

"I'm so sorry." A small canapé-laden

table between them, she positioned herself across from Isobel, and looked at her expectantly. Between two gloved fingers, Isobel picked up a paper-thin oval of cucumber and bread and nibbled at its edge.

"I hope it wasn't too close," Mrs. McInnis said finally.

Isobel nodded approval of the morsel in her mouth. Mrs. McInnis took it for an affirmative response.

"Oh no! I am so sorry." She chose a tiny sandwich herself and chewed along with her guest, demonstrating sympathy through shared action.

"I'm surprised that Ian never mentioned your loss." She finished her circlet and waited for Isobel to fill in the particulars.

"But perhaps it's too new," she prompted when Isobel failed to speak. "Or too old," she added as the silence continued.

Isobel bit into something she didn't care for and placed the offending round back on its plate. Mrs. McInnis leapt at the opportunity to change the subject.

"Oh, is that some of that awful fish

spread? I've told Clara over and over not to use it . . . ever, ever, ever. I don't know why she insists. But let's go into lunch, shall we? I hope you'll enjoy it. I asked Ian for a list of all your favorite things. I just hope his list was accurate.''

But Mrs. McInnis, having regained her conversational equilibrium, didn't appear even to notice what Isobel did or did not eat. She just talked: about the wedding, about Ian, about Ethel, Clara, Mr. McInnis, herself. Isobel interrupted at 1:30 to say she had to leave.

''Well, I'm just so glad we had a chance to have this little chat,'' said Mrs. McInnis. ''I think we got a lot of things straightened out, don't you? But I know you're every bit as busy as I am. There are so many things to think of. Where are you off to now?''

''The Capitol,'' said Isobel. ''Clara Bow's playin' in *It*.''

''Of course, it doesn't do to neglect time for relaxation.'' Mrs. McInnis didn't miss a beat, patting the weeds on Isobel's back as she walked her toward the door. ''Especially if you've been through one trying time and have another ahead. Not, of course, that there's any comparison between a wedding and . . . the other. But making arrangements, seeing to things, thinking of this and that . . ." Her voice trailed off as they reached the doorway.

As Isobel rose from her farewell curtsy, Mrs. McInnis grasped her shoulders and looked down directly into her face. "Now that we're such good friends," she said, "may I ask . . ." She took a step back and fluttered her hands in the air about Isobel's body, indicating her renewed interest in the dark garments covering it.

"Rudolph Valentino," said Isobel, gazing straight back.

Mrs. McInnis blinked rapidly several times and opened her mouth but no words issued from it. As Isobel inclined her head in a final nod, a noise sounded in the back of Mrs. McInnis's throat but it died when Isobel turned and started down the front walk. Only the ring of her stiletto-like heels cut through the silence as she moved toward the car. Mrs. McInnis struggled in the doorway to wrench her mouth into a smile. But by the time Isobel leaned forward to wave through the car's side window, Mrs. McInnis had given up the fight. She stood unmoving, jaw loose, arms hanging limply at her sides, as Isobel was borne away.

JULY 21, 1932

Whipple collected Isobel at a quarter of nine so that she could be standing before Bullock's doors when they opened on the hour. Will was stationed in the room, awaiting Rita. When she hadn't appeared by ten, he called the Hotel Housekeeper's office.

"I wanted to inquire about one of your girls."

"Yes?" The woman's voice was guarded.

"Frances Linderman?"

"Yes?"

"Well . . . I just wondered . . . I just wanted to ask if you expected her today?"

"Miss Linderman has not reported for work today."

"You mean you expected her but she

hasn't shown up?''

"That is precisely what I mean."

"I see," said Will. "Well . . . thank you, anyway, . . . thanks."

She'd decided to have the abortion today and she was, at this very moment, lying beneath the butcher's knife . . . the doctor she'd counted on wouldn't do it and she was, right now, trudging from one seamy place to another, seeking someone who would . . . she'd had the abortion last night and today she was dead. The possibilities hammered at Will, relentless, myriad. Recriminations came in similar fashion. He should have insisted on accompanying her to the filthy assassin . . . he should have forbidden the abortion altogether . . . he should have married her yesterday.

A knock on the door made him shriek and he hurried toward the repeated sound.

"Would ya take these, Willie?" Isobel thrust an armful of packages at him, her eyes flickering along the hallway into the room. "That maid canna clean. She should stick t' pictures."

"I didn't think you'd be back so soon."

Will remained frozen in the doorway.

"Dylan says ya're spendin' too much time in the room."

"Dylan says? Dylan says?" Will's efforts to smother his turbulence were wearing thin.

"Bring the boxes in, laddie."

He moved into the room and set the packages on a bed. Isobel opened one and pulled out a hat, dark lavender and feathered.

"Put on yer jacket, Willie. We're goin' t' lunch." Watching herself in the mirror, Isobel settled the hat on her head.

"With Dylan?" Will stalled, undecided what to do.

"Aye. He wants t' show ya around too."

"Seems to me he has an awful lot or free time."

"Yer jacket, Willie. Whipple's waitin'."

There was no escape. Will shrugged into his jacket and tightened his tie. "What exactly does he do at RKO?"

"He's a very busy man, Willie." Isobel reached into another box and extracted a parasol, streaked with several shades of purple, one of them matching her hat. "We'll go t' Tallulah's after lunch. Ah dinna want er t' think we've forgotten."

THURSDAY, JULY 21

Swept off to lunch at the Derby by Mr. Doyle, there to enjoy the noon repast with Connie Talmadge, Lina Basquette, Leatrice Joy and Jack Gilbert (no, those last two were not together, having decided some years back they couldn't live scrappily ever after). Afterward, Dylan headed back to the studio and Whipple whipped us over to North Stanley Avenue. Tallulah didn't recognize us at first, being as how we were wearing a Packard this time, but when she did, she jumped right into said heap, planted a smack on Isobel's puss, ditto yours truly, and sat there chewin' the rag like our best pal in the world, God love her. I thought Whipple's eyes would pop right out of his kisser!

Tonight to see *Stranger in Town* with Chic Sale and David Manners (no secret anymore who's his biggest fan). Chic personal appeared and laid 'em in the izzles.

But there's more to life than laughter and that brings your scrivener to a personal note. Moving today among some of filmland's most lustrous assets, visiting some of this town's brightest spots, he had to ask himself what it all meant. He had to ask: What would the glamour and glitter add up to without Rita? Wouldn't the gloss look pretty dull? Wouldn't it all seem an empty show? Wouldn't the gold turn into dross?

They're hard questions and yours truly hasn't got the answers. We've got a hunch there aren't any easy ones. But we do know this: You've gotta ask the questions, even when they're rough.

———————

Ethel and Ian married in early May of 1927 in a spectacle of such opulence that several guests remarked one would almost think the McInnises had deliberately tried to outdo the Claflin girl's wedding, if one didn't know better. One who didn't know better, and said so, was the Claflin girl herself. But she said it only to Herbert, who scoffed at the notion, and to Isobel, who didn't hear it.

Isobel sounded the wedding day's only discordant note by appearing in black. Ethel didn't mind — she'd long ago accepted Isobel on her own terms. Ian didn't mind because Ethel didn't. But Mrs. McInnis was outraged.

Coming down the aisle on the arm of a son, she froze when she glimpsed Isobel's weed-covered back and was unable to move for several long moments. When her paralysis finally passed, and she moved into her pew, it was evident that she was fighting for breath.

Later, at the reception, she took great pains to rationalize Isobel's appearance to the guests while, at the same time, disassociating herself from it entirely. To any who inquired, and some who did not, she murmured delicately and vaguely about a relative in Scotland — a cousin perhaps? or was it an aunt? — but then hastened to add that no matter who it was, if she'd known Mrs. Claflin planned to inject this dark accent, she'd certainly have insisted that it be set aside for the day, this one day. A wedding, after all, was a time to rejoice and you'd think, since it was her own son . . . well, she, Mrs. McInnis, had she known, would certainly have insisted.

Two weeks later, when Isobel abandoned her mourning temporarily in celebration of Lindbergh's landing in Paris, Mrs. McInnis's comments lost the modicum of restraint they'd possessed.

"The woman is a lunatic! She won't take off her horrible black for the wedding of her own son but she'll take it off for a total stranger just because he flies someplace. And why is she wearing it in the first place? Because of another total stranger. She's mad!"

For a time, Ethel tried defending Isobel. "She's not mad, Mother. She's just different."

"Wearing black to the wedding of your own son and then taking it off for some pilot whom you don't even know is not the mark of difference, Ethel. It is the mark of lunacy."

"She's just not like the rest of us," said Ethel.

"I should say she isn't, thank heaven! Variety is one thing, Ethel. Insanity is quite another."

Eventually, since her mother remained intransigent, Ethel stopped trying. By midsummer Mrs. McInnis's eruptions had withered to an occasional muttered remark. By autumn they had stopped altogether.

Will was scheduled to enter college that fall. Robert, pleading concern for Isobel, asked him to wait a year. Ian and Ethel, after staying with the Claflins for two months, moved in August into their newly built home. Since June, Jamie had been living in an apartment near school.

"Ah hate t' have er alone in the house, laddie," Robert said.

"But eventually she'll have to be," said Will. "If I don't go this year, I'll go next."

"Aye, ah know that. But we'll find a smaller place by then. Ah hate t' have er rattlin' around the big house all by erself."

"If you think about it, Pop, she's not really home that much."

"Aye, that's true too, laddie. But it's the idea a the thing . . . the idea a comin' home t' an empty house."

Eager to avoid any suggestion of coercion, Robert threw a cloak of democracy over the proceedings by insisting Will take a week to deliberate over his decision.

"I don't need a week, Pop," said Will. "If you want me to stay, I'll stay."

"It's noo me who wants it, laddie," Robert corrected him. "And take the time, fer God's sake. Ya'll want t' make the right choice."

"Don't give in, Willie," Jamie urged. "I gave in and now the best I can do is move a few blocks away."

"What do you mean?"

"Never mind . . . just don't give in."

"What choice do I have? I mean, Pop can order me to stay if he wants."

"But he wouldn't do that . . . not directly."

"And besides," said Will, "he's right about the house and Isobel being alone."

Jamie gave a snort of laughter. "Since when did Isobel mind being alone? When, do you suppose, is the last time Isobel even noticed whether she was alone or not? He's the one who can't bear it. He's the one who can't let go. But he can't ask you to stay behind for him. He could never ask that."

"Maybe he needs me?" Will had intended a statement, but his voice shot up on the last two words.

"Oh, I'm sure he does. He needs us all."

"Well then?"

"Well then . . . what about you, Willie? What do you need?"

"Is a year going to make that much difference? I've lost years before."

"It's not just a year, Willie. It's a chance . . . and I'd hate to see you lose a chance."

"What do you mean?"

"Never mind," said Jamie. "Just don't give in."

Will thought perhaps he wouldn't. He drafted in his mind a response to Robert enumerating and supporting all the reasons for continuing his education without interruption. But when he walked into Robert's office to give his answer what he said was:

"Sure, Pop. I'll stick around this year."

Robert rose from his chair and grasped Will's hand, pumping his arm up and down.

"Ya're a good lad, Willie . . . a good lad. And ah'll noo ferget it." He dropped his son's hand and threw his arms around Will's shoulders, pulling him into a ferocious embrace.

In the few brief moments he was crushed against him, Will felt his father's body wrench with a soundless sob. When they separated, however, there was no trace of tears.

"She'll appreciate this, laddie," Robert said, again clasping Will's hand. "Ya'll see."

JULY 22, 1932

"I wanted to inquire about Frances Linderman?" said Will when the Housekeeper picked up the phone.

"Yes?" She sounded even warier than the day before.

"I wondered if she reported to work today?"

"I think you'll want to speak to our Mr. Rudolph about that."

"No, no. I'm happy to speak to you."

"Mr. Rudolph is the Hotel Manager."

"I spoke to you yesterday."

"Were you one of the gentlemen who inquired about Miss Linderman?"

"Yes."

"Then you'll want Mr. Rudolph . . . or he'll want you. I'll put you through."

Before Will could ask her to clarify her statement, she'd tossed him into a humming limbo between her office and the Manager's. He was just about to hang up and call the Housekeeper back again when Mr. Rudolph picked up the phone.

"Vlados Rudolph speaking. May I help you?" The man had a thick Yugoslavian accent.

"I don't know," said Will. "The Housekeeper switched me to you."

"Yes?" He stretched out the single syllable.

"I'm not sure why," said Will. "I was inquiring about one of your maids."

"Yes?" This time it seemed even longer.

"Her name is Frances Linderman."

"You are asking for the Linderman woman?" Rudolph's languor vanished and his speech became clipped.

"Yes . . . I am." Something in Rudolph's voice caused a cold knot of fear to begin forming in Will's stomach.

"Are you calling from inside the hotel, sir?"

"Yes."

"And may I ask your name?"

"Claflin . . . William Claflin."

"Could you perhaps come to my office, Mr. Claflin? It might be best to talk here. I am just off the lobby."

"Yes . . . of course. Yes."

She was dead. Rita, his Rita, was dead, poisoned by a filthy knife, severed by a misstep, drained of her life's blood by slipshod care. How could he live with the fact of her grisly demise, knowing he could, simply and deftly, have saved her from it? Rita was dead because he had failed to act! Will felt himself sinking downward, his body crumpling in perfect synchronization with the descending whoosh of the elevator. He caught himself. He would not exhibit such impotence again! Certainly not now. Couldn't he at least be strong for Rita now? In the moment of her death?

He pounded resolutely on Rudolph's door. The man who opened it looked like an undertaker, his black clothing only slightly less shiny than his patent-leather hair and shoes.

"I'm Claflin," said Will in the sturdiest voice he could muster.

"Vlados Rudolph." He bowed, revealing a gleaming white part, like an old incision, down the center of his head.

"I know what happened," said Will, following Rudolph's extended arm and settling into a brown leather chair. "Where is she now?

"Ah," said Rudolph, drumming his fingers on his desk as he circled it, "how I wish we knew that. If only we knew that . . ."

"You mean they haven't found her?"

"Alas, Mr. Claflin, they have not."

Now, seated behind the desk, he tapped his fingers on his thin, pursed lips.

"Then how do you know she's dead?" Will leaned forward in his chair. "If they haven't found her, how do they know?"

"Dead, Mr. Claflin?" Rudolph's hand ceased its digital tattoo and fell onto the desk. "What makes you think Miss Linderman is dead?"

"You mean she isn't?"

"I assume not, Mr. Claflin. I assume she is very much alive."

"Oh, thank God!" Will collapsed back into the chair, tears of relief stinging at the back of his eyes.

"Perhaps you will feel your gratitude somewhat misplaced . . ."

"Never." Will broke in although his voice was a whisper, spent from his great effort at strength. "Not as long as Rita is alive."

"Ah," said Rudolph, "you knew her by that name also?"

"It's her stage name, her movie name." Will was impatient now. If Rita was alive, he should be out looking for her.

"Yes, of course." Rudolph's fingers

resumed their strumming, this time on the edge of the desk. "Her stage name . . . her movie name . . . and also her alias when she is working the racket."

"What do you mean *alias?*" Will sputtered. "That's a pretty cheap trick, if you ask me. Jean Arthur isn't Jean Arthur's real name but nobody says *Jean Arthur* is an alias."

"Who is this Jean Arthur, if I may ask?"

"What racket?"

"Mr. Claflin, this is a matter of some delicacy." Rudolph now clasped his hands before him and gazed at Will over the tight little sphere they formed. "But I am afraid I must ask . . . did you give Miss Linderman . . . Miss Raymond . . . any money?"

"Yes, I did." Will tried to sound firm, unruffled.

"May I inquire as to the sum?"

"It was a private matter. I don't think . . ."

Rudolph interrupted. "A private matter of an undesired pregnancy?"

"She *told* you?" Will gasped.

"No, no, Mr. Claflin. She has told me nothing . . . unfortunately. But another gentleman, another guest in the hotel, has spoken to me." His hands returned to the desk's surface and began beating on it.

"And?"

"And?" Rudolph repeated the question, obviously surprised by it.

"And what did he say? What does he have to do with it?"

"Mr. Claflin," said Rudolph, shifting about in his chair, "this is not easy for me, you understand."

Will stared at the Manager, giving him no aid whatsoever.

"In fact, it is most difficult."

Still Will stared, unspeaking.

"Miss Linderman . . . Miss Raymond . . . she is a con man."

"A con man?" Will's incredulity and confusion were evident.

"A con *woman.*" Rudolph hoped this clarification would settle the matter.

"What do you mean?"

Forced to spell things out, Rudolph tried to do so as quickly as possible. "This woman took money from you and the other gentleman to pay for an operation for an undesired pregnancy, which, I am afraid, did not exist. Each believed he was responsible; each paid. I am sorry, Mr. Claflin.''

Despite Rudolph's speed and accent, Will heard every word. He was unable, however, to respond.

''I am most especially sorry that such a thing should take place in our hotel. Perhaps at first you might think that the hotel is in some way responsible. However, you will doubtless come to agree, as the other gentleman has, that these things can happen in any place and it seems pointless to point a finger of blame. Just as it seems pointless to make any public fuss. It is quite remarkable, isn't it, what people will do to earn a living in these most difficult times?''

When Will still failed to respond, Rudolph rose from his chair and moved toward Will's.

''It is really quite remarkable,'' he repeated, arriving now at Will's side and giving him a cue by placing his hand under Will's elbow and lifting slightly.

Will stood up and allowed Rudolph to guide him toward the door.

"It would be our great pleasure, Mr. Claflin," he said, hammering out staccato notes on the door handle, "to have you and a friend as our guests at dinner tonight on the Patio Roof."

"Thank you," said Will. "That's very nice."

"So we may expect you and . . . . ?"

"Isobel."

"Very good, Mr. Claflin. And we may expect you at . . ."

"Six."

"Excellent!" Rudolph pulled open the door, his voice following Will as he moved down the hall toward the lobby. "We will expect you and your lady at six tonight."

In August of 1927 President Coolidge declared he would not run for another term and Sacco and Vanzetti were put to death in the electric chair. In September Isadora Duncan's neck snapped in the noose of her own tangled scarf and Babe Ruth hit his sixtieth homerun of the year. And in early October *The Jazz Singer,* the first talking motion picture, opened in New York.

Isobel was an avid supporter of talkies from the beginning, constantly chiding the motion picture executives for their hesitation at putting talking pictures into production.

"Ah'd like t' have heard Gloria," she sniffed to Will as they emerged from their first viewing of *Sadie Thompson*.

"Mr. Mayer should a let Joan talk," she said after seeing Miss Crawford in *Our Dancing Daughters*.

"Ah'm sure Greta's got a lovely voice," she remarked, emerging from *Woman of Affairs*.

"I guess they've got technical problems," Will invariably replied.

"Ah wish they'd let em talk," Isobel said.

Her other quarrel with the powers of the movie industry concerned the recipients of the first Academy Awards. She was pleased that Janet Gaynor had been named Best Actress. As Isobel pointed out to Will, even Gloria Swanson, being considered herself for *Sadie*

Thompson, had said of Janet: "With all my heart I want her to win." What she didn't like was that Emil Jannings had been designated Best Actor. She felt John Gilbert deserved the award for his appearances opposite Garbo in *Flesh and the Devil* and *Love.*

"Jannings is ugly as a toad and John isn't," she said, hinting darkly that Gilbert's beauty had cost him the award.

She also felt some notice should have gone to *It* ("a lotta people saw that picture, Willie"), and to De Mille's *The King of Kings* ("a grand spectacle").

Most evenings Will accompanied Isobel to the movies and if Robert minded, if he would rather have had his son chauffeuring him to Ella Finnerty's, he wasn't in much of a position to object. He had, after all, based his case for Will's postponing college on his concern that Isobel not be left alone. He was not above sputtering at the two of them, however, when they spoke their secret language at the occasional evening meal the three of them shared.

"And who're Jetta and Adolphe and

May, fer God's sake? The neighbors? And when was the last time ya spoke t' em, if ya dinna mind m' askin'?''

"Ah dinna mind, Bertie," Isobel said. "May McAvoy was Al Jolson's leadin' lady in *The Jazz Singer* and Esther in *Ben Hur* and . . .''

"Thank ya very much, thank ya very much," Robert muttered. "But never mind. Pretend ah'm noo here.''

More frequently, however, Will and Isobel had dinner at the Statler Hotel. In the early fall evenings, they strolled afterward to the Adams, the Broadway Strand, the Palms State, wherever their chosen film was playing. After the movie, they walked to Sanders Ice Cream Store where Isobel had a hot fudge cream puff and Will a black-and-white soda. When they emerged, Riley was stationed at the curb in front, waiting to drive them home. As winter approached and deepened, he transported them from one stop to the next.

Will felt terribly adult that year, working full time, entertaining a woman in the evening, walking with her on his arm along the city's boulevards, bundling her into the car when the soft night air hardened with cold. He quite quickly forgot his college plans as he became immersed in Robert's world in the daytime and Isobel's at night. This life, he felt, suited him very well.

JULY 23, 1932

Will picked up the letter from Ian on his way to breakfast Saturday morning.

Dear William:
I find it impossible to imagine why you have not replied to my earlier letters by now. I'm sure you are very busy but you might have managed to find the time.

The situation with James grows worse daily and Herbert now is not quite working to capacity as he's concerned about Alex. She's experiencing some difficulties re the pregnancy. Much as I hate to think of cutting short your trip for Isobel's sake, I'm wondering now if you shouldn't consider coming home sooner than planned. The business is now the responsibility of us all.

There's no need, of course, to mention this to Isobel, but please let me know your thoughts *immediately*.

Love,
Ian

Will stuffed the letter into his pocket. Out of sight, out of mind. Dylan arrived at ten to take them to spend the day at his beach club.

As Whipple eased the automobile toward the club entrance, a slender blonde woman stepped from a Bugatti just ahead of them.

"Ah believe that's Verree Teasdale," said Isobel.

"What's that, Izzy?" Dylan swiveled around in the high front seat where he rode with Whipple.

Will, who'd been gazing at the dazzling blonde, snapped his head toward Dylan at the sound of this unfamiliar familiarity.

"Verree Teasdale," Isobel repeated. "She played two years on the stage with

Ethel in *The Constant Wife.*"

"That's her all right," Dylan confirmed. "She's a member . . . spends a lot of time here when she's not working."

"She's Edith Wharton's cousin," said Isobel.

"And she's just the beginning," Dylan went on, as delighted as though Miss Teasdale were a tasty dish he'd prepared and served to Isobel. "Hang onto your parasol, Izzy. You'll get an eyeful today!"

His promise was immediately borne out when they almost collided with Richard Arlen on their way to Dylan's cabana.

"Say Dick," Dylan grabbed his arm, "like you to meet some friends of mine."

When Dylan made the introductions, Isobel curtsied prettily and Will shook hands silently, quite undone by hearing his mother introduced as Izzy Claflin.

"Jobyna with you today?" Dylan asked.

"No," Arlen replied, "not today."

"That's Mrs. Arlen . . . Jobyna Ralston," Dylan explained unnecessarily.

"Well . . . I'm in something of a

rush . . ." Arlen smiled politely as he began moving away.

"That's fine, Dick." Dylan gave his permission. "You go right along. Good to see you."

Isobel, frozen at the spot where she'd first glimpsed Arlen, watched until he disappeared around a bend in one of the club's long corridors.

"He looks well," she pronounced when he'd vanished.

"He's a fine fellow," Dylan boomed. "No question about that."

After settling Isobel beneath a large striped umbrella on one of the club's three patios, Dylan came into the cabana just as Will finished changing into his swimming suit.

"Turn right for the pool, straight ahead for the ocean, and Izzy's to the left on the south terrace."

Will paid no attention but blurted out a request. "Could I speak to you alone sometime today?"

"What about now?" said Dylan.

"No!" Will wasn't ready yet.

"Okay, Will, okay. There's no problem.

I've planned a surprise for Izzy later that'll give us plenty of free time."

"What's that?"

"They're shooting some scenes for an Andy Clyde comedy down the beach this afternoon. Producer's a pal of mine and he's arranged for Izzy to watch."

"Swell. She'll like that." Will hurried out before Dylan could ask any questions, turning right toward the pool.

Floating on its pale emerald surface, Will rebuffed images of Rita tugging at the edges of his consciousness. She'd been killed yesterday by Rudolph's phrases as surely as by an abortionist's knife. And he would not be haunted. Water lapping over his body began to loosen the tight knot at its center. He tried to organize the appeal he would make to Dylan for five hundred dollars.

When he felt his outline was solid, he pulled himself from the water and joined Isobel and Dylan on the patio. The morning passed slowly. Will repeated over and over in his mind the crucial points of his presentation. By the time Dylan returned from delivering Isobel to the

Andy Clyde shooting, Will's whole body was humming with nervous agitation.

"It's a business matter." The words spilled out before Dylan had even lowered himself into the chair across the table.

"Care for something wet, Will?" Dylan motioned to a waiter in the opposite corner of the lounge.

Will nodded, mute now.

"Anything special?"

Will gave a silent shrug, indicating anything would do.

"Two bourbon and soda," Dylan told the waiter, turning immediately back to Will. "Business matter, eh?"

"A matter of about five hundred . . ." Will tried to relax back into his chair ". . . dollars."

"Something to do with the foundry?" Dylan asked.

"No, no." Will's voice steadied somewhat when he saw Dylan wasn't shocked by the amount. "It's personal."

The waiter set their drinks before them and Dylan saluted Will with his before drinking. Will mimicked him and, even though he'd taken a small swallow, shuddered as it went down.

"In a tight spot?" Dylan prompted.

Will nodded, feeling the whiskey land in his stomach.

"What've you gotten yourself into?" Dylan took another enormous swallow and leaned in toward Will, confidential, chummy. "You haven't been here long enough to get a girl in trouble. What is it? Too many souvenirs? Gambling? You owe your bootlegger?"

"It's a girl." Will uttered the words in a strangled voice and then tried to clear his throat with another taste of bourbon. The shudder this time encompassed his entire body, visibly.

"Don't drink any more of that." Dylan emptied his own glass and pulled Will's toward him across the table. "You'll make yourself sick."

Will was grateful. Like an actor locked in a part, he would have continued using the prop as long as it was there.

"Now don't let this get you down," said Dylan. "I'm sure we can work things out."

Will managed a small smile now,

somewhat encouraged by Dylan's hearty assurance.

"You see, I met this girl . . ."

Rita's face suddenly tore through the barrier erected by Rudolph's words and flashed onto an enormous screen inside Will's head; her soft naked body spread across the vast expanse, turning slowly, languid, visible from all angles; her voice issued from parted red lips: "I love you, Willie boy." He felt a sob forming in his chest and struggled to keep it from breaking loose. Dylan saw his dilemma.

"It's okay, Will. It's okay." His voice was soft but his snapping fingers, summoning the waiter, cracked loudly. "Give us a brandy Alexander and one more bourbon and soda . . . fast as you can."

"Let me give it a try," Dylan said as the waiter scurried away. "You met a young lady, a very pretty one, and you thought she was just about the most special thing you'd ever come across and she felt the same about you. And then something came up — could be any number of things . . . sick mother back home . . . one-in-a-million-sure-fire investment opportunity . . . an old uncle with a failing business . . . whatever — something came up and five hundred would fix it and you gave it to her and she took a powder. Is that about the way it went?''

Will was torn. He was ashamed he'd been deceived by such an obviously common, transparent scheme. He was relieved he hadn't had to describe the deception himself. Relief won out and he nodded vigorously as the waiter reappeared.

"Take a good slug of that." Dylan pointed at the frothy mixture. "It'll go down easy."

Will swallowed deeply and felt warmth spreading through him, loosening taut muscles, tranquilizing bare nerves.

"Well, what was it? What was the gimmick?"

Will took another gulp before answering. "A baby," he said finally.

"Whose?"

"Mine."

"My God, boy! Can't you count?

You've only been in town a month!" Dylan shook his head in amazement, clicking his tongue against his teeth.

Will, the full extent of his hopelessness revealed, felt the glow of the brandy dimming, driven away by cold fact: he was in his present, bleak position because he had neglected to do a little simple arithmetic.

"She must have dazzled you something awful; dazzled you so you couldn't count."

"I would have done anything for her," said Will.

"Sounds like you pretty nearly did." Dylan gazed at Will, musing a moment on the magnitude of such an enchantment. "Just be glad she was a penny-ante operator. You got off pretty easy."

"Five hundred dollars doesn't seem so easy . . ."

"Listen," Dylan interrupted, "most of these guys won't let you through the door for less than a couple thousand."

"Still, five hundred dollars . . ."

"Don't worry about that." Dylan dismissed the rest of Will's sentence.

"We'll work it out."

"How?" Will squeaked, uncertain that Dylan understood the urgency of his plight.

"That's my specialty." Dylan patted Will's arm, trying to soothe him. "Getting things done, working things out. If somebody wants a bottle of good gin, I see he gets it; if somebody wants to spend the evening with a lovely young lady, I arrange it; if somebody needs quick cash, I find it. Put it this way, Will: If somebody needs a favor done, I see it gets done. So one guy thinks I'm his bootlegger and another thinks I'm his social secretary and another thinks I'm his banker. So? And if it involves a little conning . . . well, we all get conned in this life . . . and we all do some of it ourselves. Why, this whole town's a con in a sense. The trick is to know how to make it work for you. Now there's no question you came out on the short end this time but I bet it won't happen again, not that way . . . and I'm willing to put money on it."

Dylan signaled the waiter, asked him to

put five hundred cash on his tab, told him to clear it with the manager and ordered another round of drinks. Within ten minutes, five crisp one hundred dollar bills were resting in Will's hand. He didn't even thank Dylan. He just stared at the money.

"Of course, there's no need to involve Izzy in this," said Dylan.

"No, of course not," Will murmured, his eyes still fixed on the currency.

"As far as I'm concerned, it's *all* confidential."

"Yes," said Will, "of course."

"Everything we've said here . . . and don't you worry about paying me back."

As Will started to protest, Dylan silenced him with a raised hand.

"Your father was good to me," he said, plucking the bills from Will's hand, folding them in half, tucking them into Will's jacket pocket. "Let's just say I'm returning a favor."

SATURDAY, JULY 23

A Thought for Today: If all that glitters is not gold, at least sometimes it's brass and maybe that ain't so bad. A case in point being Mr. Dylan Doyle, late of Detroit, now of Hollywood, and a pretty fine fellow as far as we're concerned.

When Ian and Ethel's first child was born on the same June day the Republicans gave Herbert Hoover the Presidential nomination, Ethel's father suggested naming the baby for the nominee.

Isobel, herself a frequent advocate of this sort of commemoration, was appalled. "Ah'd noo name a teapot fer that mummy."

Robert, though fond of Hoover, was against it too. "One Herbert in the family's quite enough, thank ya very much."

Ian didn't want Herbert Bonine to think he'd named his son for him. He also didn't want to offend his father-in-law.

Finally, he and Ethel settled on Alfred Herbert, the former being Mr. McInnis's Christian name. Isobel always insisted, however, that the baby was named for the Democratic nominee, Al Smith. This made Ian apoplectic.

"He wasn't even nominated until ten days after the baby was born," he protested.

"It was clear he was runnin'," said Isobel.

"I wouldn't vote for him, let alone name my son for him," Ian pointed out.

"He's a merry man," said Isobel.

"He's merry all right," Ian exploded. "He'd turn this whole country into one big saloon."

"It's noo far from that now," Isobel replied.

"Well, I didn't name him for Smith," Ian sputtered. "I didn't."

"It's a lovely name, laddie." Isobel smiled at her son.

Whenever Isobel and Robert met that summer they also had words about the Democrat.

"Ah see yer *Mr.* Smith would have the

states sellin' whiskey, if he had is way," said Robert.

"Does it matter who's sellin' it, Bertie?" Isobel asked.

"*And* he'd turn the country over t' Rome, there's no doubt about that."

"The Pope'll noo come t' Washington and he canna do much from Rome."

"Well, if ya had any sense ya'd be fer Hoover."

"Ah think is collar holds is head on."

"And if it does? What if it does? At least it's there. Not like yer bloody happy warrior who's noo got one a'tall."

"Someday Hoover's'll fall right into the pot with the chicken."

Robert was rendered speechless by this macabre image.

The Claflins also debated that summer whether Will should, or should not, enter college in the fall.

Robert, watching Will's immersion in what he considered a rather sybaritic nightlife, now felt his son might be better off at school. There was no question that the boy worked hard when he was at the foundry. He wasn't lazy, thank God. And

Robert could hardly forbid him to spend his evenings as he pleased. If Will chose to spend them with Isobel, wasn't that, after all, why Robert requested he stay home in the first place? College, it now seemed to Robert, might be the only solution.

Isobel had once again become attached to Will as her companion of the evening. She liked sitting at the corner table in the Statler dining room, knowing when she glanced toward the door at six o'clock that Will would be entering. She was pleased to have a listener interested in hearing about the film she'd seen that afternoon. She enjoyed walking to the theater after dinner, leaning lightly on Will's arm, looking into windows of the shops they passed. If Robert was so pleased with Will's work at the foundry, why did the boy need to go to college? Would it make his work any better?

Will had no desire to leave his present existence. The prospect of entering a foreign environment where he was expected to study and to make conversation with people his own age had become abhorrent. He knew, however, that his father's wishes were likely to prevail, especially since Robert had the nearly unanimous support of the rest of the family. Jamie wanted Will to go as a gesture of and, hopefully, first step toward independence. Ian felt a college degree was important, good for the business. Alexine always supported Robert.

Two nights before Will's departure, he and Isobel went to the Madison to see *Four Sons*. Starring George Meeker, James Hall, Charles Morton and Francis X. Bushman, Jr., as the sons of the title, it was the story of a family shattered by war. Will felt acutely every loss, every disruption, every rent in the family fabric.

Afterward, as they strolled toward Sanders, the soft night air was touched with a tang of autumn for the first time that year.

"I could be one of those fellows," said Will mournfully. "I feel like I'm going off to war."

Isobel, her eyes directed toward passing window displays, was silent as she moved alongside him.

"So like the father," she murmured

when the string of shops ended.

"Pop? What's he got to do with it? He never went to war. He never went to college either, for that matter."

"The Bushman lad," said Isobel. "He looks exactly like is father."

JULY 24, 1932

Dressing on Sunday morning, Will's hand ran into Ian's letter in his jacket pocket. He uncrumpled the ball of paper on the dresser top and reread it.

"What's that, Willie?" Isobel, reflected behind him in the mirror, pulled on a new pair of gloves that fluted out from her tiny wrists.

"Letter from Ian," Will mumbled, keeping his eyes on the page.

"How's Alex?"

"Doesn't say." Will raised his head and watched Isobel wiggle her hat into place.

"Ah sent a picture Friday a dear Jack's bairn. She'd noo have it yet."

Will decided to test Isobel's reaction to Ian's proposal. "He thinks maybe we should come home sooner than we planned."

"Why's that, Willie?" She seemed unperturbed.

"Business problems, I guess."

"Ah canna see why he'd need us. He loves bein' in charge." She selected the one of her four parasols that most closely matched her hat, and started toward the door. "We'll go t' Doug and Mary's first and t' the Wee Kirk after that."

"You go ahead," said Will. "I'll be right down."

When the door clicked shut, he got Western Union on the phone and sent Ian a telegram: "Letter received stop considering your suggestion stop."

SUNDAY, JULY 24

A swell Sabbath kicked off by a most thought-provoking sermon at the Wee Kirk, based on a text from Galatians: "Be not deceived; God is not mocked: for whatsoever a man soweth, that shall he also reap." We concur heartily and told the preacher so afterward.

Then up the coast for luncheon on the

Santa Barbara shores and a look-see at some of the orange and avocado groves in the environs. The oranges come grapefruit size and the avocados — well, would it mean anything if I told you we saw some the size of my head (no smart remarks, please!)?

All the above was accomplished in the presence of Mr. Dylan Doyle and in his touring car as well. As was our trip to the Alexandria Hotel for dinner, a jernt so reeking of swank that yours truly felt underdressed minus soup and fish.

After dinner to *Reunion in Vienna* with Ina Claire and Donald Brian doin' their stuff. Also on hand to watch the Austrian get-together were Bob Montgomery, Connie and the Marquis, Bill Haines (if he's in town, how come Tallulah's living in his house?), Freddie March, Karen Morley, Lil Tashman (she left her Eddie at home), Kay Johnson (we're told this is one brainy lady) and Johnnie Mack Brown. Your scrivener would like to go on record as noting that Haines, Brown and the Marquis are first-rate lookers. And if you wanna argue, you can see my second. Haw!

———————————

To replace Will, Robert gave Isobel a new automobile in which Riley could ferry her back and forth to the pictures. He himself began to spend more and more time with Miss Saltonstall. This went unacknowledged until he failed to appear at one of the Sunday meals Alexine continued to insist the family eat together.

"Where's father?" she asked Isobel.

"Ah couldna say." She was surprised to have been questioned.

"I'm sure he has a good reason," said Herbert, a bit too quickly and altogether unnecessarily.

"For what?" Alexine asked, suspicious now where she hadn't been before.

"I'm sure he's gotten involved with something at the foundry." Ian's tone closed the subject.

Alexine acquiesced until the middle of the main course. "I think it's very odd he didn't call," she said then. "And even more odd that no one else seems to think so."

"Shall I call the shop?" asked Jamie. "Would that make you feel better?"

"It would." Alexine met a series of averted gazes as she glanced around the table. "I think that makes good sense, don't you?"

"Aye." Isobel's single syllable, as Jamie left the room, was more like a sigh than a specific response. "Did ya know dear Jack married the Costello girl, Alex?"

Alexine turned toward her mother but didn't really focus.

"She was with him in *When a Man Loves*," Isobel prompted, trying to help Alexine identify the new Mrs. Barrymore.

"Oh . . . yes." Alexine's murmur was noncommittal.

"She's at Warner's," Isobel added.

"Some mix-up with a shipment that was supposed to go out yesterday," said Jamie, sliding back into his chair.

"I would've taken care of it tomorrow." Herbert, automatically defensive, forgot this was a charade and responded to the fact that deliveries were his jurisdiction.

"Tomorrow's never soon enough for

Pop.'' Jamie couldn't resist giving Herbert a poke.

''What's the difference as long as it arrives on time?'' Herbert sputtered.

''Well, I'm just glad he's all right.'' Now Alexine was anxious to close the subject.

But when Robert was absent again two Sundays later and again three weeks after that, her concern could no longer be allayed by fake phone calls. Jamie took her aside to explain.

''I don't believe it,'' she said when he finished. ''He just wouldn't.''

''Think about it, Alex,'' said Jamie. ''It's not really so hard to understand.''

''There's nothing *to* understand,'' she insisted. ''He just wouldn't do something like that.''

Obviously, however, Alexine had some doubts. She needed Robert's blessing on her disbelief and presented herself at the foundry one January afternoon to receive it.

''It's true, lassie,'' he said when she completed what she called ''Jamie's horrid little tale.''

''I don't believe it,'' she said, the

reflex dying hard.

Robert came from behind his desk to perch on its edge in front of her. "Dinna be hurt by it, Alex." He reached out to stroke her cheek.

"How can you say that?" she cried, turning her head sharply away from his extended hand.

"It's naught t' do with ya," he said, letting his hand fall.

"Of course it has," she wailed. "You're my father."

"Aye," said Robert, now patting her arm, a touch she allowed, "and that's noo changed."

"It hasn't?" The question was genuine and she looked at him when she asked it.

"A course not, lassie."

"I hate her." Alexine's venom stilled the tremor in her voice.

"Katy?" Robert laughed softly. "Ya wouldna if ya knew er."

"Well, I have no interest in knowing her, I can tell you that."

"Ah didna think ya would," said Robert, melancholy undercutting his laughter.

"If I asked you to stop seeing her,

would you?'' Alexine stared down at her hands, unwilling to read any part of the answer in Robert's eyes.

"Alex," he said, after staring silently for several moments at the top of his daughter's bowed head, "we all need help gettin' through this life and we find our help in different places . . . in church, in whiskey, whimsey, tricks . . . wherever it is or whatever it is, we all need somethin'. Katy's what ah need."

"You need a lie to get through life?" Alexine was accusatory now, stung by Robert's refusal to renounce Katy Saltonstall. "That's what you're saying, isn't it?"

"Aye, perhaps it is." He returned to the chair behind his desk and slumped into it.

"Well, isn't that what you mean?" Alexine needed his unqualified admission. Perhaps wasn't good enough. "You need a lie to be able to live?"

"If ya wish t' put it that way, lassie, ah guess ah do." Robert sounded very tired. "And is it so bad, after all? We all need our lies . . . wherever we find em."

"Well, I don't." Alexine rose and

marched to the door. "Not me." She slammed it behind her and the glass pane shivered in its frame.

Three weeks later, having refused to communicate with her father at all, Alexine miscarried. Feeling responsible, though no one blamed him, Robert visited often at the hospital, welcomed tearfully by his daughter every time. They never discussed Miss Saltonstall, however, and Robert, despite his guilt, never considered giving her up.

MONDAY, JULY 25

Mommy up and at Bullock's along with the chickens while the financial wizard of this team practiced his wizardry (I went to the bank, ya rustics!). My big mistake here was leaving the gas buggy parked without (tried to take it in but the tellers objected). Some so-and-so thought the rear end was an accordion and acted accordingly. Annoying, to say the least. So our hero wended garage-ward, glimpsing Guy Kibbee and Gavin (way back when) Gordon on the way. And there the matter — and the Graham-Paige — rest, on account of because it takes a few days to turn an accordion back into a fender.

Back to the hotel — and an almost head-on collision with Sari Maritza — there to be met by another communiqué from you-know-who (and I quote: "A definite answer soonest please"). Desiring shuteye more than a night on the town (can ya believe it?), yours truly sent the Captain and Escort off to struggle along without him. Reports received here since indicate they did all right: Dinner at the Derby with Bill Powell and Carole Lombard on Mommy's right . . . *Roar of the Dragon* afterward (*Shanghai Express* minus the train, according to our gal on the izzle).

After a light repast in the room — three éclairs, to be exact — your scrivener fell into a beauty sleep (keep your opinions to yourselves, ya boneheads!) and is now about to repeat same. Anymore of this and they'll summon him to the silver screen.

When Miss Farnum died suddenly of a heart attack on May Day, 1929, Alexine and Herbert, at Herbert's suggestion, moved in with the Claflins. Someone was needed to run the household, he pointed out, and it might be just the thing to pull Alexine out of the lethargy that still lingered four months after her loss, a loss accentuated by the birth in April of Ian and Ethel's second child, a daughter.

Isobel's small body stiffened when the proud parents announced they intended to name the child for her.

"Ah'll noo have it," she said, maintaining her stand consistently for one full week.

Finally she relented but only on one condition.

"Ah dinna care what ya call it," she said, "as long as it noo calls me grandma."

And neither Alfred nor Little Isobel, as she came to be known, ever did. She was Isobel to them as she was to her own children.

That summer, with Alexine in charge of

the house, the Claflins almost recaptured a sense of family, absent for years. Will, who'd spent much of his year at school feeling alien, adrift, was especially comforted by this. Surrounded now by familiar shadows, the solace of the commonplace, he felt himself healing from invisible wounds.

Alexine dragged out of the attic the huge yellow umbrellas used years before to shield luncheons and dinners served outdoors. She reinstituted the custom of weekend dining in the yard, spurning Robert's offer to hire kitchen help, seeming to thrive on doing it all herself. Herbert was so pleased he didn't even protest what seemed to him the vast amounts Robert gave her to spend, blurring the lines between their personal budget and that of the household. Alexine was flourishing. That was more important than his pride.

Robert made a great effort to be present as often as possible. Isobel always put in an appearance when asked and Alexine learned quickly to issue her specific invitations. Even Jamie was frequently there.

When the time came for Will to return to school, he was, if possible, even more bereft than he had been the year before. Now he was not afflicted with fear of the unknown. He had a specific distaste for the sphere of strangers he must enter. It didn't matter that the world that soothed him through the summer was more shell than substance, more bones than flesh, it belonged to him and the people in it were his. More important perhaps, he was theirs.

JULY 26, 1932

Tuesday morning another telegram arrived from Ian. "Eagerly awaiting your reply," it read.

"What is it, Willie?" Isobel asked, spotting the telltale yellow paper.

"Ian again," said Will.

"Mmmmm." She rapped her toast sharply on the edge of her plate. That new man in the kitchen still hadn't gotten the amount of cinnamon right. "Will ya be comin t' the studio?"

413

"I think I'll pass today," he said.

"Aye." She nibbled at her dusted piece of toast.

Will had intended to go but as the event neared, his lassitude grew. Now he wanted only to go back to bed. Inertia had fallen over him yesterday morning as he'd deposited the five hundred dollars in the bank. His subsequent visit to the auto garage had required enormous effort. He knew he couldn't make a like effort today. He was out of power.

"I'll get a letter off to Ian," Will began, "catch up on some other . . ."

He stopped abruptly, realizing how unnecessary it was to make excuses for Isobel's benefit.

"Dear Jack's shootin' today," she said.

"Give him my regards."

She smiled at Will vaguely, threw a frown at the mound of cinnamon heaped on her place and left to meet Whipple who was waiting outside. Will went directly to the elevator, up to the room, and into his bed.

TUESDAY, JULY 26

The Captain had an early call at the studio so our hero elected to remain between the sheets and spend a lazy day.

Then to dine in the early evening at Musso Frank's with Cap and Mr. Doyle and, following the repast, to the Pantages to let the Bombshell give us an encore of *Redheaded Woman*.

Your scrivener warned Mommy that people will be babbling she's "that way" about a certain party if she continues to see so much of him. Her comment? No comment.

Robert Claflin had never believed in investing in anything but himself. What was the point, he said, of putting money into other men's ventures when he had one of his own. And a very good one. Acme Foundry had prospered and expanded as Robert poured profits back into it. As far as he was concerned, The Acme, his family and his savings account were the only appropriate repositories for his quite adequate funds. The one time he'd ever directed any money elsewhere was when he'd capitulated to Isobel's desire for Liberty Bonds, a desire created solely by the fact that Pickford, Fairbanks and Chaplin were hawking them.

So when the Big Bull Market expired, Robert's capital was intact. Will, unfamiliar with the structure of his father's finances, did not know this and seized on the general sense of calamity as the basis of an offer. He would be glad, he wrote, to leave school and come home to work in the foundry. Robert, smelling the taint in his son's altruism, refused. It was not necessary, he replied, squelching Will's hope that he might yet escape the ordeal of higher education. Robert had no plans to cut back.

This was distinctly evident to the guests at Alexine and Herbert's fifth anniversary party, held in the spring of 1930, and so grand it prompted comparisons with their wedding itself, precisely as Alexine had hoped it would.

She had left nothing to chance, including cornering Isobel the moment she heard that William Howard Taft, twenty-seventh President of the United States, recently retired Chief Justice of the Supreme Court, and the man for whom Will was named, had died.

"I know you were very fond of Mr. Taft," Alexine said, "but our party is next month and if you turn up in black I'll never forgive you."

"But he was *ill,* Alex," said Isobel, surprised.

"Well, I know that."

"And *old.*"

Alexine wasn't interested in her mother's reasoning. She just wanted a guarantee.

"You promise you won't wear black to the party?"

"Ah'd noo wear black fer im t' the grocery," Isobel said.

When, a few months later, Robert began to be concerned about business matters, he attacked with vigor. As industrial production began dropping off, and worries burgeoned, his energy seemed only to increase. In an effort to keep all his men employed, he cut slightly their wages and hours. He worked longer hours himself and stopped drawing a regular salary. He took a close interest in every aspect of the business, overseeing even Jamie's and Ian's work. He had to be certain every possible economy was in effect, every loose end tightened. That summer Will worked in the office without pay because Robert didn't want his men to feel a son of his was robbing them of work. Robert was possessed of a feverish kind of drive as he fought to stave off the misfortune he knew could be ahead. And only if one looked carefully beneath the surface of his relentless activity was it evident that something was worn very thin, stretched too tight, frayed.

Sometimes Alexine saw it when Robert came in late at night and she sat waiting for him in the parlor. It flickered behind the smile he invariably wore as he sat opposite her in his deep armchair.

"I think you're working too hard." She was slightly stern.

"Ah've worked hard all m' life, lassie."

"But there's no need . . ."

"Aye, but there is."

"You're older now . . ."

"Nonsense!" said Robert, ending it.

Jamie saw it too but knew nothing he said would cause Robert to ease up. Ian resented Robert's intrusion into his area of work and insisted on taking it as a personal affront. Will was pleased just to be working, grateful that another year of school was behind him. Herbert felt Robert might be overdoing but that it wasn't his place to say so. Nevertheless, at Alexine's urging, he finally agreed to try.

"Bob . . ." He was hesitant, hovering in the doorway of Robert's office.

"What is it, Herbie?" Robert's eyes remained on the bills of lading on his desk.

"Well there's something I've been wanting to say." Herbert moved a few feet into the room as he spoke.

Robert looked up, stopping Herbert's forward progress. "Ya think ah'm workin' too hard and ya'd like t' see me cut down. Is that it?"

"Yes." Herbert's relief at not having to deliver the lines himself was clear in his voice and in the smile that broke across his face.

"Thank ya very much, Herbie." Robert focused again on the papers before him.

"Well . . . fine, Bob, . . . fine."

Herbert reported that night to Alexine that he'd tried and that Robert seemed to understand.

Alexine, a ferocious believer in turning over every possible stone, also raised the matter with Isobel.

"I think Papa's working too hard," she said.

"He's worked hard all is life, Alex."

"But he never has a minute for himself. He's at the foundry all the time."

"It'll pass," said Isobel. "It'll all pass."

When Alexine sputtered angrily about this to Will, he pointed out she might have chosen a better time. Isobel had just come from *Anna Christie* and hearing Garbo's voice for the first time. What, after all, did Alex expect?

And in a sense, of course, Isobel was right. There was only so much that Robert could do. Those forces that determined how well or how poorly the business fared finally moved beyond his control. He could only operate when a customer requested an order. When customers stopped asking, he was forced into idleness, the hardest thing he'd ever had to endure.

JULY 27, 1932

Even in the absence of another prodding message from Ian, even though he wasn't sure what to say, Will was determined to write his brother on Wednesday morning. As soon as Whipple had borne Isobel off to the stores, Will sat down with paper and pen.

"Of course, I understand your position," he began, "and, of course, I am prepared to assume my share of responsibilities in the fall."

It seemed to Will a proper beginning but he couldn't think how to continue. Balling up that sheet of paper, he pulled a fresh one toward him.

"I'm sorry about both Jamie and Alex," he started again.

That opening also failed to lead

anywhere. He tried a third time.

"While I understand your dilemma, my main concern, of course, is for Isobel."

Will discarded that attempt and many others. When Isobel returned from shopping, he was still making false starts.

"What're the wads, Willie?" she asked, looking toward the writing table.

"Oh, nothing." Will swept the pieces of crumpled paper toward the basket, leaning over to pick up those that missed. "Correspondence . . . catching up . . ."

"Ah think people prefer cards," said Isobel. "Ah got a new batch."

"And that's not all." Will gestured toward the packages spilled onto the bed.

"Ah hate wearin' the same things t' the studio over and over."

"Well . . ." Will hesitated, "there aren't that many days left."

"Ah canna be in full sleeves in August."

"It's gone so fast."

"Dylan thinks we should stay till the picture's done shootin'." Isobel pulled a dress from one of the boxes and carried it to the closet.

"Oh?" Will was cautious.

"Or at least fer the end a the Games. He's got a box."

"Dylan's got a box at the Olympics?" Will gave an admiring whistle. "I bet that wasn't easy to come by."

"He knows a great many people, Willie."

"I'll say."

"A lovely blue." Isobel flashed another garment in Will's direction before shuttling it from bed to closet.

"Do you know exactly what Dylan does at RKO?" He draped himself in an armchair, hoping his voice was as casual as his pose.

"A bit a everything, ah think." Now Isobel unpacked a handbag matching the peacock dress.

"He *told* you that?" Will's astonishment drove his body forward in the chair.

"He's Mr. Selznick's right-hand man, Willie." She carried the purse and a pair of pale blue gloves to the dresser. "That covers a lot of tasks."

"Oh . . ." Will went limp again, staring at Isobel as she emptied the last box. "What did you say when Dylan suggested we stay?''

''Ah said there's no tellin' when we'll get back again.''

Dylan joined them that night for dinner. When Isobel traveled to the powder room, Will fired his question.

''Do you know she thinks you're Selznick's assistant?''

''So?'' Dylan's tone was gentle.

''Well . . . I just . . .''

''Does it do any harm?''

''No . . . it doesn't exactly do any *harm,* but . . .''

''I can think of things that *might* hurt her.'' Dylan paused, reaching for a cigar in his inside pocket. ''But that? I can't see any harm in that.''

''And do you know,'' Will attacked again, ''we're supposed to be thinking of leaving sooner, not staying longer?''

''I wanted to talk to you about that, Will.'' Dylan leaned in toward the table, resting his elbows on it, the newly lit cigar protruding from the knot of his hands. ''If you feel you must get back, but Izzy isn't ready to leave, I'd be happy to look after her.''

"Leave her behind?" The thought stunned Will.

"You know I'd take good care of her. Haven't I done a good job of looking after you both?"

When Will realized Dylan was waiting for an answer, he nodded.

"Remember what I told you the other day, Will?" Dylan's voice was as reassuring as a caress. "Find the lie and make it work for you? Well, Izzy's found hers. I've found mine. And you'll get a handle on yours one of these days. Who knows? If you stick around, maybe you'll even find it here."

"The attendant put me in mind a Francine Larrimore," said Isobel, suddenly reappearing. "Such a sweet face. D'ya remember er, Willie?"

Will shook his head.

"Ya may a been too wee." She settled onto the chair Dylan rose to pull out for her.

Dylan chuckled. "I get the idea Will was never *too wee* for the pictures."

"Aye," said Isobel, puzzled now. "Ya dinna remember Francine, Willie?"

425

"You'd think it'd be a cinch to get him to the studio, but I haven't seen him there yet, have you?" Dylan gave Isobel an exaggerated wink.

"Well," said Will, "count me in for tomorrow."

"Great!" Now Dylan turned the wink in Will's direction. "Just tell them you know Izzy. She and the guards are old pals."

Back in the room that night, Will and Isobel took two Chocolate Creams apiece to their respective beds.

"Do you think we're letting Dylan do too much for us?" Will asked, biting into his second roll.

"God loveth a cheerful giver, Willie," said Isobel, nibbling away at hers.

WEDNESDAY, JULY 27

Lunch at Chop'N Tweet Tweet; matinee of *Jewel Robbery,* dinner at the Biltmore, evening at a wonderful play, *Cynara,* and home to bed with our Chocolate Creams. If this ain't livin', would ya tell me what is?

And as long as you're answering questions, here's another one: Am I lucky or am I lucky?

When Will saw *The Front Page* in the spring of his junior year, he was smitten. He wanted to become Hildy Johnson, star reporter, shooting the breeze with the boys while waiting for a story to break, racing against deadlines, pitting his wits against a tough, irascible managing editor, making his mark in the rough and rowdy newspaper business. He was so stirred by the romance of the profession that he broke out of his self-imposed isolation and presented himself at the offices of the college newspaper.

He would do anything, he told the editor, who immediately offered the job of cleaning up the offices at night. Will accepted.

"Claflin, my Claflin," said the stunned editor, "where have you been all my life?"

And Will didn't mind that his task was menial. He had a foot in the door and was content to bide his time.

"You're all right, Claflin," the editor said on the last day of the term. "And you're the only son of a bitch around here who doesn't want to be a star. Maybe we'll fool 'em all in the fall and make you one anyway."

And he did, rewarding Will with a column dubbed Claflin's Corner. Intended as a repository for announcements of campus activities, the editor soon realized Will knew little about them and gave that assignment to someone else. Will would instead, at his own suggestion, write about the picture playing at the local theater. But strictly on a trial basis. The editor wasn't sure the column would catch on.

It took Will only a few weeks to prove he had an audience. He was a hit and he took his success very seriously. Often at night he was the last to leave the office, laboring over his column until long after midnight. He was still there at two-thirty one morning, writing about *The Champ,* when Jamie called to tell him Robert was dead.

He died sitting in his parlor chair. When the massive clot hit his brain, it was as though a glacial tide had flooded through his body, freezing him instantly in place. Alexine had come downstairs at midnight to see why a light still burned and there he sat, giving an absolutely perfect imitation of life. She was unable to believe death could look so ordinary. Not until Robert lay in the same room the following night, his body stretched out in a coffin, could Alexine begin to accept that her father's life was over.

Jamie took care of the funeral arrangements. Ian turned his attention to the foundry ("You'll finish the year and then we'll need you here," were his first words to Will). Isobel went the afternoon after Robert's death to a matinee of *Platinum Blonde* at the Fox. That evening, after a brief and solitary visit to the parlor, she went to see Garbo and Gable in *Susan Lenox: Her Fall and Rise* at the Adams. The following afternoon she saw *Inspiration* at the Madison and that evening, the night of the wake, she returned to *Platinum Blonde*. Will accompanied her even though Jamie offered to go in his place and Alexine objected to their going at all. Isobel would accept only Will. He was grateful to be chosen.

When they returned to the house the night of the wake, all the guests had gone, leaving behind their testimony to Robert in a leather-bound book now filled with messages and signatures. Will read through it before entering the parlor to say his own farewell.

Standing before his father for the last time, Will remembered being there when Francis X. had died and the feel of Robert's arms surrounding him as he wept. He knelt now, making himself the size that boy had been but knowing he was beyond his father's comfort. And he cried for the loss of that moment, already thirteen years past, feeling his heart would break because it could never come again.

Soon after returning to school, Will abandoned Claflin's Corner. It had come to seem only a reminder of lost dreams, nothing more. Committed now to a future in the foundry, as a memorial to his father and at Ian's insistence, Will tried dutifully to absorb the barrage of information Ian delivered by phone and letter in his effort to initiate Will into management.

Ian was keeping the foundry afloat by pouring only small castings, the most economical to produce, operating just four days a week, and cutting the work force to the bone. Jamie argued with him on this last measure, making a case for keeping more men on fewer days a week. This, he was sure, is what Robert would have wanted.

Ian disagreed. "If Pop could have seen conditions now, he'd do exactly what I'm doing. There's really no choice."

"He always thought there was a choice," said Jamie, "or at least he hoped there would be eventually."

"Well, that's a nice notion but it hasn't any place in the business as it stands today."

"No . . . I suppose not."

"And don't make me out a monster just because I don't have the sentimental streak you shared with Pop."

"You're not a monster, Ian. I

know that."

"I'm a businessman, James, something you'll never be."

"I know that too," Jamie replied, "and anytime you're dissatified with my work, just let me know."

But Ian couldn't fault him there. Jamie kept things running precisely on schedule, exactly as ordered. It mystified Ian that his brother could accomplish this while consuming a bottle of whiskey every night, but he couldn't deny that Jamie got things done.

As well as assuming control of the foundry, Ian began to take an increased and proprietary interest in Isobel. Perhaps because of his intense need to believe it, he felt she was not recovering from Robert's death as she should be. He sensed in her an unhealthy air of lingering grief and, even though this was lost on everyone else, he became convinced that she needed to get away.

In the spring several things conspired to confirm this for him. The first was the kidnapping of the Lindbergh child. Ian felt Isobel took it very badly.

When she failed to appear for a meal at which Ian was present, and Alexine said she hadn't left her room since discovery of the baby's body three days earlier, he exploded.

"Well, tell her to come down here right now. She'll waste away up there."

"I've *been* feeding her, Ian. That's not the point." Alexine didn't like the implication that she'd been letting her mother starve.

"Well, what is the point?" he blustered. "What is the goddamn point?"

"Leave her alone," said Jamie. "She'll come out."

"Good Lord!" Ian was exasperated with them all. "You'd think it happened to her."

"It did," said Jamie.

The second thing was the visit to Detroit of "The 42nd Street Special," a train sent throughout the country by Warner Brothers to promote its film of the same name. It carried such studio personalities as Bette Davis, Laura LaPlante and Preston Foster. Isobel joined the crowd that gathered in Michigan Central Station to see the Special and the stars who appeared on its rear platform.

Recalling it for Ian at Sunday dinner, she said wistfully: "Ah wish ah coulda ridden with em back t' Hollywood."

The third factor was Ian's fondness for exercising his newfound power. No longer in his father's shadow, limited to the relatively petty prerogatives of the Vice President of Sales, he enjoyed now playing the benevolent benefactor whenever it was convenient and financially feasible.

And the fourth was Ian's conviction that Will, if he had a vacation first, would be eager to come home and settle down to work afterward.

And so Ian decided. Isobel and Will would take a motor trip to California, leaving in the middle of June.

When Jamie questioned whether this was the best possible use of family funds, Ian reminded him Robert had left a decent amount of cash savings. Jamie pointed out they might need these to carry them through shaky times ahead. Ian wondered how James could debate priorities when Isobel's well being was involved. He was sure, he said, that Robert would have wanted it this way.

As for Will, he had no objection. He even felt, for the first time in his life, that Ian might be right.

JULY 28, 1932

The clerk at the front desk handed Ian's letter to Will Thursday morning as he and Isobel passed through the lobby on their way to RKO.

"Tell Whipple to hold his horses," said Will, directing Isobel toward the door. "I'll be along in a minute."

Dear William:

Since my telegrams have elicited no response, I've decided to try once more to communicate with you by letter.

James has not appeared at work the past two days; Alex miscarried and Herbert is concerned about her state of mind; two equipment failures (a cracked oven and buckled crane track) have severely depleted our cash reserves.

I'm sure, knowing these circumstances, that I needn't urge you to return at once. I'm sure, under these conditions, you would have no desire to remain where you are.

So I'll just wish you a safe journey home and look forward to your arrival at the soonest possible moment.

Love,
Ian

Will requested a Western Union blank at the desk and printed out his message: "REGRET PLANS CAN'T BE CHANGED STOP LETTER WILL FOLLOW STOP."

"See this gets off right away." He handed the clerk some change along with the form. Then he went out to join Isobel for a day at the studio.

THURSDAY, JULY 28

Our hero, coming to you with a special bulletin: He must've had rocks in his head to have been considering an early departure! We're in no repeat no hurry to blow this burg, specially since we've got a pal who's mastered the art of throwing his avoirdupois around (already I can hear the noses crackin' outta joint in the hinterlands).

Now if this flash cramps anybody's style (seein' as how this is a nize party, we won't mention names), we're sorry, but them's the breaks. We've got obligations here and we're not about to run out on them. To wit:

Who'd see *Bill of Divorcement* through its shooting schedule if we am-scrayed? Who'd be in the stands (oops, pardon me, the box) cheering Michigan's own Tolan and Metcalfe on to Olympic victory? Who'd fill the empty page Mommy's still got left in THE BOOK? Would Tallulah ever forgive us for duckin' out while she's in town? And there's more, much more, but need I go on?

We know some of our fans out there ain't gonna like this and we say they've got a perfect right to their own goût (you'd say it too, ya dunderheads, if ya had any cul-chah). But we hafta call 'em as we see 'em and we see this one as: One for Hollywood — none for the home team.

The publishers hope that this Large Print Book has brought you pleasurable reading. Each title is designed to make the text as easy to see as possible. G. K. Hall Large Print Books are available from your library or local bookstore or through the Large Print Book Club. If you would like a complete list of the Large Print Books we have published or information about our Book Club, please write directly to:

G. K. Hall & Co.
70 Lincoln Street
Boston, Mass. 02111